THE FIRST INTERVIEW

Suhl, June 6, 1636

Archie Mitchell, his wife, Marjorie, and Harley Thomas, were eating lunch in the shade of the Suhl District Courthouse. Court employees had built a small sheltered area, with some tables and benches, next to the courthouse, where they could gather for lunch and hold impromptu meetings. The area had started as a few wooden tables and benches. Over time, the employees added a roof, railings, and a raised wooden floor to cover the dirt surface. Archie's planned contribution was a brick BBQ grill to improve *der Garten*, as the area had become known.

Marjorie and Marta, the young daughter of Dieter and Greta Issler, brought lunch to Archie and Dieter. Today, the two had brought enough for Marshal Harley Thomas. Marjorie's brought her latest experiment—corned beef with cheese on a small bread loaf. Usually she had more than enough for Archie and Dieter, and a few others gathered in *der Garten*.

"What brings you to Suhl, Harley?" Marjorie asked.

"Just passing through. I had some documents to drop off to Judge Fross, and tomorrow, we're off to Erfurt."

"By yourself?"

"No, I've my deputy, Karl, and two constabulary troopers."

Marjorie looked puzzled. "Four of you? What—"

"Marj—" Archie said, shaking his head. Why Harley and the others were going to Erfurt wasn't their business.

1

"Where's your deputy?" Archie asked. Harley had mentioned him, but he's not come to the courthouse with Harley.

"Checking the horses at the constabulary stables. He said one horse cast a shoe."

"Be sure to bring him in to the office when he gets here. I'd like to meet him."

With lunch over, Dieter and Marta played a game in the courtyard's shade involving a soft, patched ball and feet. From the edge of his vision, Archie noticed a young man approaching. He shifted his seat on the bench, giving his total attention to the approaching stranger.

The man was not a local, Archie guessed from the small card inserted in his hatband that said *Press*. He elbowed Harley, then Marjorie, and nodded toward the approaching man—reporter, Archie guessed. Marjorie looked, and with a roll of her eyes, grinned back at him. Harley just shook his head and looked away.

"*Guten Tag, Herr Marshal Mitchell, Frau Mitchell, und—Herr Marshal Thomas,*" the young man said. "I am Thomas Bloem of the *Thuringia Times*. Would you have time for an interview?"

Archie glanced at his watch. Lunch hour was over; it gave him an excuse to say no. He was about to refuse when Bloem continued.

"I'm interviewing up-timers. I want their impressions of life in this time; how did you come here, and how living in Suhl, away from Grantville, has affected you and other up-timers?"

The statement stirred Archie's curiosity. Usually, interviewers asked about life up-time, how that knowledge and perspective could be used in the here and now. However, that did not seem to be what Thomas Bloem wanted . . . or so he said.

"I'm sorry. I don't have time now. Lunch is over and we," Archie said, nodding toward Harley, "have work waiting for us."

"I would be happy to buy dinner—for all of you, tonight. I understand the Boar's Head Inn has a private dining room and an outstanding reputation for their kitchen. Would you join me tonight?"

THE MARSHALS

Mike Watson

Cover designed by Laura Givens

This book is a work of fiction. Names, characters, places, and incidents either are products of the author's imagination or are used fictitiously. Any resemblance to actual persons, living or dead, events, or locales is entirely coincidental.

Mike Watson
Visit my website at https://m-watson.com/

Printed in the United States of America

First Printing: Aug 2022
1632, Inc.

eBooks ISBN-13 978-1-956015-43-0
Trade Paperback ISBN-13 978-1-956015-44-7

CONTENTS

Archie glanced at Marjorie and Harley. *Shall we go?* was his unspoken question. She returned his glance, tilted her head a moment, and then nodded, as did Harley Thomas.

"Very well," Archie said to the reporter, "We'll meet you there at seven."

"Add one more," Harley said, "I'm bringing my deputy."

✻ ✻ ✻

The proprietors of the Boar's Head Inn were very familiar with the Mitchells. Archie and Dieter had lived in an apartment in the Inn's rear when he and his deputy first arrived in Suhl. They didn't stay in the inn long, only until they bought an old bakery large enough to house both families.

Innkeeper Otto Hersch met them at the door. "Follow me, *Herr Mitchell, Frau Mitchell. Herr Bloem* has reserved the Red Room. *Herr Marshal Thomas* and *Herr Deputy Marshal Mohn* are already there."

"*Danke, Herr Hersch*, lead the way."

Thomas Bloem was sitting facing the doorway when the Mitchells entered the private dining room. A woman was with him, sitting at the table. She was dressed in a riding skirt, a small jacket, and a white blouse that seemed to match Bloem's shirt. The two were dressed similarly, with dark pressed trousers and matching jacket. Harley Thomas sat next to Bloem. Harley's deputy, Karl Mohn, Archie assumed, sat at the end of the table next to the woman.

Karl was big for a down-timer, at least six feet tall, and Archie guessed, well over two hundred pounds, none of it fat. Unlike Archie's deputies, Mohn was black—black hair, black eyes, black clothes, boots, coat, and a wide, brimmed black hat sitting on the table next to him. Completing his appearance were two .45 caliber SI-1 revolvers holstered on a black gunbelt.

Harley was laughing, enjoying a conversation with Thomas Bloem, when the Mitchells entered the room. Seeing them enter, he stood, and brought his deputy forward to meet Archie and his wife.. "Smile, Karl," he whispered. "These are friends." Karl did so, but his smile, bared teeth, was more like a grimace than a smile. That made everyone who had seen the smile laugh.

"Karl is new to the service," Harley explained after he'd greeted Archie and Marjorie Mitchell. "He's not a conversationalist," Harley said after introducing his deputy. "This trip is as much OJT training for him as it is to see the country and others in the service. He knows Max, and, when I was told they needed a courier for some special documents, I volunteered and brought him along."

Archie wished Dieter was here. He could take Karl in hand. Dieter, with badge number four, was the service's senior deputy. The next Marshal position would be his. . . if he wanted it.

"Tell me a little about yourself, Karl. What's your badge number?"

"Twelve, *Herr Marshal Mitchell*. I joined three months ago."

"Just call me Archie." Mohn didn't speak, but nodded. "Now, tell me about yourself."

"I'm originally from Ulm. Life there . . . became difficult. I'd heard that the USE, the State of Thuringia and Franconia, was much better. I joined a trade convoy to Bamberg as a guard. When we arrived there, one thing led to another, and I was offered a position as a court bailiff. *Herr Marshal Huffman* saw me and changed the offer to join the marshals' service. *Herr Thomas* was kind enough to take me on as his deputy."

With a nod to Harley and Archie, Mohn returned to the table, sitting at a vacant seat next to the woman. While Harley and the Mitchells watched, he turned to her and began a conversation.

"Not a conversationist, is he?" Archie observed as he, Marjorie, and Harley walked to the long dining table and took seats.

"Oh, he can when the situation warrants," Harley said, grinning.

Harley Thomas returned to his seat next to Thomas Bloem. Bloem took a small notebook from inside his jacket and listened to the two marshals' conversation.

"Now, tell me about Max," Archie said. "What's he up to?"

"Max has set up a boot camp for prospective marshals and deputies. Karl finished a month ago and has been with me since," Harley said.

"I've two deputies besides Dieter," Archie replied. "One, Kurt Moesch, is doing well. The other, not so much. He needs more training."

Harley started counting on his fingers. "Ya know, I've never thought about it, but three marshals and nine deputies aren't enough for what we're supposed to do."

"That's Max's primary job now, Harley. I think his boot camp idea is what we need. We can't just bring anyone in off the street. They need training with an emphasis on process and procedure. We don't want some yahoo, drunk on non-existent power, in the service.

"I'm impressed with Karl. He was the only one to finish out of his class of eight. The rest were unsuitable. Max cashiered two for soliciting bribes while doing rounds with the Bamberg watch."

"Glad that job's for Max," Archie said. "I like it here in Suhl."

The woman who had accompanied Thomas Bloem interrupted her conversation with Karl Mohn and scooted her chair closer to the marshals and Marjorie Mitchell. "I'm Maria D'Angelo," she introduced herself, extending her hand to shake theirs. Her move startled the Mitchells. Down-timer women weren't so open or socially aggressive, nor did they usually shake hands.

Mohn blinked as she did so and, following her lead, scooted his chair closer as well.

"I'm Marjory Mitchell and this is my husband, Archie," Marjorie said before Archie could respond. She caught his eye as he nodded. They'd been in unusual social situations before and this could develop into another. "And this," she nodded at, "is Marshal Harley Thomas. You've already met Deputy Marshal Karl Mohn."

"I believe *Herr Hersch* has something special for us," Thomas Bloem said before the conversation went further.

"The Boar's Head Inn is known for its kitchen and *Herr Hersch* is justifiably proud of it," Marjory said. When she took over the conversation, Archie surveyed the room and their hosts. His occupation-acquired paranoia had prevented trouble more than once. Harley Thomas and his deputy did the same. The two marshals sat facing the entrance. Mohn was sitting where he could watch the side door to the kitchen, and the rest of the room. Marjorie sat next to Archie, appearing to be deep in conversation with Maria D'Angelo. Unseen from everyone, she had a .45 caliber revolver on her lap, hidden inside her bag.

"Please, I can see you're surprised by Maria's presence," Bloem said to the men. "She's my partner—and my sister. We've started a . . . newspaper? A monthly journal of events, issues, and notable people."

Marjorie, hearing this, looked at the young woman, who sat opposite her at the table. "You're a widow, I presume?"

"*Ja*. How did you know?"

"Different names. Not usual for brother and sister, and your jacket seems to have been cut from a man's. A widow may do so in remembrance."

"Very observant," Maria replied, but didn't expand on her widowhood.

"And that brings us to why I've asked you here," Bloem said, returning to the purpose of the meeting. "Everyone wants to know about up-timers and up-time life. Your culture, your achievements, your dreams. What *we* want to know is how coming here has affected you. How did you come to live in Suhl?" he asked Archie. "And how did you become one of the city's leading civic citizens, *Herr Mitchell?*"

"Uh, I don't . . . I've not thought of us as being civic leaders," Archie replied.

Marjorie looked at him. "Archie, when the Bürgermeister has a problem, who does he come to? If Pastor Weber needs help, who does he send for? If there is trouble in Suhl, a fight or drunken mercenaries, who does Wachtmeister Frey call for help?"

"And who is also on the board of directors for Suhl, Incorporated?" Bloem asked.

"Both of you," Maria D'Angelo affirmed, looking at Marjorie.

One of the innkeeper's serving maids entered the room and prepared the table, interrupting the discussion. After covering the table with a cloth, laying out dinnerware, filling pewter mugs with the inn's famous brew, and leaving warm loaves of bread and crocks of butter, she left, leaving the occupants alone.

"*Herr Mitchell*, how did you become a marshal?" Maria D'Angelo asked.

Archie chuckled, adding some levity to the room. The atmosphere, until this point, had been growing uncomfortable. The Mitchells didn't know Thomas Bloem's and Maria D'Angelo's intentions. Were they as they seemed and claimed to be, or not? Was there a hidden agenda? Archie's suspicions had been quelled—to an extent. He looked at Harley and Marjorie for a hint of their observations. The three had discussed the invitation earlier in the day. Karl Mohn, not present for those earlier discussions, seemed to have overcome his shyness and was taking an interest in Maria D'Angelo.

Marjorie nodded. She was more comfortable than she'd been earlier. "Go ahead, Archie. I don't think I know it all, myself."

With Marjorie's assurance, Harley was being quiet, sitting with a grin on his face and taking an occasional glance at Karl. He, too, noticed his deputy's interest in the widow.

"How much do you know about up-timers?" Archie asked the two down-timers, "Our arrival, and the aftermath of the Ring of Fire?"

"Not much," Bloem said. "No one seems to know how you came here."

"We don't either. There was a flash and here we were. Some say it was God's intervention. Others say it was diabolical." Archie shrugged and took a sip from his mug. "Before the Ring of Fire, Harley Thomas, here, Max Huffman, and I were semi-retired. All of us were army retirees and needed something to do."

He turned aside to Harley. "Who was the sheriff when we moved back to Grantville?"

Harley pondered the question. "That'd be in 1990?"

" '91."

"Bill Collins, then."

"That's who I thought, but I couldn't remember his name." Archie took a sip from his mug before turning back to the two down-timers. "Anyway, we, the three of us, went to Bill Collins, our local sheriff, with a proposition. We'd heard he'd been hit with a bunch of new state and federal training requirements, and the county hadn't increased his budget to comply with them. From what we'd heard, the training requirements were the same as we conducted with our troops while in the army."

"Archie transferred to the Military Police after fifteen years in the infantry," Marjorie said.

"I retired as a sergeant major. Harley was a master sergeant, and Max Huffman had been a sergeant major. A REMF, he claimed," Archie said with a chuckle.

"REMF? I don't know the term," Bloem said.

"It means rear echelon—" Harley started to say.

"Harley!" Marjorie cut him short.

"—a desk jockey, a paper pusher, an administrator."

Marjorie reached over and patted his hand. "Good boy."

"Back to the point," Archie continued, "we'd each had at least a decade of training soldiers or military police. We submitted a proposal to the Sheriff to act as consultants to train his deputies—take the bureaucratic load off his shoulders. We were able—"

"—after a time," Harley added.

"—to convince him of the idea. We'd charge him less than hiring a professional trainer and we'd be local, always available to help." Archie took another sip.

"He agreed," Harley said, picking up Archie's story. "His only requirement was that we meet West Virginia's requirements for law enforcement officers. We did, and he hired us, swearing us in as auxiliary deputy sheriffs."

The serving maid entered carrying a large platter. "Let's eat and continue later," Bloem said.

* * *

An hour later, after they'd finished eating, and were sitting, nibbling the remnants of a cake baked by Otto Hersch's wife. Karl Mohn and Maria D'Angelo were sitting at a corner of the table, having a private conversation. Archie cleared his throat, took a sip of ale, and resumed his narrative. "When the Ring of Fire happened, Harley, Max, and I were on horseback—crowd control after Rita Stearn's and Tom Simpson's wedding. Rita was Mike Stearn's sister, and that drew almost every UMWA member around Grantville to the wedding."

"UMWA? What is that?" Bloem asked.

"It stands for United Mine Workers of America, a trade union."

"You still use horses up-time?" Maria asked from the corner, interrupting her conversation with Karl Mohn..

She must have been multi-tasking. Talking with Karl and listening to us at the same time. "Not for transportation," Archie said. "But they're useful for some events—like managing the wedding crowd. We still have—had a lot of horses up-time, especially outside the cities. I had three with saddles. Enough for the three of us."

"One was mine," Marjorie said.

Hersch's serving girl entered again, cleared the table, brought two fresh pitchers of ale, one for Karl Mohn, and another for the rest at the table. She brought a bottle of red wine for Marjorie and Maria after the ale. "*Danke,*" Bloem said to the girl, and slipped some coins into her hand as she was leaving.

When the girl was gone, Maria asked, "How does your agreement with the sheriff lead to the creation of the Marshals and the Constabulary?"

"Ah . . . that *is* a story, but it's not mine, it's Harley's," Archie said.

Karl Mohn looked up. "I'd like to hear that, too. *Herr Huffman* never said how that happened."

Harley looked back to Archie, who'd put him in this spot, and shook his head. "It's not like most think. They sent the three of us out on a simple job and we screwed it up."

PART I: GREETINGS!

Early Spring, 1633

Under most circumstances, Harley Thomas was an even-tempered man, slow to get riled and slow to cool down. This morning, before dawn, he peered into the steamed mirror and shaved a last trace of beard from his face, nicking himself once again. He growled under his breath, irritated by the harsh lye soap that caused the minor cuts on his face to sting. With a last swipe, he rinsed the straight razor and dried it carefully before storing it in the medicine cabinet behind the mirror. *Need to sharpen that thing before I cut my throat.* Rain pattered on bathroom window in the pre-dawn. The day's early morning grayness, seeping past the curtains, promised more. *A great start to a crappy day.*

Wiping his face a last time, he stepped out of the bathroom. The movement triggered a deep ache in his left knee. Once, years before, he had jumped out of a C-130 over South Carolina and had landed in a tree. A dislocated knee permanently removed him from jump status, ending, or so he thought, his military career. It didn't, but it restricted him to less arduous assignments. The knee was proof to Harley, now in his late fifties, that old injuries always came back to haunt you.

Getting late, he thought after glancing at his watch. A Second Chance vest lay on the bed. Harley picked it up and strapped it on over his heavy undershirt. This model extended below the belt line. It was uncomfortable while on horseback, but it had an upside; it protected his kidneys. With the vest firmly in place, he reached, out of habit, for his army shirt but paused.

Not today. Instead of the army shirt, he reached back into the closet for his old, faded, blue Marion County Deputy Sheriff uniform shirt. He and his two friends had been auxiliary deputy sheriffs, a part-time job that kept them active in their semi-retirement.

After the Ring of Fire, everything changed. Harley and his friends were now part-time law enforcement officers, when not on active duty with the Army. Because of the lack of Grantville PD shirts, the Chief, Dan Frost, allowed them to wear their old deputy sheriff shirts with a USA flag embroidered on the left sleeve, pewter colored Corporal chevrons on the collar points, and the retention of the deputy sheriff title. Dan Frost discovered that down-timers viewed police officers as nothing more than the equivalent of down-time watchmen. Sheriff's deputies, on the other hand, were held in higher esteem. Perhaps it was a legacy of the Old English *scīrgerefa*, a royal official, responsible for keeping the peace. The title of Deputy Sheriff helped when dealing with down-timers and minor nobility.

He pinned a Marion County Deputy Sheriff badge above the shirt's left breast pocket and gave it a quick rub, remembering the times before the Ring of Fire. Tucking his uniform shirt into his jeans and slipping his suspender straps over his shoulders, he moved to the dresser beside the bed.

On the dresser was his service pistol, a worn, blue Government model Colt .45 and three loaded magazines. He holstered the pistol, making sure the pistol rode just to the rear of his right hip. Taking the two magazines, he slipped them into the attached magazine holders on the left side of the belt, opposite of the holster. With two pounds of steel on one hip and two loaded magazines on the other, a pair of handcuffs looped over his belt in the back, he needed both belt and suspenders to support weight.

The ritual was complete. Harley wasn't superstitious, but having a ritual—a routine was . . . comforting.

Now dressed for the day, he left the bedroom and walked toward the kitchen in the rear of the house. Vina, his wife, was talking with their down-timer neighbor, Greta Issler, and Harley's mother, Emma Lou. Vina and Greta worked in Grantville's day care center, and helped, when needed, at the hospital and Grantville Assisted Living Center.

Emma Lou sat at the kitchen table sipping from her favorite glazed mug, watching and listening; she was learning German slowly. Greta was an excellent teacher, but a lifetime of speaking English made learning a new language difficult for elderly Emma Lou.

Vina was kneading bread dough when Harley entered the kitchen. Greta was teaching her how to make bread and buns in exchange for the use of the Thomas' electric oven. The heat from the stove and oven warmed the room, and the aroma of baking bread filled the kitchen.

Greta and her husband, Dieter, had been born in Vienna. She to a family of bakers and he to a family that traded in glassware. After their marriage, Dieter had become a glassware factor in Magdeburg. . .until Tilly approached. They fled, eventually finding their way to Grantville.

"*Herr Alte Thomas* was better yesterday," Greta said in German, referring to Harley's father living in the Assisted Living Center. "His heart seems to be stronger. Our German air helps his breathing." Harley's father's time appeared to be measured now that the supporting drugs had been withdrawn. It had been a difficult decision to make, but inevitable. Doctors Adams and Nichols had sent a plea to the residents and relatives of those living in Assisted Living Manor, asking that a portion of the life supporting drugs be set aside for emergencies. The elder Thomas had volunteered. He, Emma Lou, Harley and Vina had talked long into the night after the plea. Vina had felt that it was almost like asking someone to commit suicide. When the drugs ran out, there would be no refills and the result would be the same. The only difference would be how much time Harley's father had.

After much discussion and turmoil, Emma Lou and Harley agreed with the senior Thomas. Vina had quit arguing against it, but she would never agree. The decision created a barrier between them, and Harley was aware it would be a long time before it would come down.

"Are you riding today?" Greta asked when Harley entered the kitchen. She referred to Harley's occasional horseback patrol at the behest of Dan Frost as riding. Vina refused to look at Harley wearing his old Deputy Sheriff shirt. He was home on furlough from the Army, now that the internecine warfare across Germany had subsided for the winter.

"Dan Frost has no right, Harley. You already have a job and shouldn't be taking cases for him on your time off!" she said, keeping her head down as she kneaded the dough.

"We're needed, Vina," he said, in answer to her complaint. "Max, Archie, Dieter and I are going to a place near Rudolstadt. There's been some thieving and some villagers have been knifed. They appealed to the Count's man in Rudolstadt, who passed the buck to Dan Frost, who asked us to check it out."

"Will you be home for supper?" Vina asked sharply. She had flour coating her arms halfway to her elbows. At some point, she'd unknowingly deposited some on her forehead and cheek.

"I think so, if Dan doesn't come up with something else."

"Good! We're having several folks for supper; it's our turn for the neighborhood potluck. Greta has made turnip soup and I'm adding some sausage.

"Here's some willow-bark tea to get you going, *Herr Thomas*," Greta said, handing him a mug. Harley had grown used to the tea, bitter as it was. It wasn't coffee or conventional tea, but it helped to dull the pain in his knee. He had heard rumors that someone was trying to get coffee and tea imported. That would be welcome if it came to pass.

"Dieter left to get the horses saddled. He said he would meet you at the stables," she added.

Harley nodded his thanks and sipped the hot tea. *I think I'd kill for a mug of plain old Lipton tea.* He and Vina had grown to prefer hot brewed tea rather than coffee since their return from Europe and his subsequent discharge from the US Army.

"Do you want to take some willow-bark tea with you?" Emma Lou asked.

"No, thank you. My knee'll be fine." Harley finished his tea, sipped some water to clean the bitter taste from his mouth, and set the mug next to the kitchen sink. He hoped willow-bark tea would be as half as good as up-time aspirin.

His jacket and scarf hung next to the back door. He wrapped the scarf around his neck, tucked the ends inside the front of his shirt and slipped on the thick nylon jacket with *Marion County Sheriff's Office* printed across the back.

Harley, along with Archie Mitchell and Max Huffman, had been auxiliary deputies until the Ring of Fire. Now, they helped train recruits for the Army and train those who would become trainers. When home from the Army, he and the others helped Dan Frost as needed.

Keeps me out of the house. Vina will get over it. There really is no alternative. He retrieved his weathered blue trooper's hat with its blue plastic weather cover and placed it on his head instead of his usual Army headgear. Everyone seemed to have multiple roles since their arrival in Germany. Today, he was a Deputy Sheriff. Next month, he would be a Drill Instructor, again.

Harley retrieved his M1 Garand rifle leaning next to the door, a relic older than he was, and picked up his saddlebags loaded with other outdoor essentials; emergency kit, extra ammo, canteens, dry clothes, rain slicker, and enough trail food for three days.

With the saddlebags over a shoulder, Harley walked through the kitchen door. The rain was only a light mist now. He stuffed the slicker into his saddlebag before crossing the back porch, down the steps, and into the alley that led toward the center of town. Cradling his M1, he kept alert in the grayness as he walked toward the city stables. The residents of Grantville had learned the hard way that when you needed a gun, you needed it quickly. After the Croat raid, most homes in Grantville had at least one firearm, always loaded and near-at-hand.

* * *

Max Huffman and Archie Mitchell, the other two auxiliary deputies, were in their late fifties or early sixties, like Harley. All three agreed to work for Dan Frost when not on duty with the Army. They had worked together for years before the Ring of Fire and Dan Frost had decided they could help best by riding mounted patrols on the outskirts of the Ring and in the neighboring communities. Some of the neighboring towns and villages took advantage of Grantville's offer of mutual assistance. Whenever trouble appeared, they asked for help without hesitation. Harley, Max and Archie were all combat veterans and weren't intimidated by marauding packs of outlaws.

Dieter Issler had joined the Grantville Police last fall as an interpreter. Dieter spoke passable English, with Polish and Italian thrown in as well. In his early thirties, Dieter most often rode with the three deputies, gaining On-the-Job policing skills while performing his translator duties.

Harley spoke Twentieth Century German, but he had some trouble understanding some of the local dialects. Dieter helped translate when his up-time German failed him. Max and Archie didn't speak German, but they were learning, as did everyone, through necessity. That didn't help them in the here and now.

Dieter called them, the three deputies, *Die Drei Alten Soldaten,* or the three old soldiers. From Dieter's perspective, that is what the three deputies were. They didn't act like any city watchmen he'd ever met.

Max, Dieter, and Archie were already mounted when Harley arrived. Archie rode his own horse. He was a Western buff and owned the other two horses, too. They were more appropriate for use along the edge and outside of the Ring of Fire, where roads were not well maintained or didn't exist. And gasoline was scarce, a strategic commodity.

Harley slid his Garand into the scabbard on the remaining horse and stepped up into the saddle. Like Harley, the two other deputies wore Marion County Sheriff jackets and blue trooper hats. Each was armed with a rifle and pistol. Max would have liked to have a pump or auto-loading shotgun, but most of those had been given to the Army. Dieter carried one of Archie's spare pistols and a twenty-inch, double-barreled coach shotgun in his saddle scabbard. Good for close work and necessary for Dieter. He couldn't hit the broad side of a barn at ten paces with a rifle.

"Any more information?" Harley asked, ignoring the sharp stab of pain from his left knee, triggered when he mounted his horse.

"You should mount from the other side, Harley. I saw you wince," Max said.

Receiving no response from his friend, Max continued, "Here's the latest I got from Dan. It appears to be a gang. They broke into some houses and a mill. Looking for food and loot, I suppose. Beat up the miller pretty good, but he'll live. They killed a villager while leaving the mill, so they've been given outlaw status. They would have anyway, for stealing food. The Count's man, Helmut Reinart, thinks there are four or five of them."

"That's not much more than what Dan told me last night," Harley said. "Well, let's go. Vina and I are the hosts for the neighborhood potluck tonight and she wants me home for supper. They can't wait if I'm late."

"What are you having?" Archie asked.

"Turnip soup and sausage."

Glancing at Dieter, Archie leaned toward Harley and whispered, "Do you want to eat with Marjorie and me? We're having some leftover pig from my last boar hunt and Marjorie still has some potatoes from last summer's garden."

"No," Harley said softly. "Vina sets great store in these dinners. I'll never hear the end of it if I don't have a good reason for not showing up. She's adding the last of my homemade steak sauce to the mix. That'll help, and Greta is baking some fresh bread and buns. They were fixing something when I left the house. Vina was telling Greta about doughnuts and cinnamon rolls, so I hope there'll be something special."

The throb in his knee was lessening. He kicked his heels in the horse's flanks and headed down the street toward Route 250, with the others following behind.

This wasn't the first time the four had been sent out to help the neighboring towns when the local watchmen had more than they could handle. The mutual assistance agreements had a significant effect on the good will being built between Grantville and their neighbors. Sometimes a slight effort paid big dividends, and Grantville needed friendly and cooperative neighbors. The mutual assistance was one sided, now, but come summer and harvesting time, Grantville's neighbors would reciprocate.

As they rode down the road in the early morning gloom, Archie muttered, "I feel like I'm in a Western. A bunch of Sheriff's deputies riding out to catch bad guys. Where's my white hat?"

"Shut up, Archie!" Max said. "You say that every time we ride out. It's getting old."

❋ ❋ ❋

The Deputies and Dieter rode down Route 250 and past the high school. Foot traffic appeared, walking toward Grantville in twos and threes. Some were heading for the school, some toward the mine on the southwest side of town, and others to jobs in Grantville, or at the power plant beyond. By dawn, the three had reached the *Ring*, leaving the up-time highway and riding up the graded, graveled ramp to the dirt road that continued to the junction of the Saalfeld and Rudolstadt road. The right turnoff went to Saalfeld. They took the left one toward Rudolstadt..

They reached Rudolstadt by mid-morning and dismounted at the edge of the small town that backed up to the castle walls to give some rest and relief to the horses. The four continued on foot, leading their mounts.

They may need fresh horses depending on what they discovered at the crime scene.

Rudolstadt looked much like the small German towns he and Vina had visited during Harley's Army tour in Europe—narrow streets lined with well-kept houses. The Saalfield road changed into the street that led toward the center of town where the Town Hall and central market were located. Empty houses were being occupied again with returning residents, now that the threat of Tilly's marauders was gone.

Rudolstadt's town hall was the largest building outside the castle walls. It sat on the edge of the market plaza, where a few vendors were setting up their kiosks and product stands. Most of the locals preferred to remain inside. Grey threatening clouds promised rain; rain that the clouds had not delivered yet. From the Town Hall, they proceeded through Rudolstadt, heading for the Saale River waterfront and upstream to the mill. They would be met there.

The mill, powered by a water wheel, was built on the bank of the river. A large wooded building that appeared to be a warehouse was next to the mill, separated by a narrow alley. The mill serviced several small villages around Rudolstadt and the castle.

Count's man, Reinart, and a Rudolstadt watchman were waiting.

"Hello, *Herr Reinart*," Harley said, as he approached the two waiting men. "I am Deputy Sheriff Thomas. This is Deputy Sheriff Mitchell, Deputy Sheriff Huffman and our assistant, Dieter Issler."

"Hello, Deputy Thomas," Reinart replied, "and Deputies Mitchell and Huffman. You arrived quickly. *Herr Polizeichef Frost* said he would send his best deputies." He ignored Dieter.

Dieter was giving Max and Archie a running translation of Harley's conversation with Reinart. Harley noticed the snub to Dieter, but let it pass. Grantville needed good relations with Rudolstadt. "What happened, *Herr Reinart?*"

"Four, maybe five men were discovered stealing flour and grain by the miller early yesterday morning. He lives here with his family. A villager from Debra was approaching from further up the river road when he heard the miller's wife screaming. He was running to the mill when he was surprised by the bandits as he came around the corner here," Reinart said, pointing to the entrance of the alley between the warehouse and the mill. "The outlaws ambushed him. He gave us a description of them before he died. The miller's description is the same. The miller was beaten and cut in a few places, but otherwise unharmed. No serious injuries."

The Rudolstadt watchman spoke for the first time. "*Meine Herren*, I am *Wachtman Werner Anthross*. We have a description of four men of middle age; mid-thirties, the miller estimates. Three wore front and back armor and carried at least one pistol each. The fourth was more poorly dressed, no armor, and he carried an ax. I found tracks heading upriver along the river bank."

And you didn't go any further, did you? Town watchmen weren't eager to venture far from their hometown. They wanted overwhelming numbers if they were going to get into a fight. A single watchman couldn't do much by himself. Getting killed wasn't a part of his job description.

Archie and Dieter went off to speak with the miller and his wife while Max examined the scene. The morning thaw had left a thin layer of mud over still frozen earth. Too many people had trod through the alley to leave any evidence. Any attempt to distinguish the outlaws' tracks from the civilians' was impossible.

Harley asked the watchman, "How far from here did you track them?"

"Up the river to the place where a stream enters the river. The tracks continued up the stream."

"You didn't go any further?"

"*Nein*. I came back to report to the *Herr Reinart*, and he sent for you."

❋ ❋ ❋

Max and Harley met Archie and Dieter returning from interviewing the miller. The miller hadn't provided any new information.

"How do you want to handle this, Harley?" Archie asked. "You can't walk far with that knee of yours."

Harley grimaced momentarily. It was embarrassing that his knee was an issue. All three of them were getting a little old for this kind of business. They couldn't always use Dieter to walk point; he didn't have the experience. Most of the younger folk were joining the Army, or one of the Ambassadorial teams. He had his bad leg and suspected Max had a heart condition, but had said nothing. Archie had an ulcer and had lost over forty pounds in the last year. Of course, Archie said that he had the weight to spare, and that was true . . . had been true.

Dan Frost needed a younger Deputy and Dieter was the best candidate he had. Today may be the day for his promotion, Harley surmised. The decision had been left up to them. They were the best judges to determine if, or when, Dieter would be ready.

"Let's do it this way, flush and sit. Archie, you and Dieter follow the trail. Let's use this as an opportunity to give Dieter some OJT training. Max and I will ride outside the trees that line the streambed, outside the undergrowth, and see if we come across any tracks. If we do, I'll send Max back with your horses to get you. If we don't find any tracks, we'll set an ambush in case you flush them out. So, if you hear us shooting, lie low until you're sure they aren't coming back your way. I don't want you to nab them by yourself."

"Shoot, Harley," Archie replied, "I'm not that stupid. I've kept my hide intact all these years and I'm not gonna change that now." With that, Archie retrieved his rifle, canteen, and pack from the horse. Nodding to Dieter, he said, "Dieter, tell this watchman to show me these tracks and where he stopped." Dieter spoke to the watchman who, with an acknowledging nod, turned and walked off down the alley, with Max and Dieter following.

"*Herr Reinart,*" Harley said, turning to the Count's man, "we'll see what we can find."

"*Dankeschön.* I'll have Wachtman Anthross waiting for you. He can find me if I'm needed."

Harley and Max mounted their horses and, each leading one of the two saddle horses, followed Archie, Dieter, and the watchman down the alley.

"Look Max. You can see how that creek cuts back from the river." Harley pointed to a distant line of trees that ran from the river to the northwest. The ground, close to the river, had the glimmer of unmelted ice among the leafless trees. "It looks like there is a slough down there. Those outlaws won't stay there. It's too wet. Let's run up along that tree line to the ridge and see if they came out."

The two deputies rode toward the ridge in the distance, leaving the watchman standing near the edge of the river. Archie and Dieter were no longer in sight. After Max and Harley rode off, the watchman turned and walked back toward the mill. His task was over. Now, he just had to wait.

Max and Harley rode, listening, watching. "Ya think Dieter is ready?" Max asked, keeping his voice low.

"Yeah, I think so. I've been watching him. He's learning and thinking before he jumps. If he does well today, let's tell Dan to promote him."

"I agree. So does Archie. We talked about it this morning."

They rode further, until Max said, "I've still got my Sheriff's Association card . . . "

"Really? I've lost mine."

"Well, I was thinking we ought to give him something. It was just an idea . . . "

"I like it. You can give it to him if he doesn't screw up. Tell him it's his deputy membership card," Harley said with a chuckle. "It'll do until we can come up with something more official, a certificate, maybe."

"Will do."

* * *

Harley glanced upward. The clouds were rising, allowing the morning mist to thin, making visibility easier and ending the threat of rain.

"I wish we had some radios, Max. I don't like using them as bird dogs, but neither of us could do it." Max glanced at Harley, but said nothing.

They rode slowly, watching the ground and the surrounding terrain. There were tracks in several places, human and animal, but they were weathered, more than a day old. The further the two rode, the higher the ground rose until they reached the top of the ridge at mid-day. There, they found a footpath leaving the lower trees and leading over the ridge toward a cluster of buildings in the distance. Those structures appeared to be a small, satellite farming village that supported Rudolstadt castle and the town. On the path was one . . . two . . . three . . . four pairs of tracks heading for the village and not over a day old.

Was this Debra? He checked the map he'd brought from Grantville. The distant buildings were in the right place to be Debra, but he expected to see more people about if it were. Didn't matter really, so many small villages had been abandoned while armies marched back and forth.

"Max," Harley said, "take the horses and ride back and find Archie and Dieter. I'm going to follow these tracks a bit, but I'll wait for you. You get them and follow me as quickly as you can."

"All right, but don't go far, you old fart! Vina'd skin me if I let something happen to you."

"Get going, I'm just going over the ridge to the other side—don't henpeck me. You're not equipped."

Grinning, Max rode back toward the line of trees with the reins of the two saddle horses in hand. Archie swung his leg forward, over the saddle's pommel, and slid to the ground. It was easier dismounting this way. His leg was not hurting much; maybe the willow-bark tea worked.

The ground was leaf covered, masking the mud underneath. With reins in hand, he followed the tracks. On the other side of the ridge, the tracks continued toward the distant buildings.

Harley took a pair of binoculars from his saddlebags and steadied them across the back of his horse while he examined the buildings a half mile away. Smoke rose from one chimney, the white smoke of a wood fire. A door opened on the side of the building and a man stepped out, walked around to the rear of the house, and disappeared.

Someone's home.

There was an old, leafless oak not far off the path at the edge of a grove of smaller trees. Harley led his horse into the trees and tied its reins to a nearby sapling, giving the horse enough slack so that it could graze from the sparse ground cover. Finishing that task, he took his ground cloth, rifle, canteen, from his saddle, and a sack from his saddlebags. With a snap, he spread the ground cloth behind the old oak tree and sat down. He was close enough to see if anyone came down the path but far enough off it to be difficult to be seen. He crossed his legs, laid his rifle across his thighs, pulled some jerky from the sack, and chewed off a strip while settling down to watch the farmhouse.

As he watched, Harley's thoughts drifted back to the ongoing argument about his father. Vina didn't—wouldn't—understand that he was as upset as she. However, the decision wasn't theirs, it was his father's. Doc Nichols told them, Harley's mother and Vina, too, that the senior Thomas had little time.

Drugs may extend his life a few months, or maybe not. The cold facts were, there was no more. *At least Dad is the one who decided. No one took that away from him. I'm going to miss him, though.*

✳ ✳ ✳

Harley continued to watch, his rifle across his thighs, with his elbows propped on his knees, as he peered through the binoculars. He'd counted at least three people moving around the buildings, performing what appeared to be innocuous tasks. Like houses in Rudolstadt, the larger structure was two stories high, with the lower story and foundation made of bricks or stone; a house large enough for a couple of families. Its upper story appeared to be wooden with strong wooden trusses framing the exterior, with outside walls coated with mud or plaster that had dried to the consistency of cement. The sidings and roof were slate or wooden shake. He could see a door and several shuttered windows on this side, and suspected there might be other doors at the rear. Smoke continued to rise from the chimney.

The other buildings appeared to be older. One was open on one side and appeared to have been a stable at one time. The other looked more like a barn.

A low stone fence encircled the three buildings. The view toward Rudolstadt was blocked by another tree-covered ridge.

While Harley was mulling over his observations, he heard movement on the path coming from his rear. It was probably Max with Archie and Dieter, but it never hurt to take precautions. He picked up his M1 rifle and moved further behind the oak tree. From here, he could see the path and have good cover for defense if necessary. He had one eight-round clip in the rifle, two more clips in a small pouch strapped to the stock, and a fourth in his jacket pocket. Thirty-two 30.06 rounds should be sufficient against four outlaws with single-shot pistols or matchlocks.

As the sounds grew closer, Harley saw three horses and riders approaching on the path; Max and the others. A quick low whistle alerted them as he stood up.

✳ ✳ ✳

"See what you think of this," Harley said. The four had crawled up the ridge until they could see the buildings without being seen. A stiff breeze had risen from the west, ruffling the weeds and their hair, and adding a hint of windburn to their faces. A faint whiff of wood smoke arrived with the wind clearing the view across the way, and the noontime sun had burned off the morning fog.

From the ridgeline, the open area dropped into a small valley with a half-filled creek at the bottom. The area between the trees along the ridge, down to the creek and up toward the farm, was open land that had been farmed. On the far slope, the ground rose toward the house. Rain and runoff had creased with deep gullies—the evidence of heavy, untended erosion.

"Max, you and Dieter go down along the left, cross the creek and approach through the gullies. Dieter, you take the front of the farmhouse. Max, you watch the back and those stables. Archie and I will sneak down the right to that grove of trees, cross the creek there, and approach the house from the opposite side. I'll join Dieter at the front and Archie will cover the barn and the right side of the farmhouse. When Dieter and I knock on the front door, they'll bolt out the back. That's where you and Max will wait for them. If they don't take off, Dieter and I will go through the front door and the two of you come in the back. That should sandwich them between us."

Neither Max nor Archie cared for this approach. The three of them had been trained for SWAT entrances. Dieter hadn't. "Harley," Max said, "Archie would be better going in the front with you. He can cover you——"

"Max," Harley interrupted, "Dieter has the shotgun. That's what is needed. You and Archie can cover the back with your rifles, Dieter can't."

With that statement, Max paused. Nodding his head, he turned to Archie and asked, "Well, is that okay with you?"

"Don't like it," Archie muttered, still watching the distant. "Don't like it a'tall . . . but he's got a point."

"Then that's settled," Harley said. "Dieter and I will give them the standard knock and warning. If they don't come out, Dieter will kick in the door and I'll go in low and Dieter will follow. Don't forget where we are. Dieter did all right last week in that tavern brawl in Saalfeld, he'll do all right today."

✳ ✳ ✳

Harley watched Dieter from his location at the corner of the house. Dieter had crawled up from the gully and was watching the house through an opening in the low rock wall that encircled the house. Remnants of a wooden gate hung from one side of the opening. Dieter's crawl had added some camouflaging mud to his clothes. Harley wasn't any cleaner. The warmth of the day had softened the ground and Harley's jeans and jacket were now damp with a coating of dirt, leaves, and mud. The dampness sucked heat from Harley's body, making him shiver.

No one was in sight and there had been no movement since they had left the eastern ridge to begin their approach to the farm. Archie was visible from Harley's position, covering the barn. Catching his eye, Harley gave an interrogative hand-sign. Archie replied with another signal that all was clear.

Harley looked back to Dieter and, pointing to Dieter and then himself, indicating they should approach the farmhouse. This would be close work. Harley laid his M1 on the ground and drew his pistol. He rose and advanced on the farmhouse in a crouch. Dieter met him at the doorway.

The windows on each side of the door were shuttered closed. Dieter crossed to the front of the house next to the doorway, ready to kick in the door when told. Harley crouched, prepared to rush the door from the left. He would cross to the right in the interior, covering the left side of the room. Dieter would rush to the left side of the room to cover the right.

Harley looked at Dieter and pointed to his ears. Dieter nodded, tapping his ear to show he'd inserted his earplugs. Harley had done the same before joining Dieter at the doorway.

"Hello the house! This is Deputy Sheriff Thomas. Come out without weapons and your hands on your head!" he shouted in German. Harley hoped his up-time accent would be understandable to the occupants.

Harley waited for a moment, listening for movement or a reply. *Nothing. Either they're gone or lying in wait.* Finally, he nodded to Dieter to act. Dieter stood, moved to the center of the doorway, and kicked. Immediately, a shot boomed from within. Dieter spun and fell face down next to the doorway.

Damn! Dieter knew better that to stand in the middle of the door! Harley felt a surge of anger rise within him. He had been growing more irritable as the day progressed with its wet and cold. For many people, anger flared like a flaming conflagration that led to reckless reaction. For Harley Thomas, anger was cold, quiet, and controlled, a tool to be used, and Harley Thomas was a master craftsman of that tool. Time slowed, and he dived into the room.

As he passed through the door, another shot boomed. The lead ball struck the doorframe, driving wooden splinters into the side of his neck and face. Hitting the floor, he rolled onto his right side. *BAM! BAM!* He fired twice at a shadowy figure standing at the back of the room holding a wheel-lock pistol. The two forty-five caliber slugs punched through the middle of the man's breast plate inches apart. The outlaw took a step, fell to his knees and then collapsed face down on the floor.

Rising to a crouch, Harley scanned the room when a sharp blow to his back shoved him forward and back down to the floor. Harley rolled onto his side and kicked backward with his left foot, sweeping the feet out from under his attacker, who then fell on top of him.

He felt a pop and a stab of intense pain from his knee when the outlaw landed. The second outlaw attempted to stab Harley in the back with a dirk, but Harley's body armor blunted the blow. Unfortunately, the fall caused the dirk to slash his upper arm.

Dieter appeared in the front doorway, silhouetted against the noonday light. He had been grazed by the large caliber ball that gouged a groove along his ribs. The impact temporarily knocked the breath from him, but he recovered and entered the house to back up Harley.

Harley struggled with a man on the floor when Dieter rushed over and gave a vicious kick to the head of the outlaw. The force of the kick shot the man's head to the side, breaking his neck with an audible snap.

The rest of the room was empty. Dieter was helping Harley to his feet when the sound of three shots came from the rear of the farmhouse. One shot had been the boom from a down-timer weapon.

"Get your breath and keep watch," Harley ordered. "I'll check the rest of the house."

The room had two exits, one to the rear and one to the left of another room. Harley limped to the left doorway, paused, and slipped into the room. Dieter raised his shotgun to cover the door to the rear of the farmhouse just as another outlaw burst through the doorway with an ax in his hands. Dieter was ready and fired both barrels of the shotgun. The ax wielder staggered back and fell across the doorway.

The sound of the shotgun alerted Harley, and he re-entered the room at a limping run to find Dieter ejecting the two spent shotgun shells and reloading. At that moment, Max Huffman entered the room from the rear doorway, jumping over the body and stood crouched along the wall next to the doorway. Max saw the three bodies. "Harley! Dieter!" he panted. "You okay?"

"We're okay," Harley and Dieter said together.

Assured, Max leaned against the wall and slowly slid to the floor. When Max reached the floor, he was as pale as fresh snow.

"How about you, Max?" Harley said, as he knelt next to him.

"Just . . . let m . . . get my breath . . . ," he said between pants. "Archie got another one coming out the back . . . He practically ran over Archie . . . Archie nailed him, but he got off a shot and hit Archie in the leg . . . ,"

"Dieter, take care of Max, I'll check Archie," Harley said, limping through the rear door. There was another room in the back, a kitchen with a large hearth and fire still lit. There was no one else in the kitchen. With a quick glance out an open window, he continued out the back of the farmhouse.

✳ ✳ ✳

A previous resident had laid down paths of flagstones connecting the back door of the house to the barn and stable. Another flagstone path led to a covered well where Harley saw the fourth outlaw lying in a growing pool of blood. Archie was leaning against the side of the well, attempting to tie a bandage around his left thigh.

Harley hobbled over to Archie. "How bad is it, Arch?"

"Could've been worse, I guess. Damned ball ricocheted off that flagstone walk and grazed me here along my pants. It must've hit my fingernail clipper; I pulled it out of my leg." In his hand was the bloody nail clipper, bent beyond usefulness by the lead bullet. Angrily, Archie threw the nail clipper away.

"You don't look too good yourself, Harley. You're limping—did you mess up your knee, again?"

"Outlaw fell on it," Harley said, not providing more information.

The side of Harley's face and neck were covered with blood, soaking the collar of his uniform shirt and jacket. The left sleeve of his jacket had been cut above the elbow and the edges were dark with blood.

Archie had filled a bucket of water from the well and had been using it to clean his bleeding leg. Harley wetted his handkerchief and began wiping his face and neck, removing splinters from his neck as he found them.

"You should wear your knee brace, Harley."

"Can't. Gave it to Homer. He needed it more."

"Well, I guess so. He can't walk without a brace." Archie wet his handkerchief again from the bucket. "I don't trust this well water. I've a bottle of *'shine* in my saddlebags. We'll wipe down with that when we get to the horses.

Harley finished and was re-filling the bucket when Max and Dieter came out of the farmhouse. Harley wasn't sure if Max was leaning on Dieter or Dieter was leaning on Max.

Archie whispered, "Max was back of the stables when the shooting started. I think he ran flat out the whole way from there to the house. Over a hundred—two hundred yards, at least. I've never seen him move so fast, but I didn't think it would hit him this hard?"

"I think he has some heart problems," Harley replied. "He can't keep this up much longer. Vina said that she heard Doc Nichols tell him they couldn't refill some prescription. I know he's been worried about something."

A half-hour later, they had cleaned themselves as best they could with the water from the well. Dieter's wound wasn't as severe as it had first looked. In fact, all their wounds were superficial, bloody but still superficial.

"Dieter, I think you are in the best shape. Go get the horses. I have a first aid kit in my saddlebags and Archie has some moonshine we can use for disinfectant. We'll bandage ourselves up and go home." Harley looked at his watch, it was only a little after one in the afternoon. "We've had a hard day."

Before retrieving the horses, Max waved Dieter over and handed him a small card. "Ya did good . . . , Kid. Congratulations," He said between breaths.

✻ ✻ ✻

Dieter walked to the horses back at the woods at the ridgeline. From time to time, he looked at the card Max Huffman had given him. Max said he had passed the test. He'd been shot at and had shot back; he remembered his duties, and hadn't failed. Dieter held the card closer to his face. He'd show Greta when he got home tonight—and he would be home tonight. It could have been that he would not have been going home, a lesson Dieter vowed never to forget. He read the card again. It said, *Member. West Virginia Sheriff's Association. I'm a Deputy Sheriff—finally. Greta will be proud.*

✻ ✻ ✻

Dan Frost stood in the doorway of the Grantville police station watching his deputies ride toward him. They were quite a sight. All were mud-covered. Max Huffman rode slumped in the saddle, his face gray with weariness. Harley, Archie and Dieter displayed bandages on various parts of their bodies. Harley wore a bandage on the side of his face and neck with another on his upper right arm. Archie had a bandage that looked like a Kotex pad tied around one thigh. Dieter wore a bandage around his ribs, the bandage showing through a rent in his jacket.

They halted in front of Dan and dismounted slowly, all obviously in pain. "Well, well, look what the cat's drug in," Dan said. "Looks like you had a bit of a fight."

Harley looked at Dan for a moment before saying, "We caught the thieves in a farmhouse. Told them to come out. They didn't, so we went it after them. We left their bodies where they fell. The villagers can take care of them."

"Who were they?" Dan asked.

"Some out-of-work mercenaries. Appears they ran out of food and were starving, so they began stealing food to survive. I guess they figured they had a better chance taking us on than they would from the local folks," Harley answered. "I told the Rudolstadt watchman that someone had to know they were there. It was too close to Debra to be overlooked and the path to Debra and Rudolstadt was too worn for just the four outlaws. They had help."

"You're right. Well, you told him. We'll see what comes of it." Dan Frost replied. "For now, come in and get warm. There's coffee in the pot and you all look like you can use some. Besides, I have some news for you." He turned and stepped into the office and held the door open. "Go on back to my office. I want to talk to you before you all go see Doc Nichols."

"Will this take long, Dan? Vina's waiting for me," Harley asked.

"No not long. I'm coming to the potluck, too."

The four deputies walked inside. Dan closed the door and followed them down the hallway that led to his office. As Harley, Max, Archie, and Dieter entered the Chief's office, they saw Frank Jackson and Chuck Riddle, Grantville's and the NUS' Chief Judge, seated next to Dan's desk.

"We've been waiting for you boys," Frank said, "We've got a job offer for you." Judge Riddle nodded in agreement.

Harley had a sudden sinking feeling as he sat on a couch along the wall of the office. Max and Dieter joined him while Archie sat in a side chair next to the couch. They waited for Frank to continue. Max and

Archie looked guarded, as was he. Dieter looked puzzled and did not know what was about to happen.

"Did you clear up that problem for Rudolstadt?" Judge Riddle asked, speaking for the first time.

"Yes, they did," Dan Frost said before Harley replied. "All neat and tidy—no loose ends," meaning there were no survivors left to prey on people.

Frank noticed a small pool of blood collecting on the floor under Archie's chair. "Uhhh, Archie, you're bleeding on the Chief's floor."

Archie looked back at Frank with an expression of extreme irritation on his face. "F . . . ," he caught himself and said instead, "Up yours, Frank."

"Now Archie, keep control of yourself," Frank said with a smile. He turned toward Judge Riddle. "That should keep Rudolstadt happy."

Dan Frost had been pouring coffee while Frank Jackson and Judge Riddle were talking. He gave a mug to each deputy and said, "Jamaica Blue Mountain it ain't, but this is the real thing. I make one pot a week and this is the day for that one pot."

As the four held their mugs, the Judge spoke. "I have a problem. My jurisdiction will soon include all of Thuringia and Franconia not long after. Corruption is rampant, the legal system is inconsistent and its application is erratic. We've a petition from representatives of Franconia for help. They were referred to Dan Frost and me since the NUS has administrative authority in the region."

"Evidently, there are readers of up-time literature in Franconia and they've gotten some Louis L'Amour and Zane Grey westerns. They want us to establish a force like the Texas Rangers and the US Marshals. Some have seen some John Wayne films too—*True Grit* and *Cahill, US Marshal.*"

"We have limited resources—a few administrators here and there, and we've just started to understand the issues. *Shoot!* Just look at the mess that happened in Suhl. There is still a lot of potential trouble in that region that will keep our attention focused all across Franconia and Fulda, not to mention Bamberg is about to boil over."

"We need more of these folks on our side. If we can provide some stability, Thuringia and Franconia will become our base, our bastion for survival."

"There are other changes coming here in Grantville as well," Dan Frost said, interrupting Judge Riddle. "I'll be leaving by the end of the year—maybe sooner. There'll be a new Police Chief and Sheriff. Probably either Fred Jordan or Press Richards. Don't know which yet."

"We envision an organization, two organizations, really," Judge Riddle continued, "that will be a combination of the Texas Rangers and the US Marshal's service, to provide visible law and justice to the State of Thuringia and Franconia. The original Texas Rangers spent most of its time as a quasi-military force fighting the Comanches and border crossers from Mexico. It was later, after the Civil War, that they more law enforcement than militia. But that is what we need; a force to provide law and order, a mounted field force to patrol the territory, and judicial bailiffs—Marshals, to provide liaisons with the local governments, administrations and ruling aristocracies. An organization to do all the dirty little jobs that will arise, including criminal investigations."

"We know you boys are getting a little long in the tooth, and you still have Army commitments," Frank Jackson interjected, "except, of course, for you Dieter. We had planned to have you three continue as instructors and trainers for the military academies after you trained a few more drill instructors for the Army. But the more we looked at it; we realized there were younger men around in better shape that could do the job just as well. What we don't have are folks who can react to situations that the rules haven't covered. You three, and now you Dieter, are more like those old-time Marshals than anyone else around. We're not looking for a `one riot, one Ranger` hero. Just some folks who can take care of themselves when it gets down and dirty, and can train others to do the same."

"Just like you've done with Dieter, here," Dan Frost added.

"By the way," Harley said, "Dieter passed his test today. It's time to make him a full deputy."

Frost nodded, "Congratulations, Dieter."

"*Danke*," Dieter replied.

"So here's the deal," Judge Riddle said, continuing after Frost's interruption. "We're asking for the creation of a Marshal Service and a Mounted Constabulary—like the early Texas Rangers and Judge Isaac Parker's Marshals. I have my son Martin working up charters. When he and I are satisfied with it, Martin will take them to legislature for review, approval, and funding. We've been having some straw man meetings with some of the other down-timer representatives, and we think we can get it approved—later this year or early next year.

"I will head of the Marshal Service until we can find someone to take on the job full time. We have other folks in mind for the Mounted Constabulary. We want you to be marshals. When the time comes, you would be discharged from the army to accept a position in the Marshal Service. Your former army status will help with some of the local aristocracy. I want this organization to be one where anyone can call for justice, and, I want it to be a model that other states can use down the line."

"What if we turned you down?" Archie asked.

"Well," Dan Frost grinned and replied, "we hope you won't. But, if necessary, we can always draft you."

"Yeah!" Frank Jackson laughed. "Greetings! You have been selected by your friends and neighbors . . . "

Mike Watson

THE SECOND INTERVIEW

Suhl, June 6, 1636

After dinner at the Boar's Head Inn, the Mitchells agreed to another interview. "Come for dinner with us tomorrow," Marjorie asked the brother and sister. "You can meet the rest of our little family."

"*Danke, Frau Mitchell,*" Bloem said. "We'll be there. We plan to interview other up-timer residents while we're here."

"Good luck with that," Archie said. "Most of them are busier than we are."

Harley Thomas, Karl Mohn, and the two constabulary troopers left early the following morning, but not before Karl got an address for Maria D'Angelo. He asked permission from her and her brother if he'd allowed to write to Maria. Maria gave him permission. She didn't grant her brother the option of saying no. For Archie and Dieter, the day would be a court day, and both would be busy.

Maria D'Angelo and Thomas Bloem met Archie and Dieter at the courthouse the following evening and walked home with them. Suhl was not flat, like some parts of Thuringia. The route to the Mitchell-Issler home was uphill most of the way. Bloem and Maria D'Angelo were puffing when they arrived at Greta's bakery.

Greta opened the door for them as they approached and waved them inside. "I heard you on the porch. I can always tell when Archie gets home. Clump . . . clump . . . clump," she said, laughing.

Three customers remained in the bakery. Greta had a successful sales policy. Day-old bread was half-price. She limited the sale of the older bread to those greater in need. She knew who could afford full price and who could not.

Greta made her last sale. "How can you do that?" Maria D'Angelo asked, "Discount your day-old bread?" as the last customer left the bakery. "Your cost isn't less. You lose money."

"It's no secret," Greta replied. "It's what Marjorie calls *customer service*. That we do brings more walk-in customers. Most of our sales are to inns and larger residences in Suhl, regular customers who buy on a fixed schedule and amount. The continuing orders include pastries and other special items that are more profitable. Then there's market day. I never come home with anything on market day."

Marjorie appeared from the rear of the bakery. "Welcome! Archie, lock the door and we'll all go back to the dining room." She turned aside to ask Maria D'Angelo, "Do you like Italian food? I've made lasagna with garlic bread for dinner."

The down-time woman looked confused. "Ah, I've never been to Italy, but it sounds delicious. Garlic on bread?" she asked, following Marjorie down the hall.

"I'll check on Marta," Dieter said, and followed the women.

"After you," Archie said to Thomas Bloem. "Everyone will be here shortly."

❋ ❋ ❋

Archie, Dieter, Maria D'Angelo, and Thomas Bloem sat around the large dining table while Greta took little Marta, who had nodded off at the table in the middle of dinner, upstairs to bed. Marjorie, in the meantime, cleared the table. The diners finished the lasagna and the garlic bread.

Marjorie gave Maria her recipe. "It's wonderful! I would have never thought to add garlic to toasted, buttered bread."

Dieter came up from their cooler in the cellar, bringing a small keg of ale. "I've a friend, an innkeeper, brews the best ale in Suhl. I buy a half-barrel from him every month," Dieter said.

"And the innkeeper advertises his brew as Dieter's Favorite, a new brand," Archie added.

Thomas Bloem looked surprised. "Do you all have that much influence here? I'd think up-timers would have less the farther they are from Grantville."

Greta and Marjorie returned to the table and sat. With everyone seated, Thomas Bloem asked his first question. "If I've calculated correctly, an entire year passed from the fight with the outlaws near Rudolstadt, until the creation of the Marshals Service."

Archie scratched his chin, taking his time forming a response. "Yes, that's about right."

"Why so long?"

"That fight had a bigger physical impact on us—Max, Harley, and myself—than we'd thought. We all spent at least a month under Doc Nichols' care; when he was available. Max has arrhythmia, irregular heart rhythm. It had been under control with medication. He'd had surgery for it several years ago, before the Ring of Fire, but he still needed medication occasionally. He'd had an episode during the gunfight, but Doc Nichols got it running again as it should. Harley messed up his knee and spent a couple of months under PT—"

"PT?" Maria asked.

"Physical therapy. Special exercises to strengthen the muscles around his knee. Up-time, he'd have had surgery, but not here."

"And you?" she asked.

"Almost died," Marjorie answered. "The wound in his leg got infected from the water in the well that he used to clean the wound after the shootout."

"I don't remember everything Doc Nichols did on me for the first month," Archie said.

"He was feverish and delirious," Marjorie continued, "and had several surgeries to drain the infection. Doctor Nichols even used some of the reserved antibiotics to kill the infection."

"I didn't know that!" Archie said.

"The Powers that Be approved it."

"Huh. I remember him debriding the wound, removing scar tissue."

"That was later, Archie, but he couldn't get it all."

"And," Archie said, turning back to Bloem, "that's why I have a big knot in my leg from the bullet. Smarts at times."

Maria and Thomas sat quietly, taking notes while Archie and Marjorie talked. When the couple took a breath, Thomas asked, "Is that why you use a walking stick?"

"Yes, when I first came to Suhl with Dieter. Not so much now, but it came in handy after arrival."

"Really handy," Dieter said, speaking for the first time. "When we came here to Suhl, just Archie and me, we weren't exactly welcomed."

"No one knew why, nor for what reason, we were there. We weren't all that sure ourselves," Archie said. "It started with the badges . . . "

PART II: THE MARSHAL GOES TO SUHL

Early March, 1634

Judge Riddle sat behind his office desk. Harley Thomas, Dieter Issler, and Max Huffman were present, seated in well-padded side chairs. Archie Mitchell, however, was late.

Harley, Max and Archie had been discharged from the Army just three hours before. An hour after that, with their families watching, Judge Riddle swore Max, Harley, and Archie in as new SoTF Marshals, with Dieter sworn as a Deputy Marshal.

The day was bright with a light southern breeze that brought a warming hint of spring. Sunshine and its warmth, a welcome break to the cold of winter, had melted the season's last snow. Vina Thomas and Greta Issler had arraigned to have the ceremony on the Thomas' front lawn, followed by a small reception. They prepared a selection of light pastries, accompanied by a punch made from apple cider and ice cream. Frank

Jackson provided some unknown punch ingredient of approximately 100 proof.

The new officers were now in Judge Riddle's office. Everyone was present except Archie Mitchell.

Judge Riddle was about to ask Harley if he knew where Archie was when footsteps sounded in the hallway—footsteps that included the tinkle of jingle-bob spurs. The door opened and Archie Mitchell stepped into the office.

"Good God Almighty!" Judge Riddle exclaimed. "What the hell is that?"

Archie walked into the room and said, "Sorry I'm late." He wore Tony Lama boots with spurs, dark brown canvas pants, and a white shirt with an accompanying black string tie. Over the shirt was a five-button leather vest and on his head was a light gray Stetson hat. Around his waist was a wide leather belt and holster. On the right was a holster containing a Colt single-action .45 caliber revolver. A second Colt pistol, in a cross-draw configuration, rode on his left-front side. The pistol belt contained twenty-four large, fat cartridges in leather loops. Archie carried an oilskin coat called a *duster* over one arm and a cane in his other hand.

Judge Riddle glanced at Max and Harley. Max's face was turning red and his shoulders were shaking. Harley was not as constrained and was openly laughing—loudly.

Archie stepped up to the desk. "Since you've made me a marshal, I thought I'd wear my marshal's uniform."

Max spoke up, "That's Archie's SASS costume. He was a member of the Single Action Shooting Society up-time. They dressed up like that."

Riddle looked at Archie, his face turning red in anger. "Be very glad I'm not in Court. If I were, you'd be looking at five days for contempt." The judge was not sure if he was being mocked or not. "If I didn't need you—" He clamped his lips. "I'll overlook this . . . this time."

Archie's look of surprise and hurt finally convinced Judge Riddle that Archie's intent was innocent. Well, maybe not innocent, but at least not contemptible.

"Sit down, Archie and don't try my patience."

Archie sat.

After a moment to collect his thoughts, Judge Riddle said, "I have your badges here. I asked Morris Roth to design and make them. My initial thought was to make them from some silver dollars I had collected, but Morris convinced me that would only attract thieves. Morris got together with Ollie Reardon and made these. Ollie had some stainless steel and brass stock left over from some job. Morris designed these badges. I had in mind something like the Texas Ranger badge, a five-pointed star inside a circle. Morris had other ideas. He likes six-pointed stars," he said with a slight grin.

"Dieter, come here," said the Judge. "This is your badge. As a deputy, your badge is entirely stainless steel. Morris stamped your name, today's date, and the serial number on the back. Your badge is number four." Dieter stepped up, and Judge Riddle pinned the badge on his shirt.

"Max, Harley, and you, Archie, stand up," he said again. "The Marshal's badge, like Dieter's, is made of stainless steel. The difference is that the points of the star are brass, leaving the center as polished stainless steel. You are all equals as marshals, so we assigned the serial numbers in alphabetical order. Max, you have serial number one, Archie, you're number two and Harley is number three. Wear them in good health."

He pinned the badges to the three new marshals and motioned them to sit down. "After much discussion with the other Judges, Mike, Rebecca, and Frank, we decided, initially, to assign each of you marshals to some specific tasks as we build the larger service. Max, Doc Nichols doesn't want you to do much fieldwork for a while. Since you were a First Sergeant in the US Army, we believe you would be ideal as the Executive Officer of the Marshals' service."

Turning to Harley Thomas, he said, "Harley, we thought the best place for you would be the Marshal-in-Charge of training since you did most of the tactical training for the old Marion County Sheriff . . . among other duties yet to be assigned. You'll be in the field, too. Since you hurt your knee again, you're on medical leave until Doc Adams clears you for full duty."

Judge Riddle paused for a moment, looking at Archie and shaking his head slightly. "Archie, we had thought that you would be the best for the Marshal-in-Charge of Field Operations, of the district courts. I'm having some second thoughts after seeing you in that outfit, but the decision has been made. Don't disappoint me."

"Uhhh, yes . . . I mean no," Archie stammered, "I won't." *Perhaps dressing up wasn't such a good idea.*

"By the way, how's the leg?"

"Well, mostly, it's healed. Doc Nichols is being pessimistic, but he said it will get better if I continue with the PT." Archie had been wounded in the leg the previous spring and the wound had gotten infected, laying him up for months. The infection had caused some permanent muscle damage to his thigh and hip, hence the cane. He no longer needed it to walk, but he'd become attached to the cane. It was made of hickory, with an alloy, molded ball on one end and a steel cap on the other. It could be handy, he had decided—a knob-knocker his grandfather would have called it.

Nodding to Archie, Riddle agreed, "That's what Doc Nichols told me; you've been released for duty."

Judge Riddle continued, "Max, for the time being, I want you to set up an office down the hall. Your first task will be to build a Table of Organization and Equipment. All of us will be involved in that. Another first task will be recruitment."

Turning to Harley and Archie, he said, "Harley . . . don't go hurting that knee again! I know he deserved it, but next time, get someone else to kick that son of a bitch in the ass."

Judge Riddle paused and looked at Dieter. "You are the only Deputy Marshal available, at the moment, to take cases. Fortunately for us, everything's quiet at the moment."

Riddle looked at the quartet again before he continued. "Archie, I would like you and Dieter to go to Suhl and find a suitable place for a

Court. Suhl has been a thorn in our side since last year, so we think the first court should be there—establishing a presence of law and order, so to speak."

"The court system is still being designed; how many courts, how many Judges, their area of responsibility, all that. The current plan is each court will have a Presiding Judge who's in charge and two or three Associate Judges to help and take cases. You'll need to keep that in mind when you look for a courthouse. We're planning on placing a troop of Mounted Constabulary in Suhl as well, but that's not your concern once they're in place. They'll use the USE garrison barracks. It's been turned over to us. Check it out when you get there. Hire some people to clean it up and make any needed repairs. See if there is a site nearby for the court."

"How many constables will be in the troop?"

"Here is a copy of the proposed Table of Organization. It's still subject to change. Officially, it will be the 1st Mounted Constabulary Troop when it's all said and done."

Archie read the document. A headquarters platoon with one captain, a first sergeant, a line sergeant, plus a saddler, farrier, blacksmith, medical orderly and seven privates. The remaining two line platoons each contained forty-three men with a Lieutenant, two Squad Sergeants, two Corporals, a Trumpeter/Radio Operator, a medical orderly and thirty-six trooper constables.

"The troop will be larger than those that follow. It'll have to cover most of northern Thuringia, and Franconia. Some headquarters folks, like the blacksmith, farrier, and saddler, may be local people hired to fill just those functions," Riddle continued. "I would like you to spend some time with my son, Martin. He will go over everything with you and answer any questions you may have." Clearing his throat, Judge Riddle asked, "Do you think you could leave Monday for Suhl? That will give you nearly a week to get ready for the trip. A bailiff will arrive to take over the admin for the court in May."

"Yes, Sir," Archie replied. "Monday will be fine. Dieter?"

"That is fine with me, too."

"Well, that's it, everyone. Any questions? If not, then we're adjourned."

Early April 1634, Suhl

The sky was overcast as Dieter rode up to Archie's home trailing a packhorse. In front of the house was a light wagon with a horse already hitched and another horse tied to the rear. In the back of the wagon was a worn and cracked saddle, saddle bags and two of Archie's old footlockers. Marjorie Mitchell was standing on their porch, giving Archie a kiss and hug. They had been married over forty years and weren't used to being apart.

It was time to leave. "Bye, Marj. See you in a month?"

"'Bout that, I think. Be careful, Arch."

Archie nodded and carefully stepped down his front steps, using his cane to support his weakened leg. He used his cane in one hand and carried his lever-action Winchester rifle in his other.

"Where did you get this wagon, Archie? I've not seen one like it before." Dieter asked.

"I had it built in Saalfeld last year. It's called a buckboard. The wainwright built it from some pictures I had. A hundred years ago, Grantville time, these wagons were as common as automobiles were in the Twentieth Century."

"It doesn't appear too sturdy."

"It's not designed to carry heavy freight, just people and stuff like a small pickup truck. Plus, I can haul more stuff than using a packhorse. Doc Nichols suggested that I not ride a horse yet."

"What are you doing with that old saddle?"

"That was my grandfather's. He used to be a cowboy in Oklahoma before he married my grandmother. I've heard about a saddle maker in Suhl, and I'm going to have him make me a new one based on this design. I did some horse swapping last week and got a couple of good sturdy riding horses. This is mine," Archie said, pointing to the horse tied to the back of the wagon. "Marjorie's old saddle fits her roan, but mine, the pinto here, needs a new saddle. My old saddle doesn't fit."

✳ ✳ ✳

Dieter wasn't too familiar with horses or saddles. He just rode whatever was available. Archie's new horse was a mottled white and brown, a pinto, he had called it.

Archie had owned several horses before the Ring of Fire, but Dieter'd not thought much about it. Now that he'd seen the wagon, he could see how useful it could be. Maybe he should talk to Greta about a wagon and some horses? He was well paid as a Deputy Marshal. Perhaps they should invest some of that money?

"Dieter, why don't you put your gear in the back of the buckboard and tie your pack horse to it. It's forty-five miles, a two-day trip to Suhl. That'll free your hands if it becomes necessary."

Dieter did so. The pack-horse was to be his spare. Both of them had been assigned to him with his transfer to Suhl. Everything he and Archie needed for the trip, and until their wives arrived, was now carried in the wagon. He frankly stared at the footlockers and bags that Archie had loaded in the wagon.

Archie, seeing Dieter's expression, said, "One of those footlockers is full of ammo .45 Colt for my Winchester '73 and my revolvers, and .45ACP for my two Colt Commanders."

"I brought .45ACP and 12-gauge double-ought, too."

"Good, I've some 12-gauge; a mixture of double-ought and slugs. Ammo weighs a lot. That's why I want to take the buckboard—plus I can haul enough fodder for all our horses. Grazing won't be very good this time of year. Help me get this tarp over the bed and we'll be off."

Archie made sure the water-proof tarp covering the wagon bed would drain rainwater off the wagon bed before he climbed into the wagon. A thick pad covered the seat to provide more comfort than hard wood. The steel leaf springs under the seat helped soften the ride, but Archie wasn't going to complain. Marjorie made the pad using an old foam rubber camp mattress.

Once seated, he pushed the lever-action rifle against the front mudguard into a clip designed for that purpose next to his Winchester Model 1897 pump shotgun. "Let's get going." He released the brake and snapped the reins. As the wagon started off down the street, Dieter kicked his horse's flanks and caught up with the wagon to ride alongside.

✳ ✳ ✳

Marjorie watched Archie and Dieter leave, moving down the street toward Highway 250 and the road that would eventually take them to Suhl. She stood on the porch, watching, until the two turned the corner down the block and passed out of sight..

She gave a sigh and turned to Greta, who had been watching, too. "We have a lot of work to do to move two households to Suhl. Time to get busy."

Late April, 1634

Archie and Dieter arrived in Suhl in mid-afternoon. The sky had gotten darker and threatened rain. They'd been rained upon several times during the trip. Both wore their oilskin dusters and water-proofed hats to help shed the light rain. The caravan of wagons they had joined continued on into Franconia, leaving them at the gate.

After passing through the East Gate, Dieter and Archie separated. Dieter rode on to the inn where they would stay while Archie drove the wagon toward the saddler's shop.

Archie guided the buckboard through the streets toward the shop of Johann Zeitts. By prior agreement, he would leave the pinto with Zeitts to allow him to make the saddle that would fit the horse. The new saddle would cost about the equivalent of forty up-time dollars, he guessed, and the old cowboy saddle. *We'll haggle some.* Archie suspected Johann would get the better side of the deal with a template for a new style saddle. *I wonder if I could get a new saddle for Marjorie if I traded that old McClellan cavalry saddle?*

Johann Zeitts' shop was on the southern side of town. He had started life as a cobbler. In fact, his son, Hans, still worked as a cobbler in a corner of the shop. Johann had become a saddle-maker by accident. One of the leading members of the Suhl council wanted a new saddle, and Johann made a bid. Zeitts made saddles using techniques learned as a cobbler. His technique, using small brass nails and hand stitching, was new. Several competitors in the area were copying his methods, but Zeitts was more skilled. His business had grown, and he was able to acquire a combination shop and home for his wife, married elder son, Hans, and a younger son, Christian.

The wagon pull up in front of the shop and Hans, the middle Zeitts son, walked out to welcomed the marshal.

"My father isn't present at the moment," he said. "Please follow me. We have a stable in back." Hans led Archie with the wagon and horses through the gate into the fenced-in area behind the shop where a small stable was located. The stable had room for several horses, three already present.

Hans waited while Archie watered his two horses. "Your wagon and horses will be safe here while you meet with my father," he said. "My younger brother, Christian, normally takes care of the horses and the stable, but he's shoeing one at the moment. He's a farrier and journeyman blacksmith," Han explained.

Johann arrived after they finished with the horses. The elder Zeitts entered the front of the shop at the same moment Archie entered from the back, followed by Hans carrying an old saddle.

"*Wie Gehts, mein Herr! Guten Tag.* I'm Marshal Archie Mitchell from Grantville."

"Welcome, welcome, *Herr Marshal Mitchell.* I see you have arrived safely."

Why would I have not arrived safely? There's been no outlaws anywhere near here. The comment surprised him. He thought Suhl was mostly peaceful after the late unpleasantness with the gunsmiths and the CoC the previous year.

He dismissed the comment and followed Zeitts into the main workroom, where Hans placed the old saddle on a wooded trestle that could be adjusted to meet the size of different horses. Johann lifted the stirrups, examined the leather fenders, skirt, cantle, and seat.

"Hmmm," he muttered and flipped the saddle upside down on a nearby table to see the saddle's wooden tree, visible through holes in the rotten leather. He rubbed his chin and hummed again.

"Ja! Now I see the differences. It is like some Spanish designs."

"True," Archie agreed. "The design evolved from saddles used by Mexican vaqueros up-time and they had Spanish ancestors. It is a working design to allow a horseman to ride comfortably all day."

"Do you want any embellishments? Any silver?"

"No!" Archie chuckled, "I'm not rich. I just want a good working saddle . . . well, maybe a bit of leather tooling and embossing if it isn't too expensive."

"Very well." Johann seemed a bit disappointed.

"When could you give me an estimate for cost and delivery?"

"Oh, yes, uh, tomorrow? Noon?"

"Noon, it is. I'll be here. I've other business in Suhl, but I'll make a point of being here at noon or as close to it as I can."

"Would you be available for dinner tonight, *Herr Mitchell?*" Zeitts asked. "Our quarters are above the shop and I would like you to meet my wife and family."

"Thank you! I would be grateful, *Herr Zeitts,* but I'm not alone. Deputy Marshal Issler is with me."

"Bring him, too. We would like to have both of you. Besides, it does me honor to host the new marshal and his deputy."

Archie drove his buckboard back into town to the Boar's Head Inn, where Dieter waited. The State of Thuringia-Franconia had a contract with the innkeeper to house them, their horses, and gear until permanent quarters could be found. Noelle Murphy had arranged it before she left Suhl. The innkeeper, Otto Hersch, was being exceedingly helpful. He wanted them to remain at the inn as long as he could keep them. The SoTF was paying half again his current rate. More coins in his pocket.

Noelle had asked for a ground floor room explaining to the innkeeper the nature of Archie's injury. When Archie arrived, the innkeeper led him and Dieter to the rear to an area of the inn where three rooms awaited them.

It's a suite! Archie thought when he entered. The front room contained a desk, chairs, a table that could be used for conferences, a sideboard that appeared to be well stocked, and floor to waist-high cabinets. The innkeeper had built a strong-room in a small, windowless closet-like room for storage of their guns and ammo. It would also keep secure the coins that had been given to him for the purchase of the new SoTF courthouse, and other associated incidentals. Off the central room were two others made up as individual bedrooms. A door on one side of the central room led to the inn's bath, jakes, laundry, and an exit to the inn's stables in the rear. Noelle Murphy made an excellent choice when she chose this inn. He was surprised the innkeeper was so accommodating.

Otto Hersch appeared and asked for permission to take Archie's buckboard and horses to the rear stable. "My stable-boy will feed and groom your horses, *Herr Marshal Mitchell*. They will be in the stalls next to *Herr Deputy Marshal Issler*'s horses."

"*Danke, Mein Herr.* I appreciate your courtesy."

The innkeeper left.

"Nice place, Dieter," Harley said.

"*Ja.* He bowed to me when I arrived." Dieter chuckled. "I almost thought he was going to add a *Von und Su* to my name. I think he's glad to see us."

"I got the same impression from Johann Zeitts. It makes me curious. Everyone is glad to see us . . . wonder why."

"Perhaps I should wander around and listen to gossip? No one would think twice about me . . . at least for the next day or so until I become known."

"Start tomorrow . . . and dress like you live here." Dieter was dressed much like Archie: an oilskin duster, Western-style boots, pants, shirt, leather vest and a copy of Archie's Stetson hat—Archie's unofficial idea of a marshal's uniform. "Tonight, we have dinner invitations with Johann Zeitts and his family."

✳ ✳ ✳

Dusk was falling when Archie and Dieter arrived at the Zeitts' shop and home. Darkness came early this time of year. Johann Zeitts welcomed them and introduced his wife, Elizabeth, his son Hans and his wife, Lena, and the saddlemaker's younger son, Christian. Hans' and Lena's two small children were already in bed.

Johann and Elizabeth's ages were betrayed by their white hair, but both appeared to be quite fit. Hans and Lena were in their late twenties. Christian was several years younger.

Christian had the shoulders and grip of a blacksmith. Hans was slighter than his brother, although his hand was as calloused as that of the elder and younger Zeitts, Archie noticed.

"Welcome to our home," said Elizabeth. "We are very happy you accepted our invitation. Follow us, please."

She led them upstairs to the family area, a larger room than he'd expected, given the size of the building. Johann and Elizabeth had separate rooms for themselves. Christian had his room, and so did Hans and Lena. The rest of the upper floor was a common area for the entire family.

Dinner went well. Elizabeth and Lena had prepared a leg of roasted mutton, with bread-pudding for dessert. They were finishing dinner when, from the stables outside, they heard a scream from a horse. Everyone headed downstairs, led by Hans and Christian, who grabbed a lantern before leaving the shop. Hans saw two men in the stables standing next to one horse. One man held a knife.

Christian outran his older brother and yelled at the two intruders. One ran out of the stable into the darkness. The other, the one with the knife, was slower. Christian threw the lantern at him and it hit with an audible *clonk!* The man stumbled, dropped to his knees, and fell.

Dieter arrived next and rolled the man over. The lantern was heavy brass and the bloody dent in the man's temple caused by the lantern was clearly visible.

Christian ignored the other running man who had disappeared in the darkness. He ran into the stable to check the horses.

"He was trying to hamstring the horses!" he called, pointing to a slash on the leg of one of Zeitts' horses. Christian soothed the shivering horse and inspected the wound. "It's a deep cut, but I don't think any tendons are cut. May need stitches. I'll see in the morning when the light is better."

Dieter checked the other horses. "The rest appear to be all right. I don't see any wounds."

Archie and Johann were the last to arrive. Hans picked up the lantern, relit it, and held it close to the face of the body. He, like Christian, who was vomiting next to the stable after seeing the damage to the intruder's skull, appeared to be shocked.

"Christian clearly did not intend to kill him," Archie said to Johann, "just stop him from hurting the horses."

"*Danke*," the elder Zeitts said. "Will the watch believe that?"

"With a SoTF Marshal and Deputy Marshal as witnesses? Yes," Archie assured him. "You know him?"

"No," replied Johann, looking at the body.

"Nor I," added Hans.

Christian, wiped his mouth, spit, and looked closely at the body. "He's one of Achen's men. I've seen him around."

"Who is Achen?" Dieter asked.

"He's . . . well . . . I . . . ," Christian hesitated to say more.

"Friedrich Achen," Johann began, "is . . . uh . . . a . . . he calls himself a businessman. He has what he calls 'a private security firm.' You pay him a fee and he guards your home and business."

"If you don't, things happen," Christian explained.

"His men came around wanting me to sign up for their protection," Johann said. "I refused. That is what the watch is supposed to do."

"Except the watch is seldom seen after dark," said Hans.

"It isn't seen much during the day, either," Christian added.

Archie nodded. *The old protection racket.* He hadn't expected to see it here, in this time, but there was no reason it shouldn't have occurred to someone.

"Did you report it?" Dieter asked.

"No. Why? It isn't illegal." Johann replied.

"It is if it includes intimidation and extortion."

"What do we do with the body until the watch comes?" Archie asked?.

"Leave him there," Christian said. "The watch will show up, eventually."

"Okay," Archie agreed. "Be sure it's reported in the morning if they don't come tonight."

❋ ❋ ❋

Dieter Issler rose early the next morning. The sky was gray just before dawn. He dressed as a down-timer, hiding his pistol inside his knee-length coat. His wide-brimmed hat would not draw attention. His boots were of up-time design, but many USE and National Guard veterans wore similar boots. They'd not draw attention.

He left the inn and headed toward the river-side gate, not the one they had passed through yesterday. He was curious if it was manned at this time of the morning. Some cities in the SoTF had become complacent and failed to keep their gates guarded. As he walked, he kept an eye out for anyone about to dump their night-soil. He didn't want to get splashed.

* * *

Archie, having finished an early breakfast, had one of his Colt Commander pistols disassembled on a large cloth on the table when the innkeeper announced a visitor. "*Herr Marshal, Bürgermeister Feld* would like to see you."

"Send him in," Archie said, rising to greet the Bürgermeister.

"*Guten Tag, Herr Marshal.*"

"And to you, too, *Herr Bürgermeister.* I'm glad to see you. I had planned to see you later this morning, but now will do," Archie said. "Please sit. Excuse the mess. I like to clean my weapons after they've gotten wet. It rained often on our way here."

Feld glanced at the pieces of the pistol, a collection of small, finely machined pieces of a Model 1911 pistol, laid out neatly on the thick cloth. "Ruben Blumroder would like to get his hands on that."

"Ruben Blumroder?"

"He is the . . . guildmaster . . . no, that's not correct, there is no guild here. He's the informal leader of Suhl's gunsmiths and our representative to the new SoTF legislature. Ruben is quite influential."

"I wouldn't object if he wanted to examine it. The pistol is easy to copy, the springs aside. It's the ammunition that is difficult. How did you know I was here?"

"Word gets around. The militia guard on the gate sent word that you had arrived. *Fraulein Murphy* said you were coming, but we didn't know when."

"Well, it isn't any secret. My deputy and I are here to secure a site for the new SoTF District Court."

"Court?"

Feld appeared to be surprised, Archie noted. "Yes. It will provide justice and legal services for the district—administer SoTF law. The judges will report to Judge Riddle, the Chief Justice of the SoTF Supreme Court." Archie removed a wax-sealed envelope with Judge Riddle's official court seal, from his saddle bag on the floor.. "I have a letter for you and for the city council."

Feld took the envelope and read that it was addressed to him and to the Suhl council. He weighed it in his hand and appeared to be impressed. The envelope was heavy paper.

Feld looked up to see Archie watching him. "Should I open it now?" he asked hesitantly.

"If you wish . . . as soon as you sign this receipt," Archie replied, extending a form letter and pen to Feld.

Feld looked at the receipt as if it were a serpent. After a silent moment, he reached for it and signed with Archie's pen.

"Thank you, *Herr Bürgermeister*," Archie said, slipping the receipt into his saddlebag. "I've already given you an overview of its contents," Archie said, nodding toward the envelope in Feld's hand.

"I suppose our . . . difficulty last year is why the court is being established here."

"I wouldn't know. There are difficulties in Franconia and I assume the Mounted Constabulary will be sending many patrols there."

"They won't stay here?" Feld said with alarm.

"Some will always be here, the headquarters and support troops, but most of the troopers will patrol the main roads and areas away from the larger cities."

"We don't have many watchmen. The militia guards the gates and the city wall."

"That reminds me. I noticed the militia on my arrival. Who is the Wachtmeister? There was an incident last night. A man tried to hamstring some horses and was killed during the commission of the crime."

"Crime! Uh, we don't have much crime. *Herr Heinrich Buch*, one of our council members, oversees the watch and represents them, among others, in the council."

"How many watchmen do you have?"

"I'm not sure of the actual number. *Herr Buch* is the *de jacto* Wachtmeister. I think they're thirty-five or forty."

"That's all?"

"Well. the militia protects the city. The gunsmiths take care of their part of Suhl, and the rest of Suhl is quiet. There have been no complaints, and the cost . . . is . . . expensive."

"Suhl looks to be prosperous. You shouldn't have any difficulty raising the funds to add more."

"There are . . . concerns."

Archie watched the Bürgermeister sitting across from him. The situation wasn't new. Cities always seem to shortchange their safety, whether external or internal, especially when there was no danger on the horizon. "Neither the SoTF court, the Marshals' Service, nor the Mounted Constabulary are responsible for running Suhl. You are. It's up to you and the council."

"Yes, yes, we know. We didn't know about the Court coming. All we knew was the rumor about the Mounted Constabulary. We thought . . ."

Archie said nothing. He now understood why he and Dieter were being welcomed so enthusiastically. "My deputy and I work for the Court, and answer to them. Suhl is your responsibility. I would suggest you and the city council review your needs. I believe you have some. That said, to whom should I report the incident?"

"Oh! Well, *Herr Buch*, I suppose. We rarely have anything untoward reported."

"Very well. I'll pay him a visit. By the way, would you suggest someone I could see about what is available for a courthouse? The Constabulary will use the former USE barracks."

Feld seemed startled at that last piece of information. "I'll check with the council. One of them should know. I'll ask them to see you."

"Good, good. I appreciate your help."

Feld glanced at Archie, looked down at the envelope still in his hand, and nodded. "I'll present this to the council," he said, rising. "*Guten Tag, Herr Marshal.*"

"*Guten Tag, Herr Bürgermeister.*"

* * *

Dieter found the river-side gate manned by a very young militiaman, an apprentice of a local gunsmith, he discovered. The youngster had a blue cloth tied around his sleeve, and he was watching a farmer pass through the gate in an ox-drawn cart. The gate-guard was unarmed as far as Dieter could see. He was just standing at the side of the gate, watching people come and go.

After a brief conversation, Dieter discovered the name of the inn favored by the journeymen and master gunsmiths, *Das Matchlock. Useful information if we want to meet with them.*

He watched the early morning traffic while continuing to surreptitiously interrogate the gate-guard. A journeyman gunsmith arrived to check on the guard and, when finding nothing unusual, left to check another guard.

As least the guards are organized. I'll check the cavalry barracks next. Without doubt, the barracks would need minor repairs; being unused over the winter.

* * *

After Feld left, it was time for Archie to visit Johann Zeitts. He shifted in his chair, groaning lightly. The hard wooden chair in their quarter's central room made his hip ache. He hadn't slept well the previous night; the bed was a simple pallet on a wooden frame. His sixtieth birthday was coming up, and he seemed to feel every one of those years.

God, I miss the 20th Century. Marjorie was bringing some of their furniture when she and Greta comes to Suhl. He hoped she could bring his recliner. Hard beds made him restless and cost him sleep. Sleeping on the ground these last couple of travelling days, hadn't helped, either. It seemed, more and more often, the only time he could sleep well was in his recliner.

The innkeeper's wife cleaned up the remnants of breakfast and swept the floor, and the hallway leading to the stable. Archie made a mental note to tip her for her care and efforts.

Archie reassembled the Colt Commander, inserted a loaded magazine, chambered a round, and set the safety before slipping it into his shoulder-holster. The other Colt Commander was already on his belt. Rising from the table, he picked up his hat and walked through the inn's common room and out the front door. Archie hadn't taken but a few steps out of the inn before he saw a familiar face.

"Hi, Archie. How are ya?" Anse Hatfield asked. "I heard you were in town so I came over to visit."

"Anse! Good to see you. It's been, what, a year or more since we last met?"

"Yeah, 'bout that. It's good to see a familiar up-time face."

"I was just going out. I have an appointment."

"That's okay, I'll come along if that's all right? We can talk along the way."

* * *

Dieter approached the former USE barracks and was surprised to see several workers on the site. They appeared to be tearing down the palisade walls. He walked up to the one who seemed to be in charge. "What's going on?" Dieter asked,

"None of your business," the man said.

"I'm Deputy Marshal Issler.," Dieter said exposing his badge. "That is SoTF property and soon to be the barracks of the Mounted Constabulary troop that will arrive shortly. That makes it my business."

"Don't know anything about that. I was told to tear down the walls, and that's what I'm going to do."

"Who's your boss."

59

"That's none of your business, either. Now go or we'll make you go."

Dieter saw he was outnumbered by six to one. He'd better pass this to Archie. "I'll be back. I strongly suggest you have your boss here when I return."

✻ ✻ ✻

" . . . Noelle Murphy left a few days ago," Anse Hatfield said. "I've been recalled, and I'll be leaving in a few days to rejoin the army with my folks. There won't many up-timers here after that, just Pat Johnson, the Reardons, Gary and Gaylynn, and maybe one or two others."

"Marjorie is coming in a few weeks along with Dieter's wife, Greta. I don't think there will be any more up-timers coming here after she arrives."

"I plan on coming back," Anse said. "I like it here . . . and I've found someone."

"Oh? Local lady?"

"Well, yes, and no. She's a down-timer, but not from here, originally."

They reached the street that would lead to the Zeitts' saddlery. Archie glanced at his friend walking next to him. "You just didn't come to see me because we're old friends, Anse. What's on your mind?"

"There's a problem here, a gang," he said, looking down to side-step some manure in the street. "I thought I had a handle on it, but now I'm leaving, my detachment and the other army folks, too." Anse looked back up, "I wanted to fill you in and ask if you'd look into it."

"A gang that's running a protection and extortion racket?"

"Yeah, among other things."

"I've heard. I met some of them last night. They were trying to cripple a horse, and I understand they were Achen's men. Who is this Achen?"

"I don't know too much. I've heard that he's the new son-in-law of one of the city councilmen. They don't try much in my part of town, but they work the rest of Suhl and outside the gates. The watch never seems to be around when something happens. When they finally show up, they do little. They catch no one and things just seem to get worse. It's getting so that it's not safe on the streets after dark."

They turned onto an uphill street. Archie leaned on his cane more often; the pain in his leg had increased. "I thought the Jaegers were helping to take care of things?"

"Only in our part of town and most of them are gone."

"That's twice you've said, *my part of town*. What do you mean?"

"Where the gunsmiths are, their shops and homes. After the, ah, incident last year, they've kept the peace in their area. The city council is supposed to handle the rest of town. They don't. They think the militia is enough . . . you can't keep the peace by manning the walls and gates with unarmed boys."

"And the watch?"

"They seem more interested in patrolling the 'better' parts of town. The homes and businesses of the council members and the like."

"I met *Bürgermeister Feld* this morning. He said they only have thirty-five to forty watchmen for the whole town."

"I know. It's one problem Suhl has. Saves them money, don' cha know. I'm surprised the council hasn't called for help. I've heard rumors they are deadlocked on that. They need about seventy-five to a hundred men if they are to have good day and night patrols," Anse said. "They think the militia will fill in for their lack of watchmen. The militia has to provide their own weapons, and most militia members work for the gunsmiths and their families."

"Where have I heard this before?"

"Yeah. Almost like old times."

"Dieter Issler is my deputy—do you know him?"

"No . . . don't think I do."

"He's out scouting the town, getting a feel of the place. Before you leave, I'd appreciate it if you'd have a talk with Pat and Gary, ask them to keep their ears open, and give us a holler if they hear anything we should know."

"I can do that. I'm glad Pat and Gary aren't in the army," Anse said, slowing to match Archie's pace. "I don't really want to go but I don't have a choice."

"They kicked me, Max Huffman and Harley Thomas, out and made us marshals. Frankly, I'm glad I'm not in anymore."

They were approaching the saddlery. "I better get back," Anse said. "I'll drop by again before I leave."

"Thanks, Anse, I appreciate it."

* * *

Ruben Blumroder looked up from his workbench when Anse Hatfield walked through the door. "Did you meet him?"

"Yep. I think ol' Arch will do. He asked me about Achen before I brought it up. He's already put out feelers gathering information."

"Tell me about him."

"Archie's hard to describe. He's a SoTF Marshal now. Up-time, he'd been a deputy sheriff, an army vet—up-time, not just here—plus, he's a combat vet, too."

"What's he like?"

"Well, like many up-timers, Archie has some . . . eccentricities. He has always been a cowboy fan. Have you heard about Westerns?"

"*Ja,* but I don't think I understand."

"Westerns are stories about the American West in the 19th Century— the American Frontier. Archie lives it. Up-time he was a member of a group that had action shooting matches using old-style weapons— revolvers, rifles, usually lever-action, double-barreled shotguns, weapons that were common in the 19th century. They had shooting matches, some even shooting from horseback, and they dressed up in costumes like those from the Old West. Archie lives it. He even dresses like it."

"Is he crazy?"

"No. Absolutely not. But, when we arrived here in the middle of what we called the Thirty Years war, it was a shock. People reacted differently.

Some did well, some did not. The Ring of Fire affected everyone in some form or another. Living as a real Old West Marshal is Archie's way of coping—but don't doubt his competency. That would be a mistake. His, uh, eccentricity aside, he's a tough lawman."

"Good! That makes me feel better, we need someone like that."

"I think Archie will do."

"I have a meeting tonight with some of the other craftmasters. I'll tell them about our new marshal."

❊ ❊ ❊

"*Guten Tag, Herr Zeitts,*" Archie said as he entered Zeitts' workshop.

"*Guten Tag, Herr Marshal.*"

"Well, what do you think?" Archie said, pointing to the disassembled saddle on Zeitts' workbench.

"I can do it," Zeitts affirmed.

When the haggling was over, Zeitts and Archie had an agreement. Zeitts would finish the saddle in two weeks unless there was an unforeseen circumstance to delay delivery.

Archie and Johann Zeitts were shaking hands on the deal when Christian Zeitts entered the workshop with the help of his brother. He was badly beaten, with one blackened eye almost closed.

"What happened?" Johann asked, rushing to Christian's side.

"Achen's men caught him outside. They were looking for their man who didn't come home last night. It was their two on Christian until I arrived."

"Where are they?" Archie asked, referring to Achen's men. "Are they still around?"

"They ran up the street. I don't know where. Don't go after them," Han said, "they outnumber you."

"I think I can handle them." Archie said, leaving the shop. Outside, he surveyed the scene. Zeitts' shop was next to the city's wall. A ring road ran parallel to the wall, with homes and shops lining the cobblestoned

63

street. Several people were out walking along the street, but none appeared to watching Zeitts' shop.

"They ran that way," Hans said pointing to the left. The street ended several hundred yards away where it met another that led to the eastern gate.

"*Danke*. Tell your father I'll look into this." With that, he stepped into the street and proceeded in search of Christian's assailants.

The buildings on the left side of the street abutted the city wall, but did not touch it. There was a ten-yard separation between the wall and the buildings. This gap provided space for wall maintenance and easy access in time of need. The right side of the street was like that of the left, with narrow alleys appearing from time to time giving access to another alley to the rear.

I need a map. This place is a maze. You could hide an army in these alleys and no one would know.

Archie reached the intersection, seeing no one or anything suspicious. He had stopped a few passers-by asking if they had seen two men running down the street and no one had . . . or at least would not admit that they had. That was the problem with a gang. They intimidated people. Individually, people like Zeitts' family were at the gang's mercy. If they united, the gang would be ineffective and would soon be removed or would leave for easier pickings.

Leaning on his cane, Archie headed back to the Boar's Head Inn. He'd not had any lunch, and he was getting hungry.

After a late lunch, he visited Ruben Blumroder. He seemed to be the actual leader of Suhl. Maybe Blumroder would have more information.

❇ ❇ ❇

Achen's two men watched the Marshal walk past the alley where they had hidden themselves. Their boss would not be pleased with their failure to extract information from the younger Zeitts.

Friedrich Achen sat in a corner of the taproom in *Der Bulle und Bär*, his favorite inn, when his two men entered. They walked over to his table and sat.

"What did you find?" he asked.

"Nothing. We were interrupted. Zeitts' brother and some neighbors came before we had the younger one softened up. The new marshal was there, too, so we left."

"Conrad's dead," Achen said. "One of the Zeitts, maybe the marshal, killed him."

"How did you know?"

"Feld told my father-in-law who told me. Also, the other marshal, the deputy, was nosing around the barracks. He told the men to stop working. They refused, but the deputy said he would be back, with the marshal, to stop them."

"Shall we be there, too? Together we would have enough to take both of them."

Achen thought the suggestion over. "Do so. Keep watch. When the workers refuse, join them and overwhelm the marshals. Don't let either get away."

"You want them dead?"

"No, not yet. I need to know why they're here."

"Your Father-in-law doesn't know?"

"He says not. I'm not sure I believe him."

"We'll find out. The Marshal doesn't look all that strong. He uses a cane."

"Go. Wait for them as long as it takes."

✷ ✷ ✷

After following the directions garnered from several people, Archie arrived at Ruben Blumroder's shop, that was on the same street as was Pat Johnson's US Waffenfabrik. A shot echoed from the rear of the shop. Instead of entering the shop's front, Archie walked down the adjacent alley to the rear, where he found Blumroder and a couple of men testing long arms.

Archie stood watching them load the long guns with patched balls. Rifles, he assumed. The target, a wooden board attached to a large square post, was filled with bullet-holes.

Bam! one man fired the rifle, which produced a cloud of white smoke. The rifle produced significant recoil.

"*Guten Tag!*" Archie called, as another shooter stepped forward to the line.

Ruben Blumroder, at least that is whom Archie assumed the older man was, appeared startled when Archie called. He turned his head swiftly and gave Archie a quick inspection. The older man stepped away to walk toward his visitor. The other two ignored Archie's interruption.

"*Herr Marshal Mitchell*, I presume?"

"The same. I assume you are *Herr Ruben Blumroder*?"

"The same," he said with a grin. "I was going to visit you when I had some time. *Herr Hatfield* told me you arrived yesterday. And here you are. What is the occasion for your visit?"

"I don't want to interrupt your work, but I would like to talk with you about Suhl. I understand you will be the city's representative to the SoTF legislature."

"*Ja*, that's so. The craftmasters and their people elected me. We outvoted our opponents."

"The craftmasters were able to control fifty percent of the votes?"

"Not alone . . . but with some other allies, we did."

"Politics?"

"Politics," he confirmed. "Come, let us go inside. I have some cider in a cooler that I've been thinking about all day."

Archie chuckled and followed Blumroder into the rear of his shop. Inside the door, he let his eyes become accustomed to the gloom of the unlit room. The sole light source was the open door and two windows facing the alley. To one side of the room were three rifling machines next to a small forge used to make small metal pieces that would eventually become parts of the rifle's lock.

Blumroder walked down the aisle, stopped at a table where rifles and long arms were assembled. He picked up a rifle and handed it to Archie. "This is a copy, as best we can determine, of your Kentucky rifle. It's .50 caliber. Pat Johnson had a . . . magazine? . . . catalog? . . . that had an exploded view of this rifle. We created our molds from that and refined the final product to be this rifle."

To Archie, it appeared to be very much like a flintlock Kentucky rifle he had once fired. The smooth honey-colored wooden stock, forearm and ramrod were expertly finished and varnished with fine checkering at the grip behind the trigger and at two points along the sides of the forearm. The brass side-plates and patch-box were polished to a mirror-sheen that brought out details of an engraved hunting scene. Archie hefted the rifle and found it to be perfectly balanced. "A fine piece of work," he told Blumroder.

"*Danke*. It is intended as a gift for the Landgrave of Hesse-Kassel. A working rifle, not some pretty piece that will never be fired. I can't say who ordered it, but the commission was very welcome."

"I repeat, a very fine piece of work."

"A man who knows his weapons, I see."

"Of necessity. A reliable, accurate firearm can mean life or death. A man can be known by his weapons. I'm used to mine."

"If I may ask . . . "

Archie chuckled. "I've nothing fancy. He pulled his duster aside to reveal a Colt Commander in a belt holster, then pulled the other side of the duster open to reveal a second Colt Commander in a shoulder holster.

"Ah, yes, the Colt Model 1911A1. Anse Hatfield carries one."

"Almost, this is the Commander version," he said pointing to this two pistols. "The 1911 has a five inch barrel, the Commander a four and one-half inch barrel. It's not much shorter but it can make a difference if you have to draw quickly."

Blumroder walked into the shop where he had an office—a side room from a larger space where his apprentices and journeymen worked small pieces of metal to insure they fit exactly into molds. This was the current method of standardizing parts. It worked well enough and helped keep parts interchangeable, more or less. Using molds wasn't as precise as using a milling machine but would do until those tools became available.

After they had seated, Blumroder asked, "What can I do for you, Marshal?"

"I came mainly to introduce myself. Anse Hatfield, whom I've known for years, paid me a visit this morning. He mentioned you were one of the city leaders. I've found it's best to know the PTBs."

"Excuse me, *Herr Marshal*, PTBs?"

"Powers That Be. Folks like *Herr Feld*—and you. I keep forgetting few here know all out language foibles."

Blumroder chuckled. "I'm not in the same category as *Herr Feld*. I'm just a local craftmaster."

"Who effectively controls at least a third of the city."

"Um, uh, well, yes."

"And is the recently elected member to the new SoTF legislature."

"True, as well."

"I think that qualifies you as being one of the PTBs, don't you, *Herr Blumroder*?"

"Anse said you were different, *Herr Marshal*."

"Just call me Archie, if you would."

"Very well . . . Archie, and please call me Ruben."

"Thank you, Ruben."

"Now, what can I do for you, Archie?"

"Information, really. Anse alluded to some troubles here in Suhl—different from last year. A gang, he said."

"Yes, Friedrich Achen. He arrived a year ago and married the daughter of Heinrich Buch, one of the city council members. No one seems to know from where he came. He has, as Anse has said, no visible means of support. Achen hangs out at the *Der Bulle und Bär*, one of our more disreputable inns. He has a gang that extorts money from the shop-keepers, selling protection. The watch—the city council—has done little to curtail Achen's activities. It's not our, the militia's, responsibility, either. Achen knows better than to bother us."

"Your militia?"

"The city's militia. However, we, the gunsmiths and the remaining Jaegers, are the largest contingent of the militia. The Jaegers answer to us . . . me . . . for the moment. Patrolling is not a responsibility I—we—want. It's been thrust upon us. We ensure our people are safe. That's all we can do."

"I see. It's not my responsibility, either. But, like you said, sometimes it's thrust upon us."

"Have you met the council yet?"

"I met with *Herr Feld* this morning. He arrived on my doorstep bright and early. I had some documents for him—for the council and gave them to him. The SoTF will establish a district court here in Suhl. I'm here to find a suitable building for the court. The SoTF will also station here a troop of the Mounted Constabulary in the USE barracks."

"I suspect the documents may disappear if he doesn't like their contents."

"I don't think so. He signed a receipt . . . and I have copies."

"I see *Herr Feld*'s reputation has gone before him."

"Don't know about that. It just a standard precaution."

"I wouldn't wait to meet the council, Archie. I've been told there are workmen dismantling the barracks. If you don't lay claim, there may be no barracks, shortly."

Archie sat silent for a moment. "*Danke*, Ruben. I'll get on that."

"I have a meeting tonight with other gunsmiths and craft masters. If you don't mind, I'll tell them about the new Court and the Mounted Constabulary."

"Feel free. It's no secret."

"Thank you for coming, Archie, but if you don't mind, I have some apprentices to oversee. Some need to be constantly supervised."

Archie chuckled. "I understand, Ruben. That is true even up-time. *Guten Tag.*"

"*Guten Tag*, Archie."

* * *

Dieter arrived at the Boar's Head Inn in time to see Archie enter before him. "Archie!" he called. "We've a problem."

Archie turned at the entrance to their rooms and asked, "The barracks?"

"*Ja.* It's being torn down."

"I know. Ruben Blumroder told me. He's the head of Suhl's gunsmiths and would be the *guildmeister* if there was one."

"I told them to stop, but they refused and there were six of them to my one."

"Get your gear. Let's pay them a visit."

Dieter disappeared into his room to reappear a few minutes later dressed much like Archie—boots, canvas pants, white shirt and badge, leather vest, gunbelt, shotgun on a sling, and covering all, his duster. "I'm ready. Let's go."

They arrived at the barracks a half hour later. "There they are. That one," Dieter said, pointing to a man in a leather coat watching the others, "is the leader." To one side were two other men leaning against a partially dismantled palisade wall.

Archie walked up to the man in the leather coat. "Are you the boss of these men?"

"I'm their overseer. So what?"

"Then I'm ordering you to stop work and leave—immediately."

"I don't take orders from you."

"You do now. That's SoTF property, and it's my responsibility. I have my authority here," he said, exposing his badge.

The man turned and yelled to the other workers, "Get them!" and drew a large knife from under his coat.

Archie stepped back, shifted his grip on his cane and swung, knocking the knife from the overseer's hand. He slide his hand down the shaft to the other end of the cane, and on the backstroke hit the overseer's forearm with the cane's alloy head breaking both lower arm bones. The overseer shrieked at the sudden surge of pain.

Archie heard a click behind him. Dieter had switched off the safety of his shotgun that had been unseen under his duster. He had it leveled at the rest of the workmen. From the corner of his vision, Archie saw the two *leaners* running toward him. He turned and punched one in the stomach with the steel foot of his cane. That one bent double from the punch, blocking the path of the other, and fell to the ground in a huddle. By the time the last attacker stepped around the first, the cane's alloy head was swinging toward the attacker's jaw. It hit with a crunch, and both attackers were out of action and on the ground.

The fight was over. Two men on the ground. One standing clutching a broken arm and five others with hands up, eying the muzzle of Dieter's shotgun. Archie was panting and wheezing. *I'm outta shape.*

"Do you know if Suhl has a jail, Dieter?" he asked between pants.

"No."

"I don't either. Let's tie their hands and march 'em to Ruben Blumroder's place. I think he'll have a place to put them, or tell us where's the jail."

Archie only had one pair of steel handcuffs. Instead of handcuffs, he and Dieter carried rawhide thongs. Between the two of them, they had enough to restrain the six men still standing.

"Archie, I think this one is dead."

Turning to Dieter and then looking at the man on the ground, he said, "Well, crap."

Archie checked to two on the ground. The first one, the one he'd punched with the steel foot of his cane, was dead. He open the man's shirt to reveal a purple splotch covering most of his stomach. The cane must have ruptured some internal organ, and the man had hemorrhaged to death. Checking the second man, Archie found him dead, too. The alloy head of the cane had impacted the hinge of his jaw, caving in the side of his skull. *Hit him too hard. I need to practice with this cane more often.*

"Dieter, take the boss man's coat and cover these two. We'll send someone for 'em later."

❊ ❊ ❊

Anse Hatfield was standing in the doorway of Ruben Blumroder's shop when he saw Archie and Dieter approaching with their prisoners. "*Ruben!*" he yelled. The urgency in Hatfield's voice brought Blumroder to the front of the shop.

"Archie's been busy," Anse said, "Told you so."

"Ruben, do you have somewhere to stash these folks?" Arched asked when they reached the doorway.

"I could find a place, a storeroom I suppose."

"Neither Dieter nor I know if Suhl has a jail. I assume there is one?"

"Yes, below the council chambers in the Rathaus. I don't think it's been used much, not since last year."

"I don't think that jail would be the best place just now. Can you keep these people out of sight for a while? Week, maybe, until the mobile constabulary arrives."

"I can do that."

"Good. Dieter, go with them and get our cuffs back. I think we're going to need them."

Blumroder spoke briefly with one of his journeymen. He and a couple of apprentices armed themselves with pistols and marched the six down the street.

Archie sighed. "There are two dead men at the barracks, Ruben. I hate to ask, but could you send someone to get them?"

"What happened?"

"They were waiting for us. The one with the broken arm was the crew boss of the ones tearing down the barracks. He refused to stop work and drew a knife on me. I have a sneaking suspicion the two deaders may have been a couple of Achen's men. While Dieter and I were taking care of the workmen, those two joined the fight. They rushed me and I got careless. I hit them too hard with my cane."

Ruben eyebrows rose. "You killed them with a cane?"

"Unintentionally. I hit one too hard in the head with this," he said raising the cane to reveal the round alloy knob, "and punched the other too hard with this," pointing to the steel capped foot of the cane. "They got too close to me. I had to use what I had; I was rushed."

Ruben nodded. "I understand."

"Does Suhl really have a watch? I've been here two days, and I have seen none yet."

"They do, but I don't know their patrol schedules. They don't come here because we take care of ourselves. The council has not asked the militia for help. Truthfully, I haven't paid much attention, The watch rarely comes around here."

"I'm thinking it, the watch, should be rebuilt from scratch with a professional wachtmeister who can properly train, organize and lead the watchmen. The only ones I've seen on watch are your militiamen at the gates."

"There are some on the walls, too."

"Guess I didn't look hard enough," he paused, a thought occurred. "While I'm here, I need someone to help me survey the barracks and see how much damage has been done. I'll need to hire some workmen to fix it up, repair any damages, and ready the place for the constabulary troop.

"I'll speak with some of the other craft masters. It's about time for our weekly meeting. I'll ask them to send you a man or two—tomorrow?"

"*Danke*, that'll do. Tell them we're staying at the Boar's Head Inn. If I'm not there, Dieter Issler, my deputy, will. Feld will arrange a meeting for me with the council sometime tomorrow."

* * *

A messenger from *Bürgermeister Feld* arrived early the next morning. The council would meet with him in a couple of hours. Archie sent a messenger to Anse Hatfield and asked him to come to the meeting. Anse knew, at least by reputation, many of the council members.

Archie would have preferred Ruben Blumroder there, too. But that would appear to be too much political favoritism, Ruben being a SoTF official. If he needed a local representative, it would not surprise them for Archie to have Anse standing next to them. These folks understood family ties. As up-timers, they viewed Archie and Anse to be kith, if not kin.

Ruben had been good at his word. A master carpenter arrived early. He and Archie discussed the issue with the barracks. "*Herr Heinrich Buch* owns the barracks property," the carpenter said. "I heard he bought it from the council. He said he planned to build a warehouse on the site. It is prime property."

"I'm going to find out about that. It wasn't the council's property to sell. It belonged to the USE, and they transferred ownership to the SoTF."

"I only know what I've been told."

"Is that going to be a problem with you? *Herr Buch* claiming it?"

"*Nein*. You said you would pay for the survey. It's guilders in my pocket either way."

"How long will you need for the survey? A day? Less?"

"Not a day. A couple of hours at least."

"Could you finish this afternoon?"

"*Ja*."

"You've met my deputy, Dieter Issler?"

"*Ja*, when I arrived."

"I have a meeting later this morning. Dieter will go with you and keep anyone off your back in case someone objects."

The carpenter left. Archie glanced at his watch. Time to meet Anse at the Rathaus.

Archie was limping when he arrived at the Rathaus. He'd been more active than usual and had not been in a fight since he'd been wounded the previous year. Age was creeping up upon him.

Anse Hatfield was waiting when Archie walked up to the Rathaus entrance. "Hurtin', Archie?"

"Some."

"Feelin' mean and ornery?"

"Yeah, why?"

"You'll need it with these folks."

The Rathaus was a three story building, the tallest in Suhl, Anse said. Its ground floor was an open space used for large meetings, weddings, and festivals. In a room on the next floor above ground-level, was the city council. Offices for city officials, bureaucrats, and departments, were on the top floor.

Archie's leg hurt more after climbing the stairs. If he needed to be feeling mean and ornery, he was ready when he and Anse walked into the council-room. *Herr Feld* sat at the head of the table. Six other councilmen sat along both sides leaving Archie and Anse to sit at the end, opposite of Feld.

"Welcome *Herr Marshal*, and you, too, *Herr Hatfield*," Feld said. Without giving Archie the opportunity to respond, he introduced the other six members of the council. Heinrich Buch sat to Feld's right, Archie noticed. Each councilman nodded as he was introduced.

"We are here at your request, *Herr Marshal*," Feld said.

"I appreciate you acting so swiftly," Archie said. Turning to the rest of the councilmen, he began. "I am SoTF Marshal Archie Mitchell. I assume you have read the documents I gave *Herr Feld*?" he paused, and turned to Feld. "Has the entire council read them?"

"No, I've not had time to make copies. A couple of the councilmen have read them but not all."

"By chance, I have a copy with me. I'll read it to the council," which he proceeded to do.

Several councilmen interrupted as he read, asking to clarify one point or another. When Archie came to the part about renovating the barracks, Councilman Heinrich Buch interrupted. "That's my property!"

"No, it isn't. It is owned by the government of the State of Thuringia and Franconia. The USE transferred ownership to the SoTF.

"Noelle Murphy transferred ownership to the city council. I bought it from the council!"

"Noelle Murphy didn't have that authority," Anse replied. "She was very aware of the limits of her authority. As far as she knew, the barracks belonged to the USE. No one knew the USE had transferred it to the SoTF until Marshal Mitchell arrived."

"I have the document here. Right here! It's proof that she did, whether she had the authority or not. You can't take back what she has done."

"May I see that document?" Archie asked.

"No! It is my only proof."

"It is a transfer of ownership to Suhl, not you Heinrich," Feld said. "Give it to him."

Grudgingly, Buch gave the document to the councilman sitting next to him. It was passed, councilman to councilman until it reached Anse Hatfield.

Anse glanced at the document and looked up. "It's a forgery."

"What!" exclaimed Heinrich Buch, jumping to his feet and turning over his chair in his excitement.

"Look at it, Archie," Anse said. "Look at the signature."

"What about it?" Archie asked.

"Look at it. Is it written by someone who is right-handed or left-handed?"

Archie looked down at the document again. "Right-handed. Why?"

"Noelle Murphy is left-handed. I carried messages for her whenever I went back to Grantville. Whoever wrote this was right-handed."

"You're a liar!" Buch shouted.

"If I am, it can be refuted in a few days. I can send a radio message for samples of Noelle Murphy's signature. They can get here by courier in a couple of days."

"They'll be fakes! You just want to steal my property."

"Now why would we want to do?" Anse asked. "How could we, when no one outside Suhl even knew you claimed the barracks?"

Buch stood white-faced, trembling. Abruptly, he sat, and muttered something to Feld who said, "We await your proof, *Herr Hatfield*."

"In the meantime," Archie said, "I'm having the barracks surveyed to determine what is needed for its full restoration. No work will be done until the council has proof the transfer of the barracks to Suhl was fraudulent. I also warn you now that the Court of the State of Thuringia and Franconia will be very interested how this all happened."

✳ ✳ ✳

" . . . that was the end of the meeting," Archie told Dieter as he and Dieter sat at the table in their quarters. "I'm very glad Anse was there. Otherwise we'd be in a mess, a big lawsuit probably. Just the thing to kick off the new court. So? How was your afternoon with the carpenter?"

"Interesting. A stonemason joined us at the barracks. Apparently, the USE had built a stone armory for their munitions and a stone outbuilding that could easily be converted to be a jail, guardhouse, whatever you call it. It had strong, fitted stone walls and floors, and iron-studded doors. A little dark, no windows, but the stonemason said he could be added those if we wanted."

"I think we'll have to do that. If we make that the holding prison for the court, the prisoners will need access to light and air."

"He's coming by here tomorrow. I can tell him then. He and the master carpenter will draw up some estimates for us, cost, time, and materials, for the renovation."

"Good. Now, we have to find a courthouse."

"I think I found one."

"Oh? Where?"

"Right next to the barracks. You remember that stone building right next to the place where the wall had been torn down?"

"Vaguely."

"It's part of the barracks, quarters for the cavalry officers and their headquarters. They didn't like the spaces in the barracks proper so they included that building when they appropriated the property for the barracks. I was told Buch had owned it before it was seized by the USE."

"That explains much," Archie said.

"Yes, it does. I didn't go in it today, but I think we should give it a look over as soon as we can," Dieter said.

"I agree. Tomorrow?"

"Let's see, the carpenter and stonemason are coming in the morning. We could go with them. I don't remember any other appointments, do you?" Dieter asked.

A knock on their door interrupted their conversation. The innkeeper entered. "*Herr Marshal*, this message just arrived for you."

"*Danke*. I appreciate your promptness."

The innkeeper left to return to the taproom in the inn's front. Archie tried to read the message, but it was hand-written, and poorly at that. "Can you read this, Dieter?"

"Well. Uh, it's from Heinrich Buch. I think he is offering an apology, and would like to meet you tonight at . . . ," he glanced at his watch, a gift from Greta, "at around nine this evening, if I'm reading this right. His handwriting is terrible!"

"Huh! I wonder what he wants? After the meeting today, I wouldn't think he'd want to meet for hugs and kisses."

"What?" Archie's witticisms continued to surprise Dieter.

"Never mind. Ask *Herr Hersch* to send a messenger to Buch and tell him I'll be there. Remind me, we need to budget for messenger service."

"I'll do that. Is it alright if I don't go with you? One of my horses has cast a shoe. I'd like to take it to Christian Zeitts and get it shod."

"Go ahead. I don't think Buch is going to try anything, not now that all has been exposed."

✳ ✳ ✳

Dusk came early that evening. A storm line had passed over Suhl earlier in the evening with a light, intermittent rain. Friedrich Achen, and three of his men, hid in the shadows, watching the old man walk down the alley. He used a cane, leaning on it from time to time, and wore a wide-brimmed hat with a long coat of some heavy cloth that shed the rain like feathers off a waterfowl. He was softly singing to himself.

Compared to the watchers, the old man was richly dressed, easy prey for those in need. A short run, a shove, some blows, sift his pockets, and take his purse and that coat. A knife would be the finish. They were four to his one. It would be easy.

"Go," Achen said softly. The others slipped past him to stalk their quarry.

* * *

Archie thought he heard someone behind him. His leg ached with every step, but his destination, a cabinet shop, was only a dozen yards ahead; a few more steps in the alley and across the cobblestoned street to the storefront two doorways down.

Something splashed behind him. A foot had stepped into a puddle; too loud to be an animal. The sound caused him to pause and turn to look back behind him, back down the alley where he had walked a few moments before.

The overcast from the earlier rain shower was leaving. Light from the three-quarter moon suddenly filled the alleyway. A shadow flitted in the alley, crossing from one side to the other.

Ambush. Archie opened his duster to provide free access to his pistols before glancing over his shoulder to the street, estimating the distance to his stalkers. *Could he reach the shop before the shadows reached him? No,* he decided. No one was around to help, and it was too far to reach shelter in the shop. His chances were better here, to stand and wait, facing those who approached. He dropped his cane, turned to face the alley, and drew his Colt Commander.

Moonlight filled the alley again. Three men were running toward him, not over twenty yards away. Two of them had knives in their hands; the other a bludgeon or some sort of metal shod truncheon. Their intent was obvious.

Archie brought up his pistol and aligned its sights on the nearest attacker and fired. The report was loud, sharp, and distinctly different from the boom of a down-time weapon. The sound echoed off the nearby buildings. He shifted his aim and fired again . . . and again.

The last attacker staggered, tripped, and fell only a few feet away, his knife skittering across the cobblestones to slide to a stop against Archie's boots. Archie remained slightly crouched, his pistol sights sweeping from side to side, searching for any further threats. There were none, and he heard nothing other than the ringing in his ears from the reports of his pistol.

Archie stepped forward, ready for any movement, and checked the bodies. *Young men, out for an evening's fun, mayhem and profit. Or . . . mercenaries, perhaps?* He looked closer; they were not as young as he thought, and were well muscled and well fed. No, they were not ordinary cutpurses. He kicked the knives and bludgeons away from the bodies in case one was shamming.

He scanned the surrounding buildings. Some were dark, abandoned, not uncommon in this part of Suhl. No faces peered from windows, no lights appeared in darkened rooms, no sound of someone running to investigating the shots in the night. *Curious. And where is the watch?*

Archie looked again at the bodies. They had sought a victim and had found something else. He replaced the half-empty magazine with a fresh one and holstered the pistol. Next, he stooped to pick up his cane, and the scattered, fired brass. Grunting softly, he straightened and placed the spent brass in his coat pocket. With cane in hand, he continued toward his destination, where Heinrich Buch was waiting. *Someone there can fetch the watch.* As he walked, he resumed singing *St. James Infirmary*, alert for others who might wish to interrupt his walk. Archie did not notice his leg no longer ached.

✳ ✳ ✳

Friedrich Achen watched silently from the shadows. He cursed, stepped further into the darkness, and slipped quietly away.

✳ ✳ ✳

Archie entered Buch's shop. The smell of burned powder still lingering on his duster and clothes.

Heinrich Buch approached from the rear of the cabinetry shop. "*Herr Marshal.*"

"*Herr Buch.* I think you have a mess out front. There are three dead bodies."

"I heard." He sighed, motioned for Archie to follow him into the rear of the shop, where a table and chairs waited. Buch sat without offering Archie a seat. "I need to confess," he said, looking down at the floor.

Archie stepped forward and sat in a chair across from Buch. "Luring me here to be killed?"

"No! No, I . . . I didn't know what was planned. My son-in-law told me to invite you here. He . . . uh . . . he forced me."

"How?"

"My daughter. She's six months with child. Achen beats her. I—I'm afraid he'll kill her."

"Isn't that frowned upon?"

"Yes. No. The church won't interfere. It's not against the law if it's just a beating. There's no one."

"I know how that can be. I've seen it often enough. Back up-time, if something like this occurred, a man gathered his friends and family, and fixed the problem; puts the son of a bitch in the hospital. No one talks, nothing can be proved."

"I don't have anyone that I could trust to not talk. This whole scheme with the barracks is his idea. He told me to build a warehouse and storefront at the barracks. When finished, I could sell it and the building next to it for three times what it cost me."

"And what did it cost you to buy the barracks?"

The price Buch gave was astonishingly low. "Who pushed this through the council? You?"

"Feld. He gets a percentage of the profit when the buildings are sold."

"Somehow, I'm not surprised."

"Now, where can I find your son-in-law?"

"He's usually at *Der Bulle und Bär* this time of night. He lives, sometimes, here with my daughter. They have rooms upstairs, but most of the time he's there."

"Will he be there tomorrow?"

"He should be."

"Don't warn him I'm coming."

"No—no, I won't."

"I think Suhl needs a new councilman and Bürgermeister, don't you?"

Buch didn't speak, just nodded and hung his head. He'd be lucky to get off with some jail time and a heavy fine. He and Feld both. The SoTF was said to be hard on public corruption.

❊ ❊ ❊

Archie wished he hadn't given Dieter time off to get his horse shod. He wasn't up to bracing Achen in his own territory this time of night, and he didn't know how many men Achen had. Six of them were now pushing up daisies, but Achen could have more. Tomorrow would do. Then, he and Dieter would scout *Der Bulle und Bär*. If Achen was there, they would arrest him . . . one way or another.

He headed back to the Boar's Head Inn, feeling fine. An adrenaline rush had made his aches and pains slip away.

When Archie walked through the Boar's Head Inn doorway, instead of heading back to his rooms, he walked over to a table in the corner and sat. Normally, he drank little, but every once in a while, he liked a beer. "*Ein bier, mein Herr*," he called to Hersch, the innkeeper. In minutes, the beer arrived in a large foaming mug. Otto Hersch brewed it himself.

When the Ring of Fire had occurred, the up-time supplies of beer were the first item to disappear. Archie didn't like the current brews. However, in the time since the Ring of Fire, he was becoming accustomed to down-time offerings, especially Hersch's brew.

* * *

Archie slept late the next morning. He left Dieter a note on his bedroom door the previous evening to postpone the follow-up with the carpenter and stonemason. He and Dieter would have law business in the morning.

A visit to the jakes, a bath, and he felt ready. From their makeshift armory, Archie retrieved his Winchester Model 1897 shotgun and dumped a handful of double-aught shells in his side coat pocket. Next, he reached into his ammo box and loaded the shotgun's magazine with five more shells of double-aught buck. The Winchester shotgun was once known as a trench gun. It had a twenty-inch barrel, and, at one time, a bayonet lug, but Archie had never had a bayonet for the shotgun. He was well off without it. All a bayonet did, in close quarters, was get in the way.

Dieter stood, waiting. He, too, had his double-barreled shotgun, loaded and ready, and his Colt 1911 on his belt. The two walked out through the front of the Boar's Head Inn, Archie in front, with Dieter following. Otto Hersch did a double-look as they passed. They were armed and appeared ready for business.

Der Bulle und Bär, nestled against the city's northern wall, was in a section of Suhl that Archie had not yet visited. He and Dieter walked up to the entrance. Dieter opened the door and stepped aside to let Archie enter first.

Archie walked in and stood at one side. Dieter followed and stepped to the other side. Neither was silhouetted against the open doorway.

Schlick-schlock. Achen looked up at the strange sound that interrupted his conversation with his last two men.

"Friedrich Achen," Archie said. "You are under arrest for fraud, extortion, assault on a SoTF Marshal, and murder. Place your hands on your head and stand up!"

Achen looked into three shotgun barrels; the double-barrels in Dieter's hands and the one in Archie's. Both Marshals stood covering the inn's common room, their six-pointed badges visible in the inn's dimness.

No one moved. Then, Achen, face turning pale, slowly raised his hands, put them on his head and rose. The other two sitting at his table didn't move, scarcely breathing.

"Step forward and turn around."

Achen did so.

"I'm using my good steel handcuffs on you, Achen. The rest of you—don't interfere. Stay where you are and don't move until we're gone. Don't follow us either. We can take you all out if necessary."

The room remained silent. No one appeared to doubt his word. Archie and Dieter backed out of the room pulling Achen with them. Dieter kept watch on their rear as they headed for Ruben Blumroder's shop.

"We REALLY need a jail, Dieter." Archie said, as they neared the gun shop. "This is just getting repetitive."

Mid-May 1634, Suhl

A mounted constabulary trooper dismounted outside the entrance of the Boar's Head Inn. The inn's stableboy took the horse's reins and led it to the stables in back for watering while the trooper went inside the inn. "Where may I find *Herr Marshal Mitchell?*" he asked Otto Hersch, standing inside near the front door.

"He's in back. Wait. I'll get him," the innkeeper replied, and disappeared into the rear of the inn to reappear a few minutes later with the marshal.

"I'm Marshal Mitchell." Archie told the trooper.

"Sir, the First Mounted Constabulary Troop, with *Frau Mitchell* and *Frau Issler*, should arrive in two hours. Captain Gruber sent me ahead to tell you."

"That's wonderful news, Trooper." Archie walked back to the rear doorway, "Dieter!" he shouted. "They're here. Want to ride out to greet them?"

"Yes!" Dieter replied, unseen from their rooms.

Archie returned to the trooper and said, "Have a beer on me while we saddle our horses. We'll ride back with you."

"*Danke, Herr Marshal.*" No trooper ever refused a free beer. By the time he had finished his beer and walked out the front entrance, Archie and Dieter appeared around the rear corner of the inn on horseback with the stableboy leading trooper's horse. The stableboy had fed and given it a quick combing.

"Lead off," Archie said after the trooper mounted his horse.

The three riders trotted down the road from Suhl that ran along the river until they found the troop and several accompanying wagons rolling toward them. Archie saw Marjorie sitting on one wagon, next to a trooper, driving it. Greta sat on another one. Both heavily loaded wagons were covered by waterproof tarps.

"I think Marjorie and Greta brought everything but the kitchen sink," Archie said to Dieter as they approached the troop. He identified himself and greeted the officer in the lead before riding down the column to Marjorie's wagon. Dieter rode on the next wagon and Greta.

"Hi, Marj, I've missed you," Archie said.

"Arch, I missed you, too . . . I'm glad to be here. You're looking good."

"Feel good, too. I was really whupped when I first got here. Dieter and I had some troubles, but that's all cleared up."

"I see you have a new saddle."

"Yeah, I made a good deal. Where're our horses?"

"Mine and the gelding are in the string back behind the wagons with the constabulary's spare horses. I rode most of the time, but too much made my rear hurt. I'm not up for long rides on horseback anymore."

"I hear ya. Dieter and I found a nice house in town. It needed a bit of work, but it's two stories and big enough for all of us with room to spare, and it's close to some new friends of mine, Johann Zeitts and his family. I think you'll like them."

"I brought your recliner and our bed. I had to disassemble them to get everything in the wagon but I knew you'd want them."

"Thank you. I really miss that recliner. The beds here are okay, but my leg starts hurting in the middle of the night."

Captain Gruber rode up next to Archie and introduced himself. "Is the barracks ready, Marshal?"

"Almost. The workmen should finish up today—just minor stuff. The trooper's barracks, beds and bedding, plus the stables, were finished first. I left two tall trees standing for the radio antenna according to the instructions I received. The army unit took their radio when they were recalled a few weeks ago."

"Good. I brought a permanent radio with me and two radio operators. They'll work for the court. Did you find a blacksmith, farrier and saddler?"

"Yes, I did. Johann Zeitts and his son, Christian. I have them under contract to give you twenty hours each, each week. Johann Zeitts is a saddler. He made this saddle I'm sitting on. His son, Christian, is a journeyman blacksmith and farrier. I don't think you'd need them more than twenty hours a week."

"No, that should be sufficient. I brought one hundred and twenty horses. They were all shod before we left."

"Before I forget, I made one commitment for you."

"Oh?"

"There's been a shakeup in the Suhl city council. The city watch was pretty much useless. They've not been competently led and lacked training. The militia has been manning the gates and walls, but that's all. The new city council has asked Bamberg for some suitable Wachtmeister candidates. I told the council that you would provide a half squad of troopers to help train the watch and patrol the city until a new Wachtmeister takes over or for two months, whichever occurs first."

"Hmmm. I think I can do that. We'll always have the headquarters squad posted here. Some of them can do double-duty for a while."

"I'm glad you agree. The city council put me in a spot, and I hate to make commitments for other people. My deputy and I have been helping to improve the watch's overall capability, and some on-the-job-training with a few promising watchmen. We've been making random patrols throughout the city with them, but we're just two, and when the court is established, we'll have our own work to do."

"I must start sending out mounted patrols as soon as I can, but we'll need some time to get everything set up and rest the horses and men before we start. I think we can work something out."

"Thank you, Captain."

"You are very welcome, *Herr Marshal*." Gruber kicked his heels into his horse's flanks and rode up to the head of the column. Archie stayed, riding next to the wagon and Marjorie.

They travelled silently for a time, he on horseback, and she on the wagon seat next to the wagon driver. Archie broke the silence. "I really missed you, Marj. I don't like living alone."

"What? No dancing girls in that inn?"

Archie laughed, "No, no dancing girls. I hope you like the place Dieter and I found. The building was a bakery at one time and that's what caught Dieter's eye. I had some walls added to divide it into two apartments, one for us and the other for Dieter and Greta."

"It sounds good, Arch . . . Arch, I'm ready to go home."

"Me, too, Marj, me too."

Mike Watson

THE THIRD INTERVIEW

Suhl, June 9, 1636

Two days after Maria D'Angelo and Thomas Bloem interviewed the Mitchells and the Isslers in their home, Judge Fross, the Presiding Judge, declared a half-day for the Court. Normally, he held court from Monday through noon Friday. That didn't mean the court employees had the rest of the day off. But, occasionally, like today, they had finished their usual tasks and paperwork, too, allowing the employees to take advantage of a half-day of freedom.

Der Garten was an outdoor lunch and meeting area nestled along one side of the Court's courtyard. The long-term plan for the *der Garten* was to transform it into a park. Judge Fross found some unbudgeted funds to help with expenses, with the understanding that the park would be open to the public. When Bloem asked for another interview session, Archie thought of *der Garten*.

"Welcome," Archie said when the two down-timers approached. Archie and Dieter had secured one of the covered tables for the meeting. Marjorie and Greta were present and unloading two baskets with lunch. Marta played with the children of other court families.

While Marjorie and Greta prepared lunch, Maria began the interview. "What happened to Achen, Feld, and Buch?"

"Feld and Buch were fined and given three years of community service," Archie said.

"Community service?"

"The SoTF doesn't have prisons . . . at least not yet. There is a jail in the basement of Suhl's Rathaus, but the city isn't equipped, or funded, to keep prisoners for a long period—neither is the Constabulary. Feld and Buch sleep at home, and during the day, work for the city . . . picking up nightsoil for the nitrate beds."

Bloem had been listening and laughed. "I think that would be fitting. But, what about Achen?"

"They hung him a week after his trial," Dieter said. "Judge Fross sent the trial transcript to Judge Riddle for review—"

"Although he didn't have to," Archie said.

"—since it was the first capital crime tried in Suhl."

"Bamberg did not comment, and the sentence went forward."

✲ ✲ ✲

Greta and Marjorie joined the four. Maria had been watching Marta play with the other children. She blinked and wiped her eyes.

"Are you all right?" Greta asked, sitting next to Maria.

"I lost my husband and daughter to Tilly's murderers. She would have been Marta's age." After a pause, she looked at Greta and added, "You're so blessed."

"Yes, we are. We lost our first daughter fleeing Tilly. She got a fever when we fled Magdeburg."

Maria was watching Marta again. Greta laid her hand on Maria's and squeezed lightly. "Dieter's family had a glass factorage in Magdeburg," Greta said, continuing her tale. "When the city refused to surrender, we ran. We knew what would happen."

"We stayed," Maria said. "Our mistake."

"I've thought whether we should have stayed," Greta said. "They robbed us of everything we had when we left Magdeburg. Then B . . . B—"

"It's still hard for Greta to say Bella's name," Marjorie explained.

Maria looked again at Marta. "I don't understand, Marta is—"

"Too old? Yes. She joined us last . . . almost two years ago."

"That sounds like a story," Bloem said. He had been listening to the women talk.

"It is," Archie said. "I sent Dieter on a—you tell it, Dieter. It's your story."

Mike Watson

PART III: THE SEARCHERS

Meiningen, Friday, September 8, 1634

Guenter Bettin lay on the floor of his cell waiting for the warder to come with his supper, a bowl of whatever leftover was available from the nearest Meiningen inn. He looked up to the narrow window set high in the cell's wall. Too narrow for an escape route, he concluded. Bettin didn't think it was wide enough to pass a hand, much less his entire body. The window was just wide enough to let in sufficient sunlight light to dispel the gloom.

I have to escape! He knew he'd get short shrift from the magistrate; a local against a stranger. Regardless of innocence; the stranger was always guilty. He may be a pickpocket and a thief, but he was no murderer. The locals, however, wouldn't see it that way. The warder told him they would take him to Suhl for trial, followed by the gallows.

Bettin admitted to himself that he was cheating at bones. Unfortunately, he had been caught. When his opponent objected and attacked Bettin, it wasn't his fault he'd hit his head on the flagstone of the fireplace. He admitted that he'd ducked the man's swing—and helped him along as he stumbled by, but it wasn't his fault he'd fallen, hit his head and died. It was an accident!

As the light through the window waned, he heard the warder walking heavily toward the cell, the young one, he realized. The older warder who brought him breakfast was cautious and suspicious. He would have no chance against him. The young one, now . . . Bettin searched the cell for something to use . . . something . . . the chamber pot.

The chamber pot wasn't pottery, just an old wooden bucket that served the purpose. When the old warder came, he made Bettin place the bucket by the door where it could be reached. Bettin was forced to sit against the far wall of the cell, out of reach, or he wouldn't eat. The warder moved the bucket outside and replaced it was a bowl and a mug of cheap beer. The bucket was returned when he retrieved the bowl and mug. Occasionally, he'd bring a second warder for safety.

The young one, however, wasn't as strict. He didn't make Bettin move to the far wall. When he set the bowl and mug on the floor in the doorway after opening the door, he would be vulnerable—and he was always alone.

DAY ONE

Suhl, Tuesday, September 12, 1634

Marshal Archie Mitchell watched his deputy, Dieter Issler, enter his office. He'd dispatched a messenger earlier that morning to deliver a note asking him to report to the Marshal's office.

The walk from the stables to the courthouse was through a light morning rain. Dieter's oilcloth duster and waxed leather hat shed the falling raindrops. His task that morning had been to check the horses, his, Archie's, and those of the district's other two deputy marshals, stabled at the constabulary barracks. The messenger had found him there.

Archie had a small office in the rear of the Suhl District Courthouse; one that he shared with the Court's Chief Bailiff, Karl Wagner. He waited until his deputy had hung his dripping coat and his hat on a peg, and was seated, before telling Dieter why he'd been called.

"I've a job for you, Dieter, a fugitive warrant," he said, extending the warrant to his deputy, "for Guenter Bettin, wanted for theft, assault, and murder. He escaped from custody in Meiningen where he was being held pending pickup by the bailiff's wagon. They said he's gone into the 'Wald."

Dieter read the warrant, a simply written document and not filled with legalese that Archie had said was the case in up-time warrants. "Umm, I'll need some help. Can I hire a tracker to go with me?" Dieter asked.

"One, if you can find one—standard rates. Any more is out of your pocket. Take Kurt with you and give him some on-the-job training." Kurt

Moesch, along with Dieter Feitel, or *Two* as Archie called him, was one of the two probationary deputy marshals recently assigned to the First District Court in Suhl.

Dieter was the senior deputy. In fact, Dieter's was badge number four, making him the most senior Deputy Marshal in the entire service, not that there were all that many deputies yet. Kurt Moesch was from Erfurt and had some knowledge of the Thüringer Wald. Feitel. . .Two, from Vienna, was not a woodsman and knew nothing of the Wald.

"Two has court duty for the next two weeks," Archie explained. "Else I'd sent both with you for some field experience and training."

Dieter nodded, rose, and had turned toward the door when Archie spoke one last time. "If he wasn't charged with murder, I'd let the locals handle this, but murder is a capital crime and that comes under our jurisdiction."

Dieter nodded. "We'll get him or it won't be for lack of trying."

❋ ❋ ❋

To find a tracker, I need to go where there are some. Maybe a Jäger. Ruben should know where I can find one; people who would go with us. Ruben Blumroder was the leader of the Suhl association of gunsmiths. He was also Suhl's representative to the SoTF legislature.

Dieter was approaching Ruben Blumroder's gun shop when he remembered Ruben wasn't there. He was in Bamberg for the legislative session. *But Pat's here.* Pat Johnson's U. S. Waffenfabrik was a few doors from Ruben's shop. *And maybe my rifle is ready.* Dieter, like all the deputies and constables, had been issued a standard SRG. rifle. Since then, the SoTF was converting SRG rifles from flintlock to caplock. Deputies and the local constabulary troopers would be the first ones to receive the upgrades.

Standard SRGs were flintlocks and had a forty-inch barrel. Carbine versions, to be issued to the Marshals Service and Mounted Constabulary, not only included the caplock action but came with a shortened barrel of twenty-two inches. Dieter and the deputies had been practicing with one of the first conversions, learning the modified manual-of-arms for the converted SRGs.

Dieter stood inside the doorway of the U. S. Waffenfabrik. The September morning shower had tapered off to a light mist by the time he arrived at Pat's shop.

Pat Johnson sat behind a desk writing in an account book. He looked up, and when he noticed Dieter standing in the doorway. motioned for him to enter. "Come in out of the weather, Dieter. What can I do for you?" he asked, rising to shake Dieter's hand.

"Do you know who the local Jäger leader is? I need a Jäger for a job."

Pat thought for a moment, "I think that would be Konrad Heimbrecht."

"Where can I find him?"

"This time of day . . . try the market. He brings in game that his hunters have bagged. If he isn't there, someone should know where he can be found."

"*Danke*, Pat. I need a tracker for a job."

"He should know of one, Dieter. By the way, you *do* know some Jäger are a bit . . . eccentric."

"So I've heard. I think I can work with one."

"Good."

Dieter turned to leave, but before he'd taken a step, Pat called after him. "Uh, Dieter, what kind of job is this?"

Dieter hesitated, but, as Archie was wont to say, *it isn't a secret.* "I have to find a man. I've a fugitive warrant for him and he's supposed to have gone into the 'Wald."

"What kind of long-arm do you have?"

"The usual, an SRG—unless you have my carbine ready?"

Pat chuckled. He was one of several gunsmiths in Suhl who had a contract for SRG conversions. Converting them to caplock and shortening the barrel; making them carbines. Pat's contract was to convert the local SRGs, including those issued to the Constabulary and Marshal's Service.

"It's ready. I'm delivering the constabulary carbines to Captain Gruber this afternoon. You can take yours now."

"*Danke*, Pat. Kurt is coming with me. Keep his here; I'll send him along to pick it up."

Pat nodded. "I just sent a messenger to Captain Gruber and Karl Wagner. I'll keep Kurt's." He hesitated. "Are you familiar with this rifle? Enough to take it into the field?"

"I've been practicing with one of the initial conversions and so has Kurt. The new SRGs aren't all that different from the flintlocks. They're still muzzle loaders."

✻ ✻ ✻

Dieter found Konrad Heimbrecht in the city market. Dieter introduced himself and presented his problem. "I need a tracker who's also a good rifle shot, but being a good tracker is more important. Do you know someone who would go? I think the job will take a week to ten days. He'd be temporarily deputized while on the job."

Heimbrecht had been hanging a gutted deer carcass when Dieter arrived at the market. He walked over to a tub of water next to the stand, washed his hands and arms, and then motioned Dieter to sit with him at a small table nearby. "Hmm. I know of one who fits those requirements, especially the tracking part. But, I have to tell you, he isn't the friendliest person to come down the mountain."

"Where can I find him?"

"He has a cot on the other side of that mountain at the edge of a mining hamlet," he said, pointing to a high, rocky ridge north of Suhl. "It's about a five—six mile ride. He'll need a horse if he goes."

"A horse isn't a problem." The Marshal's Service owned several horses for official uses. Each deputy had a horse for their official use and several horses remained that could be used for other purposes.

"He'll make demands."

"Like what?"

"Whatever you plan to pay him won't be enough. Be ready to haggle."

"I'm from Vienna. I can haggle." Dieter grinned. Either way, he told himself, he was going to have that tracker riding with him on this search.

"Good, you'll have to. Be sure to tell him I sent you."

DAY TWO

Wednesday, September 13, 1634

Dawn came early this day, or so Dieter thought. He was not an early riser. Getting up before dawn, waking Greta, his wife, and the rest of the household, couldn't be helped. Greta rose, wrapped herself in a robe, and went down the stairs to the kitchen they shared with the Mitchells. Greta had baked some travel food the previous evening, including several small loaves of apple-nut bread that would keep well on the road. Marjorie, Archie's wife, was up, too, to help Greta. Dieter could hear Archie faintly snoring in the Mitchell's apartment.

When Dieter and Archie were assigned to Suhl the previous spring, they shared this house; a former bakery. The previous owners had died and left no heirs. Archie worked a deal for the house. The large common room in front was now Greta's bakery shop. A short hallway led to the rear, to the kitchen and oven. Archie and Dieter subdivided the rest of the ground floor into several smaller rooms that comprised the Mitchell's apartment. Off the kitchen were stairs that led to the upper floor and the Issler's apartment.

Marjorie gave Dieter a breakfast taco she'd made the previous evening and had warmed in the oven. When the women were finished, Marjorie went back to join Archie. Greta watched Dieter eat while she ate her own taco and nibbled on some crumbs of leftover apple-nut bread.

"You can go back to bed, Greta. Thank you for breakfast and please thank Marjorie, too."

"Of course I'll thank Marjorie. You shouldn't be surprised she got up with us. You know she and Archie think of us as family."

"I know. I'm still getting used to them and all the up-timers. You think you know them and then they'll do something completely unexpected."

Greta chuckled. "Time for you to go."

"Yeah, I'm meeting Kurt at the stables. If I can hire this tracker, we'll continue on. Else, I'll look for another. I may be gone awhile."

"You've a job to do. Do it."

"Yes, Greta, as always."

He gave her a peck on her cheek and left by the back door to the small stable behind their house. Dieter, when he'd arrived at Suhl, had taken Archie's advice and bought two horses; one for him and another for Greta.

Johann Zietts, a local saddler, made two saddles patterned from the ones owned by Archie and Marjory Mitchell. The *western* saddle, as Archie called it, was much more comfortable than down-time saddles.

Inside the stable, Dieter saddled his roan mare, slung his saddle-bags across the saddle, and slid his SRG carbine into the scabbard. A short time later, he rode into the mounted constabulary stables where Kurt Moesch was waiting.

"*Wie Gehts, Kurt.*" The greeting was an up-time German phrase Dieter had picked up from Archie.

"Good, Dieter. I have the spare horse ready and I put the revolver, holster, powder, caps and balls into the pack like you said."

"Good. Did you find a map?"

"Captain Gruber let me copy his." Moesch was, amongst his other skills, a talented artist. At one time, he had been apprenticed to a portrait artist. Unfortunately for his mentor, Moesch preferred to be outdoors, to being cooped up inside formulating pigments for his master. Moesch would never be a master portraitist. However, he was much better than amateurs and better than many journeyman artists.

"I hope we won't need it. But . . . if we can't get this tracker to join us, it'll be just you and me."

"I'm not that good a tracker, Dieter."

"You're better than me. If this tracker recommended by Konrad Heimbrecht won't go, you better get in practice very quick."

"*Jawohl, Dieter.*"

*   *   *

The trail over the mountain ridge was steep. They emerged from the forest above Suhl into a rocky, grass-covered summit where the soil was thin. A few stunted, twisted, lightning blasted trees graced the grassy landscape but not much else. The trail continued down the other side into the valley below. Rows of green mountains, hills, and ridges, continued into the hazy distance—the Thüringer Wald. The two deputies followed the trail down the other side until they were at the edge of the valley forest. When they reached the forest's edge, the trail continued further down to a small mining hamlet. At that point, a second path led to a small stone and slate roofed cot. Smoke rose from its chimney.

Stengel emerged from the cot as the two approached. "Hello," Dieter called. "Are you Walter Stengel? Konrad Heimbrecht recommended you for a job with us."

"Who wants to know and what kind of job?" Stengel asked.

"We're SoTF Deputy Marshals. I'm Dieter Issler and this is Kurt Moesch. We have a warrant to arrest a fugitive who escaped custody in Meiningen. He was waiting for transport to Suhl for trial. We want you to help us find him."

The haggling begun. A small woman stepped out from the cot's interior to stand in its doorway. She watched the men and held a rifle cross-wise in her arms. Stengel's wife, Dieter assumed. She could probably shoot as well as Stengel.

In the end, Stengel agreed to go for the standard daily-rate, plus Dieter's help in getting Stengel a new rifle. He wanted a cartridge rifle like the Sharps or one similar to it. Dieter knew Pat Johnson was working on a breech-loading rifle, one based on the Remington design. He hoped he could convince Pat to let Stengel *field test* one before Gary Riordan put the rifle into production.

Stengel gathered some trail food, his rifle, a different one than that held by his wife, Dieter noted, and a camp pack. He strapped the pack and food to the back of the horse they had brought for him.

Kurt Moesch retrieved the H&K pistol, holster, powder, ball and a small cap box from his saddlebag and gave them to Stengel. "Just in case," he said. Stengel nodded, ran his belt through the holster and slid the pistol into it.

"It's unloaded, I presume?" Stengel asked.

"Yes, of course. I wouldn't give you a loaded pistol without telling you. I'll show you how to load it when we break for camp tonight. You shouldn't need it before then."

Stengel laughed. "I have everything I need right here," he said, lifting his rifle.

Stengel's confidence was assuring. Dieter felt he could use some during this assignment. "Let's go. We need to get to Meiningen and pick up Bettin's trail."

DAY THREE

Thursday, September 14, 1634

The three riders reached Meiningen just before noon. Meiningen wasn't far from Suhl, about fifteen miles if they could have ridden in a straight line. But the road wound through valleys, along creeks and up and down enough hills to make the trip longer. With the low overcast and mist, plus an intermittent light rain, all three were ready to find a nice dry inn out of the weather. Whether that happened depended on what they discovered from the local watch.

Meiningen lay in a valley between two lines of mountains through which the *Werra* River flowed. The town, built at a bend of the river, was surrounded by three moats and walls. Dieter led the three across the bridges, entered the town, and rode to the Rathaus. There, they found *Herr Peter Vorholzer* of the Meiningen Watch. He was the one who had sent the message about Bettin's escape.

". . . the guard, one of our younger militiamen, took Bettin his evening meal. Bettin attacked him and locked him inside the cell. We didn't know he had escaped until the next morning," *Herr Vorholzer* explained. "We found some people who thought they saw him cross the *Werra* and head north into the Wald."

"Did Bettin get any weapons? Food? A horse?" Dieter asked.

"He took a truncheon from the guard and some coins, a few pfennigs. Nothing else. There's been no report of anything missing, no food, no clothing, nor any horses. He's on foot."

After Dieter was satisfied they had gotten as much as they could from Vorholzer, he asked Moesch to get a detailed description and make a sketch of Bettin's face. They needed something to help identify the fugitive in their search.

Bettin was a bold one. After he had locked the militiaman in the cell, he'd calmly walked out of town, ignored by everyone.

"I'm more curious about Bettin's clothing and shoes," Stengel said.

"As best anyone could remember," Vorholzer said, "Bettin wore lace-up boots with heels. Most of our people do not have heels on their boots." The Wachtmeister gave them the names of two farmers in a small neighboring hamlet on the north side of the *Werra* who may have seen Bettin.

The three rode out of Meiningen, crossed the *Werra* and headed north on the trade road. Bettin had a three-day head start. They were mounted and Bettin was not . . . unless he'd stolen a horse that hadn't yet been reported.

The farming hamlet was only three miles north of Meiningen. The two farmers who had spoken with Vorholzer repeated their stories. Given their description of Bettin's clothing and with the aid of Moesch's charcoal drawing, Dieter was convinced the person the farmers had seen was Bettin.

"Walter, do you know the towns north of here?" Dieter asked Stengel.

"Walldorf is the next large town. There are some small hamlets here and there along the road, but I don't know any of their names, if they have any," Stengel said.

"I would think he'd head to Walldorf since he's going north," Dieter said. "What do you think?"

"Possible. We don't know Bettin's history or where he's from. I suspect he's not from the Wald. It's logical that he'd head for the bigger towns. Given that, I think it would be prudent if I scouted a bit, see if I can pick his trail. It'd be cold by now but there hasn't been any heavy rain since he escaped, just this fog and mist."

"Go ahead. Kurt and I will follow the trade road. We'll stay in Walldorf overnight. You can join us there."

Moesch had been listening to the conversation. "Dieter, do you think it's wise for us to split up? I know the armies have gone west, but there are still bandits and gangs of mercenaries roaming around."

"I think we're safe if we keep alert, Kurt. We should have enough firepower to fight off any attacks from bandits. If there are too many, we'll run. Mama Issler didn't raise any fools."

"*Herr Marshal Mitchell* would . . . "

"Archie Mitchell is sneaky and one of *Die Drei Alten Soldaten*. There aren't too many like him. He isn't a fool, either . . . besides, he isn't here."

✱ ✱ ✱

Dieter and Kurt Moesch proceeded along the tree-lined dirt and packed clay trade road. The paved metaled road ended a mile north of Meiningen. Moesch was more of a woodsman than Dieter and took the lead, while Dieter followed with the packhorse. From time to time, they would see the tracks of a single horse crossing the road from one side to the other—Stengel looking for signs of Bettin, Dieter thought.

While they hadn't seen Stengel, they knew he was there. At one time, a feral pig was flushed from the underbrush. It ran away from them, up the road and then back into the underbrush on the other side. Moesch said he'd seen a flash of a mounted rider in the brush where the pig had lain hidden.

They continued riding, Moesch leading, examining the road for footsteps along the way. He reined up and waited for Dieter to come alongside. "Cots, ahead."

"You think they may have seen Bettin?" Dieter asked.

"Possibly. This is the only road I've seen and the mountainsides are steep. He has to follow this valley to Walldorf. I don't think he would go over the mountain, alone and on foot."

When they arrived at the small hamlet, Stengel was waiting.

❊ ❊ ❊

"Bettin was here," Stengel said as Dieter and Moesch rode up. "He tried to steal one of their plow horses." Tilting his head momentarily toward the villager standing next to his horse, he added, "Tell them, Helmut."

"It was just before dusk," the villager said. "We had been pulling stumps to clear a field, and we had just finished stabling the horses when we found this stranger hiding in the hayloft. He gave us a story, but we didn't believe it. Then he asked if he could stay for the night. We would have agreed, but I saw him hiding a bridle he's taken from the tack room. He then jumped on a horse and tried to ride away on it, but we stopped him. The last we saw of him, he ran that way," the villager reported, pointing toward the *Werra* River that flowed north to Walldorf from Meiningen.

"Can you track him, Walter?" Dieter asked.

"If his tracks haven't been blotted out by others, yes."

"Move out," Dieter said. "We're not that far from Walldorf. You lead, we'll follow."

Stengel rode out, with the villager trotting next to his horse to show Stengel where the villagers had lost sight of the fugitive. This close to a village, the undergrowth had been cleared and Stengel soon found Bettin's tracks. Dieter thanked the villager and rewarded him with some coins he carried for that purpose. "Go home," he told the villager. "We'll take up the chase from here."

Bettin had been chased out of the hamlet the previous evening. When Dieter, Kurt, and Stengel started the hunt in Suhl, they were three days behind. They had made up a couple of days; Bettin was not that far away. He must have gotten lost and wasted his lead wandering along the *Werra* River. Stengel led the deputies along Bettin's path to the river and found a cold campsite where two trees had fallen that had provided Bettin with some slight shelter. Stengel examined the site carefully.

"Bettin may not have gotten a horse at that village, but he got some food," Stengel said, pointing to some pork bones and a few breadcrumbs that had escaped Bettin's attention. The *Jäger* checked the sun's position, a dull glow in the overcast, estimated the time and pronounced, "He's in Walldorf by now, if he hasn't gotten lost again."

* * *

Walldorf, while smaller than Meiningen, was large enough to have several inns, a busy marketplace, a Rathaus, and a watch. Although Walldorf wasn't all that far from Meiningen, according to Kurt's map, it took the deputies and Stengel the rest of the afternoon to reach the town. Dieter told Moesch and Stengel to find a suitable inn and to ask if anyone had seen any strangers that day.

Wachtmeister Jacob Eichel welcomed Dieter. He had heard of the Marshal's Service, although he admitted he didn't understand its function. He did understand an organization whose purpose was to find criminals. Although that was an imperfect understanding, Dieter didn't bother to correct him. Eichel reported his watchmen had seen no stranger. That didn't mean there wasn't one; he'd said, just that one hadn't been reported.

With the troubles still lingering in the west along the Rhine and in the south around Bamberg, the road through Walldorf was the major trade route from Grabfeld and points south to Eisenach to the north. Traders constantly traveled the road during the summer months. But now, with the coming change of season, traders were fewer. None had been seen in almost a week. Eichel agreed to pass the drawing of Bettin to his men and would make rounds during the evening with the deputies.

Dieter rejoined Moesch and Stengel. Moesch had their horses stabled in the rear of an inn. Stengel suggested he sleep there to keep watch on the horses. Bettin needed a horse and here were four just waiting for him. Neither of the two deputies objected; if Stengel wanted to sleep on straw, on the ground, it was his choice. For themselves, they preferred a bed.

"Not all that friendly, is he, Dieter? I don't think Stengel has spoken more than a dozen sentences today."

"He does his work and follows orders. That's enough for me."

"Still . . ."

"I think he's spent too much time alone in the 'Wald. I've known people like that. After a while, they don't know how to act with people. He'll do his job, don't worry."

That evening, Dieter, Moesch, and Wachtmeister Eichel visited all the inns and shops that were still open. No one admitted to seeing Bettin. Moesch made several rough copies of the drawing and left one at each inn. The drawings weren't *Wanted* posters, but they would do.

DAY FOUR

Friday, September 15, 1634

With no reports arriving about Bettin, Stengel left to ride the perimeter of Walldorf looking for Bettin's tracks. Dieter and Moesch, each with an accompanying watchman, left to make the rounds of the town while Stengel searched.

Kurt Moesch and his assigned watchman were talking with a shopkeeper when they were interrupted. A farrier had had a horse stolen from his stable overnight. It had lost a shoe and had been left to be shod. The farrier intended to shoe it today but discovered it missing this morning. Kurt's companion watchman took the report and made a copy for Moesch that included the size and color of the horse. The horse had a clipped ear, some old injury, that should make it easy to identify. The watchman left to report to the Wachtmeister. Moesch thanked the farrier for his report and went to find Dieter.

Stengel returned to report that he had found several tracks, most following the road north and south. Two tracks headed west toward Fulda. One horse heading west only had three hooves shod.

Stengel found the tracks again, of two horses, one with a missing shoe. The horses did not appear to have traveled together. In many places, Bettin's horse stepped on the tracks of the other. A short distance from Walldorf, the trail split. Bettin continued west. The other horse followed the branch toward the south-west. Dieter asked Stengel to ride point fifty to a hundred yards ahead. They were getting closer to their quarry.

Stengel watched the trail and the brush on both sides. He had no intention of being ambushed by anyone, much less some thief unused to the 'Wald. The tracks from Bettin's stolen horse were easy to follow. Stengel thought the thief didn't know how to hide his tracks or make them harder to find and follow.

By his estimate, Bettin was two—maybe three hours ahead. The trail wandered through the thickening forest. The cloud cover of the previous day had lifted, along with any breeze, to dispel the growing humidity. By this time of September, the *Jäger* expected much cooler weather with a prevailing wind out of the North and Northwest. Today, the marginal breeze was from the south and southeast out of France, Spain, and the Mediterranean coast.

Stengel glanced at the sun through the tree cover overhead. *Nearly noon.* The trail ahead passed through a small man-cleared meadow and turned southwest, following the valley. The open meadow allowed a fresher breeze and with it . . .

Stengel halted and waited for the deputies to catch up. "Smoke," he reported. "Bettin left the trail here and headed upland along the side of the valley. I think he is bypassing a village up ahead; I can smell their smoke," he said. "His tracks are very fresh. Fresher than I expected."

"Lead on," Dieter said. "Let's finish this."

Bettin's tracks lead to a small copse of trees, rocks, and thick underbrush. Stengel left the deputies to work his way around the copse. All three believed Bettin was hiding inside, but they weren't sure why he had stopped, nor why he traveled around the village. He'd made a mistake. Now they were about to reach him. Stengel was their blocking force. Dieter and Moesch would go in and flush Bettin out . . . or not if he chose.

They waited until Stengel had time to get to the other side of the copse. The deputies dismounted, tied the three horses to a sapling, and retrieved their rifles. Moesch checked his H&K pistol to insure the caps were still in place and did the same with his SRG carbine. Dieter checked his H&K pistol, the two loaded cylinders secured in loops on his gunbelt, and his rifle. He was ready.

Walking softly and quietly, the two deputies approached the copse, Moesch walking a few yards to Dieter's right. They heard a horse whinny. Bettin was certainly there. Entering the copse, they saw the horse, the same one stolen from Walldorf according to its description, clipped ear and all. Bettin was standing next to it stroking its nose to quiet it.

The two deputies cocked and aimed their rifles. Dieter shouted, "Guenter Bettin! You are under arrest for escaping custody at Meiningen, assault, theft, and murder. Raise your hands and slowly turn around."

Bettin froze at the sound of Dieter's voice. He turned his head and saw the two rifles aimed at him and raised his hands. "Please be quiet!" he whispered. "The demons may hear you."

"Demons?" Dieter asked.

"I got here a little before dawn. I smelled smoke and thought about getting some food in the village. Instead, I found the village on fire. People were burning and screaming. I could see the demons running around killing people, tossing them in the fire. It was horrible!"

"And you think the demons are still there?"

"I don't know!" Bettin's voice quivered. "It got quiet, but I didn't want them to find me, so I hid here . . . then you came."

Stengel arrived while Bettin was telling his tale. "Something's wrong," Stengel said. "I could see some cots burning and there's a big fire in the center of the village, but I didn't see anyone moving."

"Okay, saddle up," Dieter ordered. "We'll investigate. We can run if we're attacked and outnumbered."

Bettin's stolen horse didn't have a saddle. Moesch slapped manacles on Bettin and then Stengel boosted him up on their packhorse. It wasn't the most comfortable arraignment, but the packhorse had a rudimentary saddle with stirrups and it was an easier ride for Bettin than bare-back.

✳ ✳ ✳

Stengel led them back the way they had come, back to the road from Walldorf. The brush along the hillsides was too dense for riding. Stengel halted and listened. After a moment, he turned to the deputies and whispered, "Arm yourselves." He dismounted, checked the powder in his rifle's frizzen pan, gave the reins to his horse to Moesch, and walked slowly forward.

Dieter dismounted, removed the holster hammer loop from his pistol, and drew his rifle from its scabbard. He passed the reins of his horse to Moesch, too. Kurt drew his H&K pistol, his other hand being encumbered with the reins of the horses.

Dieter gave Stengel a ten yard lead and then followed the tracker. The closer they approached the hamlet, the stronger the smell of wood smoke.

He could see some burned cots through the trees. Stengel was looking closely at the trees and brush on his left. He raised his rifle to his shoulder; he had spotted something off the side of the road. Dieter cocked his rifle as a figure appeared from behind a tree. Stengel fired, the figure dropped. Another figure appeared and fired a wheel lock cavalry pistol at Stengel. It missed. Dieter, with Archie's shooting instructions firmly in mind, aimed and fired. The figure lurched backward but didn't fall. Dieter dropped his rifle, drew his pistol, and fired again. This time the figure fell and by falling exposed a third figure. Dieter fired once more. The third figure grunted, leaned against a tree and slid down its trunk.

Moesch, after settling the horses, walked up next to Dieter with his pistol ready.

Silence. The only sound was Stengel stamping his rifle butt on the ground, reloading while watching the trees and brush on both sides of the road.

Dieter walked forward, watching, until he reached Stengel. "Think there are any more, Walter?"

Stengel finished reloading his rifle. "I'll check." He crouched and walked into the brush toward the three figures.

"Watch Stengel and the right, Kurt," Dieter ordered when the other deputy arrived with Bettin in tow, still atop the packhorse. He would cover Stengel in case there were more men in the woods on the left, while Dieter reloaded his carbine.

Stengel appeared and motioned for Dieter followed him into the trees. The *Jäger's* mount was a trained mounted constabulary horse. When its reins were dropped, it would stay in place until its rider returned.

When Dieter arrived, Stengel was standing over two bodies. A strong aroma of liquor filled the air. Several empty bottles littered the ground. Although their clothes were worn and ragged, their few pieces of armor and their buff coats were well maintained. The fired wheel lock lay on the ground next to one—its lock shattered by Dieter's first bullet. The second bullet had struck the man in the throat. Stengel's bullet found its mark in the middle of the first mercenary's face. Stengel stooped and searched the bodies.

Dieter knelt next to the third man slumped against the tree trunk. The man turned his eyes up to Dieter. A trail of blood from his mouth showed that he had been shot in the lung. He was drowning in his own blood.

"Who are you?" Dieter asked.

The man coughed, turned his head, and spit a gobbet of blood. "Bruno Beck . . . of Herter's band." He coughed again.

"Who—what is Herter's band?"

"Mercenaries. Herter said the Bishop wouldn't pay, so we left Cologne . . . ended up here."

"How many are in Herter's band?"

"Few now," his voice whispered. "Desertions . . . said they were soldiers, not bandits . . . twenty . . . maybe." he coughed again.

Dieter could see he was going fast. The wounded man appeared to panic, his eyes moving as if searching for something. He returned his gaze to Dieter's face, coughed one last time, and slumped.

Stengel finished his search of the other bodies. "Nothing," he reported, "nothing worth keeping. Even their powder is fouled."

"Think there are more in the trees?" Dieter asked.

Stengel stood and scanned the surrounding trees. "I don't think so. They would have come by now . . . or we'd have heard them running."

"I don't think three could take an entire village."

"I don't either. I think these three went off to get drunk and were left behind." Stengel shook his head, looking at the bodies, "Drunk. Idiots." He looked at Dieter. "We were lucky. They could have hurt us if they hadn't been drunk."

Dieter considered that. They were lucky. These three, from the smell of them, were too drunk to do much of anything. They couldn't have been very good mercenaries to be drunk while in the field.

After the exchange of shots, the forest had become quiet. As thick as was the ground cover, no one could move through it silently with any speed. He nodded. "Let's check the village."

✳ ✳ ✳

Dieter mounted and followed Stengel, leaving the corpses behind. They rode forward, following the smell of smoke.

The village, not more than a collection of a dozen cots, still smoked. Flames flickered here and there, but most of the cots had burned to the ground. They found the residents, thirty-two, by later count. A stake still burned in the center of the village, surrounded by bodies. It was unclear if the bodies had been burned at the stake or tossed on the flames later. Stengel and Moesch searched the cots and found more bodies.

The smoke had settled into a thin layer hanging just below the bottom boughs of the trees. There was no breeze to dissipate the haze—nor dissipate the smell. Dieter heard Moesch retching behind him. Bettin, too. Stengel was made of sterner material, but Dieter could see him clench his jaw. Dieter had seen worse in the aftermath of Tilly's horde that had cut a murderous swath through Germany, but not recently. He was ever thankful the up-timers stopped Tilly's rampage. Stengel rode through the village, searching for the tracks of the marauders. He said he wanted to see how many *demons* were involved and where they had gone. In a short time, he found their tracks and disappeared into the trees.

Dieter unshackled Bettin and put him to work laying out the bodies in the center of the hamlet. Bettin balked at first until he saw Kurt's face. He quickly got to work, interrupting it periodically to vomit.

Before Bettin was finished, Stengel returned. "I think there were twenty or twenty-five of them, heading south, off the road. All the food in the village seems to be missing. They may have attacked the village for food." Stengel paused before continuing. "They appeared to split up about a mile south. Fifteen headed west, back to the Rhineland, I'd guess. The rest continued on south. If the split is permanent, they're too few to endanger the larger towns . . . too few to threaten even the larger villages."

Dieter nodded. "We'll have to warn Walldorf and Meiningen so they can prepare. I worry about the smaller villages, but if they remain divided, even this small village could have driven them off . . . if forewarned." Dieter watched Bettin collecting the last few bodies under Kurt's watchful eye. "I think the Constabulary can deal with them if they can find them before they escape over the border."

Stengel agreed. He was about to reply, but paused and looked toward the edge of the village. "Someone is watching us," he said quietly to Dieter. "I caught a glimpse in the brush over there." He pointed with his chin across the burned village toward a small thicket."

"How many?"

"I think only one. I just saw a flash of color; someone is squatting down in the brush."

"A villager?"

"Could be. Hard to say. Whoever it is, they aren't big. Might be a woman."

"Where did you see them?"

"See that tree with a notch about head level?" Stengel said, referring to a tree behind him.

"Yes."

"Just to the left of that tree, maybe ten-twenty yards into the brush behind it."

Dieter looked where Stengel directed. He didn't see . . . wait . . . something moved, close to the ground. "I see them. Let's split—you to the right, me to the left, and we'll see who that is . . . maybe a survivor who fears us. We need to know who did this."

"Kurt! We're going to check on a survivor. Keep an eye on Bettin."

Moesch was leaning against a tree, having retched again. He straightened and nodded, acknowledging Dieter's order.

Dieter mounted his horse and rode slowly, watching the brush in the thicket where he had seen movement a few moments before. Stengel was circling the brush from the right when Dieter saw the survivor, a small child. The child, a girl Dieter now saw, screamed and ran.

He dismounted and ran after her. She saw Stengel appear from around the other edge of the brush and hesitated—deciding which direction to run. That gave Dieter the opportunity to reach her. She screamed again as he scooped her up and held her in his arms.

He held her, whispering, until her screams and trembling had finally quieted. Stengel watched, saying nothing. "You're safe, *Mädchen.* You needn't fear us." The girl hugged his neck in response.

"How old do you think she is, Walter?"

"Hard to say, four, maybe five years old. She *is* pretty small."

"She doesn't seem to be poorly fed, I think four is right."

"What is your name, *Mädchen?*" Dieter asked the girl.

At first, she didn't respond, and then she softly said, "Marta."

"And your father's name?"

"Poppa."

"Your mother's name?"

"Momma."

Dieter sighed. Her answers didn't help. Right now, they had other problems. "Walter, would you ride back to Walldorf and fetch Wachtmeister Eichel with a burial party? Maybe he will know if Marta has any family or relatives around here. Take Bettin's stolen horse and return it to the farrier."

Stengel nodded and turned his horse around. He gathered the reins of Bettin's stolen horse from where it had been tied and trotted back down the road toward the town they had left earlier that morning.

Dieter hoisted Marta up and lifted her to sit on his shoulders. He had once carried his daughter Bella in that fashion. She had been gone three years now, dying of a fever and dysentery when they were forced to flee Magdeburg and Tilly's horde.

Greta missed her too, he knew. He often awoke in the night to hear her crying softly in another room. He missed Bella, too. Maybe, someday, they would have another.

He clasped Marta's ankles to steady her while he walked back to the village. Moesch and Bettin had made a slower, closer inspection of the burned cots and the village's surroundings, looking for other survivors. They found none.

Noon came and went. Marta was hungry, and so was Dieter. They led their horses and Bettin, once more shackled astride the packhorse, down the road toward Walldorf and away from the sight and smell of the burned village. There, several hundred yards from the village; they stopped and made a temporary camp while they waited for Stengel's return.

Dieter searched his saddlebags and found half a loaf of apple-nut bread Greta had baked and some cheese. Marta, between sips of water, gobbled down the apple-nut bread while Dieter ate the cheese. Bella had liked Greta's apple-nut bread, too, he remembered. He wetted a cloth from his canteen and washed the soot and dirt from Marta's face. She looked much like Greta—light brown hair and green eyes. *So much like Bella*, he thought.

Stengel, with the Walldorf Wachtmeister and the burial party, arrived a few hours later. Wachtmeister Eichel had resisted coming but Stengel had used, inappropriately perhaps, his authority as a temporary Deputy Marshal, to convince the man to gather a burial party and come. The Wachtmeister hadn't liked the order, but he obeyed. When Dieter asked if he knew Marta, he denied any knowledge of her. "She's no family around here. She's your responsibility, now, Deputy. Take her to Meiningen or Suhl. The Church will take care of her."

DAY SIX

Sunday, September 17, 1634

Dieter and Kurt Moesch returned to Suhl late in the morning with Guenter Bettin in tow. Marta rode in front of Dieter, sharing his saddle. Walter Stengel had left them at the city's gate to go home, but not before reminding Dieter of their agreement on a new-styled rifle. He said he would bring the borrowed horse back in a day or two. He had to make his accounting with the Marshal Mitchell and the Court. Dieter suspected Stengel hoped the H&K revolver he had been given when they started on their search would be overlooked.

Dieter watched Stengel ride away. "Let's get on and report to Archie, Kurt. I want to tell Captain Gruber about the bandits. If he's quick, he may catch them before they can escape."

They heard church bells ringing across Suhl. The searchers had left the city the previous Wednesday, and both had forgotten today was Sunday. "It seems like forever since we left, and it's only been a few days," Moesch remarked.

Dieter glanced down at Marta sitting in front of him. "Yes, it does."

* * *

Dieter walked into Marshal's office with Marta in tow. Archie looked up from his paperwork and tilted his head in a silent question. "Pull up a chair . . . all of you and tell me what happened."

" . . . I have Bettin in a holding cell," Dieter reported. "He didn't try to escape. I think the Meiningen warders put a scare into him. From what the Meiningen Watch said and Bettin's story, I don't think the murder charge will stick. Manslaughter, maybe, but not murder."

"That's up to the court," Archie said

"I know, but that will be my opinion in my report."

"What did Eric Gruber say?"

"I gave him a full verbal report and returned his map. He was saddling up to go with one of his patrols that was about to leave. He's leading the troopers and hopes to catch both bandit gangs. *Deal with them in detail,* he said."

"Gruber's good. So are his constables. Want to go with them? Finish the job?"

"No. I've seen enough."

"What about her?" Archie asked, nodding at the little girl who was munching on a small wedge of cheese that Archie kept in his desk for whenever he skipped or missed lunch.

"She's an orphan we found. I'm off to see Pastor Weber next. The Meiningen churches said they send orphans here."

"Pastor Weber is a good man," Archie agreed. "He'll do what's right."

✳ ✳ ✳

"I'm sorry, Deputy Issler. I have no place to keep her and I can't keep up with a small child. There is no one I can think of who would accept responsibility for her," Pastor Weber said. He and Dieter were sitting in the Pastor's study discussing deputy's problem. Weber had been severely injured at one time and hobbled around with the aid of canes.

"You have no orphans here?"

Weber sighed. "No. We send them on to Jena, Erfurt or Magdeburg, one of the larger cities. They have the facilities and funding for orphanages. We do not."

"But . . . what do you suggest?"

Weber looked at him. He knew of the Issuers by reputation. They were becoming one of Suhl's more popular citizens . . . and they were frequent attendees of his church. Yes, they were the solution.

Dieter rode up to his home and noticed that Archie had installed a hitching rail and water trough in front of their house. The bakery, with its ever-present smell of freshly baked bread, was growing and he could hear the Mitchell's horses whinny in the stable behind the house. It was good to be home.

He rode up to the hitching rail, lifted Marta over his saddle's pommel, set her carefully on the ground, and dismounted. After tying his horse to the rail, Dieter picked Marta up and sat her on his shoulders.

"Hold on," Dieter said to Marta as he walked up to the door, opened it, and shouted into the open doorway, "Greta! I'm home."

Greta was in the kitchen where she and Marjorie were kneading dough for tomorrow's bread. She looked at Marjorie.

"Go," Marjorie said.

Greta walked down the hallway to the front of the house and saw Dieter silhouetted in the doorway. He was not alone.

She walked up to him, put her hand to her lips and breathed, "Oh!"

"Greta, this is Marta. She's been orphaned and is alone. I thought . . . Pastor Weber said . . ."

Greta stood looking at Dieter, then at Marta sitting on his shoulders. She stepped forward, tears running down her face, took the girl from Dieter, and held her. "Hello, Marta. Welcome to our home."

Mike Watson

THE FOURTH INTERVIEW

Suhl, June 9, 1636

Thomas Bloem had been taking notes as Dieter told his story. When Dieter paused, Bloem said, "I think that is one difference between up-timers and us, their generosity. We, us down-timers, would have done as that wachtmeister said, passed Marta on to the church or some other group. But you didn't."

"I'm—we're not up-timers," Dieter said, "but we, those of us who work with them, have learned much . . . to be better people."

"Not every up-timer is a saint," Archie added. "We've our criminals, too."

"No doubt," Bloem said. "People are people. But over all—"

"Archie! Got a minute?" a voice called. A tall up-timer walked across *der Garten* toward Archie and the group.

"Sure, Gary. Come here and I'll introduce you to Thomas and Maria."

After exchanging greetings, Gary Reardon said, "I don't want to interrupt your free time; just that I've moved the board meeting to the Boar's Head Inn, the upper room."

Maria and Thomas glanced at one another. Archie could tell they wanted to ask, *what board meeting?* They didn't ask. They were too polite to interrupt the exchange between Gary Reardon and Archie.

"Same time?"

"Yes. We've a new order from Nasi that the board must review and approve."

"Okay, we'll be there."

When Reardon had left, Thomas Bloem asked Archie, "Is that *Herr Reardon* of Suhl, Incorporated?"

"Yes. Not only of Suhl, Inc., but of several companies."

"He doesn't look like the richest man in Suhl."

Archie blinked. He glanced at the departing up-timer and then back to the two reporters. "Uh, I don't think he is. There are many—"

"He owns Suhl, Incorporated, doesn't he?"

"Gary? No. He's just a stockholder like Marjorie, Dieter, and me. Pat Johnson, another up-timer, is a stockholder, too. Gary and Pat are corporate officers. Marjorie and I are just board members; corporate directors. But, no single person owns the corporation."

Bloem expressed surprise. "Like the Dutch traders? Selling shares on their cargos/?"

"Yes, something like that. Shared profits, shared risks."

"How did that come about?"

Marjorie leaned over toward Bloem. She'd been talking with Greta and had only one ear listening to Archie's conversation with the reporters. "The whole thing started in our home when Pat Johnson came to see Archie while he was reloading."

"Reloading? That's another term I don't know," Bloem said.

"Up-time ammunition is reloadable—the brass, the shell casings," Archie said. "You need four things to reload: clean fired brass, a primer of the appropriate size, powder, and a bullet. Put them all together and you have a cartridge ready to be fired."

"You just put them together? It seems too simple."

"Putting them together is simple. We've machines at the Reservation—"

"That's where SMC, Suhl Metallic Cartridge, makes ammunition," Dieter said.

"SMC is a subsidiary of Suhl, Inc. Getting back to making cartridges, the problem isn't making the machinery to make cartridges, it's making the components, like primers."

"What's a primer?" Maria asked.

Archie stood and pulled a cartridge from a loop in his gunbelt and handed it to her. "See that round button on the bottom?" Maria fingered the cartridge and then looked at the flat base. "Yes, that," he said, pointing to the round button. "That's the primer. When struck, it fires, shooting a small jet of flame into the cartridge, igniting the powder within."

She passed the cartridge to her brother. "So small." Handing it back to Archie, he asked, "And this was the hardest to produce?"

"Yes, by far. There were some primers being made elsewhere, but they're very poor quality, and unstable. Many were not properly sized and were useless, or would fire when inserted into a brass casing. We needed something better. When Pat Johnson came to visit, I was close to running out of up-time primers and powder."

"So you decided to make primers yourself." Bloem stated.

"No. Not me. Pat Johnson got the idea, and he took it to Gary Reardon. Suhl, Incorporated and SMC, is the result. The creation of SMC and Suhl, Inc., is their story."

PART IV: SUHL, INC.

Mike Watson

I

July 1634, Suhl

Archie Mitchell was about to pull the lever on his reloading press when he heard his wife, Marjorie, call from the front of the house, "Pat's here!" Archie was in what the family called the gunroom, a room off the Mitchell portion of the two-story jointly owned house.

Dieter Issler was Archie's senior SoTF Deputy Marshal. He and Archie had come to Suhl the previous spring when they were assigned to the new district court.

The house was divided by floors. Archie and Marjorie had the ground floor, less the large room in the house's front that was the storefront for Greta Issler's bakery. Dieter and Greta had the upper floor.

The door of the gunroom was thick, and iron-strapped for security. Additional thick, hardwood paneling covered the walls, and iron bars covered the room's two windows. It was not as secure as an up-time safe, but it was the best strong-room that Archie could make until his up-time safe could be hauled from their house in Grantville. Inside the room was a wooden reloading table that faced one window. On that table, securely mounted, was a single-stage reloading press. Along one wall was a rack containing rifles and shotguns.

Archie's up-time oak desk, swivel chair and two wooden newly made captain's chairs faced the other window. He had commissioned the chairs from a local cabinetmaker who used photos from one of Archie's *True Tales of the West* magazine as a guide.

Pat Johnson walked into the gunroom and stopped when he noticed what Archie had in his hand. "Whatcha doin', Archie?"

Archie turned to face Pat in the doorway. "Decapping brass, Pat. Take a seat and tell me what's up."

Pat walked into the room, pulled the swivel chair from Archie's desk and slid it around to face Archie at the reloading table. "Got a delivery for you. This just came in," he said, giving Archie the box he carried. The box had been delivered to U. S. Waffenfabrik, Pat Johnson's gun manufacturing company. "It was delivered to the shop. One thousand large pistol primers from the Hart boys," Pat said.

Archie looked at the box in his hand. It was a plain, wooded box, flimsily made with *LP* written by hand on the top. "LP . . . large pistol? Did they size 'em right this time?" The last box of primers from the Hart Brothers was supposed to have been sized for Large Pistol, the primer size used in .45ACP cartridges. Unfortunately, the last batch from them wasn't sized correctly. When Archie tried to seat the primers into some brass, they wouldn't fit. They were too large and had detonated. The detonation hadn't damaged Archie's reloading press, but it destroyed the cartridge brass in the press. Archie had quit trying to find one that was the correct size after a half-dozen failures. Forty-five caliber brass was too valuable to be wasted trying to seat primers that were oversized.

"Well, so they say. I guess you'll find out when you try to seat them. I'd use my old brass first."

"You better believe it," Archie agreed.

Archie pulled the lever of the reloading press, finishing the act he had started when Pat arrived. The fired shell casing slide upwards and disappeared into the reloading die. Pat saw something shiny fall out of the bottom of the press and drop into a wooden box at Archie's feet. Archie returned the lever to its usual upright position, and the brass slid out of the decapping die with the spent primer missing. Archie took the decapped cartridge brass and dropped it into another larger box on the floor.

"Uh, what are you going to do with your spent primers?" Pat asked. He picked one and examined it.

"Haven't decided yet." Archie glanced at the box at his feet. It was filled inches deep with spent primers. "They are metal. Should be worth something, I suppose," he mused.

"Can I have some?"

"Well . . . okay. Why?"

"I just had an idea . . . well, it might be an idea," Pat explained. "I'd like to have some used up-time primers to play with. See if my idea is something I'd like to try."

Archie waited for Pat to expand on his statement. When he didn't give one, Archie reached down, picked up the box with the spent primers littering the bottom and extended it to Pat. "Here, take all you need." Pat reached into the box, took a handful of the spent primers and put them into his pocket.

Archie looked at the box of Hart Brothers primers and then back to Pat. "I hate using the Hart boy's primers. They use fulminate of mercury and that makes the brass crack and split after a few reloads. It cuts their reloading life in half, if not more." Archie muttered, " . . . wish I had a new supply."

"What was that, Archie?" He hadn't heard Archie's muttering clearly.

"I said I wish I had a new supply of cartridge brass. I think I'm going to run out of .45 Colt brass in a year, and then what? Back to cap 'n ball?" He looked at the box of primers and shook his head, "I hope not."

Pat stood. "Well, see you later, Archie. Let me know how those primers work."

"Will do, Pat," Archie said. He stood and walked with Pat to the front door. Archie watched Pat walk down the street for a moment, then closed the door and returned to the gunroom to decap more fired brass.

✻ ✻ ✻

Archie's wish gave Pat ideas. He needed to think on it for a while, do some research. When the time was right, he'd need to talk to Gary Reardon, maybe Ruben Blumroder. There could be opportunities here.

Pat's walk home took him past the Boar's Head Inn. His mind was still working on an idea that had formed when he visited Archie Mitchell. Pat Johnson was in the business of making firearms. He, like several gunsmiths in Suhl, was introducing up-time technology to the Seventeenth Century. The design of the SRG rifle in use by the USE army used two technologies, rifling and the flintlock ignition system. Neither technology was new. Both existed before the Ring of Fire. However, the arrival of Grantville and up-time firearms had sped up the development and use of technology earlier than had happened in the old time line.

The thought was still in his mind when he turned a corner and entered the street where the Boar's Head Inn was located. The inn had become the favorite watering hole for Suhl's up-timers when it was the temporary residence of Marshal Archie Mitchell and Deputy Dieter Issler the previous spring. Archie and Dieter had moved out when the two found permanent housing. Since that time, the inn had become *the* place favored by the city's up-timers. It had also become a cop bar, having become the chosen place to meet, eat and drink by the city's watch, the militia and members of the Mounted Constabulary stationed in Suhl.

Gary shifted direction and entered the Boar's Head Inn to discover his favorite table, in a corner next to the fireplace, empty. He sat with his back against the wall, ordered a stein of beer, and took a spent primer from his pocket.

He rolled the primer in his fingers, not seeing it. His mind was elsewhere. The idea that had started during his visit with Archie Mitchell was percolating. He looked closely at the primer. On one side of the primer cup was the face of the primer with the center dented by the impact of a firing pin. On the other side, the primer was an open cup with . . . Pat took his lock-blade knife from his pocket, flicked it open and used the tip to pry a three-legged, star-shaped piece of copper out of the cup—the primer's anvil. When a firing pin hit the smooth face of the primer, that face was pushed into the primer, crushing the primer compound against the anvil and igniting the compound. The shape of the anvil directed the burning primer compound into the powder of the cartridge. It was a simple concept, a simple design, but very difficult to make.

"May we join you, *Herr Johnson*?"

Gary looked up to see Osker Geyer, Suhl's temporary Watchmeister, and Mounted Constabulary Captain Eric Gruber, standing before him. The two habitually had a beer here in the Boar's Head Inn after making their joint walk around Suhl in the late afternoon. Their frequent walks were a public display of cooperation between the city watch and the Mounted Constabulary. Occasionally, they would have a third party, Marshal Archie Mitchell or Deputy Marshal Dieter Issler, or another one of Archie's deputies, with them. "Certainly. Take a seat," Pat replied.

"What have you there? You were studying it so much that you never saw us come in," Gruber asked, sitting next to Pat in the vacant chair that allowed him to watch the common room and its entrance.

"It's a spent cartridge primer. Archie Mitchell gave me some." He reached into his pocket, retrieved another spent primer, and gave it to Gruber. "Here, look."

Gruber took the primer and rolled it in his fingers, just as Pat had done minutes earlier. He inspected it and said, "I've never seen one that wasn't in a cartridge. So little for what it does. Here, Osker, take a look."

He passed the primer to Geyer, who made the same examination. Then he looked at the disassembled primer on the table before Pat.

They were interrupted by the barmaid with Gary's stein of beer. Gruber and Geyer gave their orders and returned to their examination of the spent primers.

Pat took a swallow from his stein while Gruber asked, "What makes the primer work?"

Pat completed his swallow and replied, "The most important part is the primer compound. It's a small piece of explosive that ignites when it is crushed in the primer cup by the firing pin. The Hart brothers use fulminate of mercury. Fulminate of mercury is extremely dangerous. The Hart brothers have already had one explosion in their factory that I know of. Their finished primers have to be carefully handled, too. I've heard tales of their primers exploding in people's hands."

Gruber nodded. He knew that rumor was true. An acquaintance who was reloading some up-time cartridges had a hole burned into his hand when a Hart primer ignited while he was handling it. It wasn't a disabling injury, but still . . .

"Looking at this, it seems so simple," Geyer observed. "Every time I see a piece of up-time technology, I think to myself, 'Why didn't I think of that?'"

"Me, too," Gruber agreed.

"I'm with you," Pat said. "I lived with up-time technology. I didn't think about it and had no idea how the technology worked, I just used it."

The barmaid returned with two more steins of beer for Gruber and Geyer. Pat was still nursing his first.

"Much of your technology is simple, once you understand the principles," Geyer said. "Before the Ring of Fire, I was content to just make iron—cast iron, some better wrought iron. I made ingots and shipped them out. Iron was what factors wanted, and I supplied them. Since the Ring of Fire, factories now want steel. I have been corresponding with some of my . . . uh . . . competitors about how they make steel. They don't see me as a competitor, yet, so they've been very informative. I know now what mistakes not to make. I'd rather learn from their mistakes than from ones I make through ignorance. Recently, I've started making steel. Now, I can't meet all the demand."

"How much different is making steel and making brass?" Pat asked.

Geyer paused, took a deep swallow from his stein. "In concept, not very much. Both are alloys, a mixture of two or more metals. For steel, it's iron and carbon, for brass, it's copper and zinc. The real difference is the temperature and how you manage extracting the metals from the ores. You need higher temperatures for iron and steel."

Pat nodded, absently. His idea was still percolating. He remembered Gary Reardon, the owner of Suhl's Bolt and Nut Company, saying that he needed to make more milling machines. He had started with one from Ollie Reardon and had made several more. But his stock of high-grade carbon steel was dwindling. Geyer's mention of making steel entered the mixture of thoughts in Pat's mind. He could almost see how Geyer's comments merged with his idea. He needed to talk with Gary.

More customers were entering the inn and the noise level was increasing. The afternoon was over and shadows were stretching along the streets. Time to go home, Pat decided. He'd have to face Ursula when she smelled beer on his breath.

Pat changed the subject, and the three finished the last of their beer. They had talked through the last of the afternoon and evening was approaching. The three left the inn. Gruber and Geyer turning left toward the center of town and Pat turned right.

Ursula will be waiting, and she'll smell the beer on my breath. He sighed, his mind returning to his discussion with Gruber and Geyer. *I'll sleep on this and talk with Gary tomorrow.*

II

August 1634, Suhl

Pat Johnson didn't meet with Gary Reardon the next day as planned; the unexpected intervened. Pat's company, U. S. Waffenfabrik, received a new order for twenty rifles. A letter from Grantville followed that order. The letter said Anse Hatfield had been severely wounded during the Battle of Ahrensbök and was now recuperating in Grantville. Anse was a friend and investor in Pat's company. He had been a part-time employee until the army recalled him the previous spring. Ordinarily, Hatfield should have been in a support position. That didn't happen. Somehow, Pat was told, Hatfield became involved in the battle and was wounded. His wounds weren't life threatening but, apparently, he was suffering from PTSD . . . *Post-Traumatic Stress Disorder.*

Anse Hatfield was a friend—a good friend—and his condition worried Pat. He jotted a letter to Hatfield, assuring him that his job was waiting whenever he returned to Suhl.

One interruption led to another. July slipped into August. Weeks passed before Pat finally had an opportunity to sit down with Gary Reardon and discuss his idea.

Pat still hadn't fleshed it all out; everything was still a bit nebulous. Pat was a visionary. He was good doing things, imagining things and working in his shop with his hands. What he wasn't, however, was a planner. Planning and organizing was one of Gary Reardon's skills. Pat's method of operation was straightforward, *see the hill, take the hill*, as Archie Mitchell would say. Gary, given the same situation, would see another approach, usually a better one, plan it out in excruciating detail and get it done. Pat needed Gary. Gary had the drive, once he understood the endgame, to get there quicker, and with less effort, than could Pat. Pat was the idea man. Gary was the man who could take the idea and make it a reality.

❋ ❋ ❋

Gary Reardon sat in Pat's office. For the last hour, Pat had been describing his idea, how it had occurred, the benefits, and what it could become. At the end of the hour, Pat had run down, finishing with, ". . . that's the idea, Gary. What do you think?"

During Pat's near monologue, Gary added to the vision with some of his own ideas. He wanted tungsten carbide to make harder, stronger dies and tools. With the inclusion of tungsten carbide, they saw a need for better steel, better than was currently available. Pat sat back in his chair and blinked. *Scope creep was setting in*, Gary realized.

The endgame vision was now much more clear after their meeting. How to get to that endgame still needed more thought. The two of them listed five things that had to be made and assembled to make the final product. Determining those five things was the easy part. How to make them was the real task ahead of them. Pat got up, went to his office door and asked someone to go to the inn down the street and bring back two steins of beer. Pat reached into his pocket and gave the other person some coins. " . . . and tell them to fill the steins with the cool beer in the cellar."

He returned to his desk. "I was getting thirsty and I expect you were, too."

Gary laughed. "I can count on you knowing your priorities, Pat."

Pat hung his head for a moment. It was true. His momentary attack of ADHD had been appeased.

Gary stood and paced. He habitually did so when he was wrestling with a problem. He had said that more than once. As he paced, he talked, clarifying their joint vision of the endgame. His method, now, was to work backward from his vision, detailing every item needed to make the vision a reality. "Well, we can get all the raw materials, I think. We have copper here in Suhl. We can get zinc to make brass from the Clausthal-Zellerfeld mines up in the Harz Mountains. Maybe tungsten, too. What we don't have are the tools to make the tooling and the dies . . . and the power to operate the machines. We need better steel, good hard carbon and tungsten carbide steel." He continued to build his list, mentally organizing them—what had to be done first, what they needed, and when.

He stopped before Pat's office window. The messenger Pat had sent for the beer was approaching with a large stein in each hand. They needed one more partner, another partner for the enterprise that would be built on Pat's initial idea.

"I think Osker Geyer would be interested." Pat said. "I know he wants to make carbon steel instead of cast and wrought iron. I know he's experimenting with crude carbon steel. He told me so. And, he mentioned wanting a powered hammer forge and stamping mill, too."

Gary stopped pacing for a moment and considered Pat's statement. It mirrored his own thoughts. "Could be, Pat. If Osker Geyer wants to upgrade his iron foundry to a steel mill, I don't see why we can't help him— in exchange for him helping us." Gary returned to his chair in front of Pat's desk. "We'll need power for our factory, too, if we want to get into commercial production—more output than can be made by hand."

Pat agreed. "How about Schmidt steam engines? Maybe we can get a price-break if we make a volume order—combine our order with one from Geyer?"

"It's worth asking, isn't it?" Gary said.

"Let's go visit Geyer and see what the thinks . . . after we finish our beer."

"Good idea," Gary agreed as Pat's messenger appeared at the door with two steins. It was a hot day and, Gary thought, a nice cool beer would be an enjoyable interlude before bracing Geyer in his lair.

✳ ✳ ✳

Osker Geyer was sitting on a stool behind a tall desk in Suhl's watch office, writing in a ledger, when Gary Reardon and Pat Johnson found him. Geyer was tiring of the city council stalling to fill his temporary position with a permanent appointment. *I have work to do at my foundry. If the city council doesn't act soon, I'll give them an ultimatum. I'll give them a week and if nothing is done, I'll resign. It's too much to ask . . .*

"*Herr Geyer, Guten Tag,*" Pat Johnson said. "How are you on this fine day?"

Geyer glanced out the windows to the gray overcast. Returning to look at the two, he simply said, "*Herr Johnson,*" Geyer then looked at Gary Reardon, "and you, too, *Herr Reardon.*" Geyer was known for his bluntness, but his greeting was more blunt than usual. Geyer was, if not quite friends with the two up-timers, he was at least a good acquaintance. He knew quite well that Pat Johnson and Gary Reardon wouldn't appear before his desk without wanting something. What was it Archie Mitchell had said? *Keep your hand on your purse when talking with these two.*

"Pat and I would like to discuss an idea we have with you." Gary Reardon said.

"What do you want the watch to do?"

"Absolutely nothing. This is a business proposal for you. Well, not a proposal, yet, just an idea."

Geyer looked sharply at Gary and then at Pat. "*Humph!* Come back into my office." With that, he got off his stool and walked into his office at the rear of the room.

✳ ✳ ✳

". . . we thought that a combined order may get us a volume discount and save us all some money," Pat explained. "It'd help you with your upgrades and expansion, and we'd get what we need from you—at a discount, of course."

Geyer silently listened to the two seated across from his desk. He had only asked a few questions, but Pat could see the wheels turning in Geyer's head. He had a hungry look, but was too cautious to go further until he'd calculated his risk.

Pat continued, "And, of course, we would sell shares in our new . . . consortium. We've already spoken to some who may be interested and have some funds to invest."

"Who?" Geyer asked.

"We can't disclose that at the moment," Gary said.

Pat knew only too well that the only investors so far were Gary and himself. He knew of others who would invest when asked, but they needed more money. For that, they needed a plan, something they could show to the potential investors that would convince them the concept was feasible, and that Pat, Gary, and the . . . consortium were the ones who could make it possible.

"We need to develop a plan, a financial plan, business model and a project plan for all of us. There are a number of interrelated tasks and dependencies that we have to manage if we bring this off."

"Determine the critical path, determine what has to be done and when it has to be done," Gary added. "The critical path is those tasks that had to be done, in sequence, for the plan to progress. We can do some tasks in parallel without affecting the critical path as long as we finish them as planned. If the plan works, we could be millionaires."

The three talked throughout the afternoon, interrupted occasionally by a watchman. They had not totally sold Geyer on the idea. He wanted to do some research and analysis himself. Toward the end of the day, he sent a message to the city council by a watchman to say that he was taking a few days off.

"Ambitious, aren't you," Archie Mitchell said. Pat and Gary entered his office in the Suhl District courthouse just as he was about to quit for the day. They recounted their conversation with Geyer and were about to expand on their need for funding when Archie interrupted, "Let's talk on my way home."

Archie led the three out a side-door. His office, one that he shared with court Bailiff Karl Wagner, was in the rear.

The courthouse was next to the Mounted Constabulary barracks. As they passed the barracks, a mounted constabulary troop approached toward them to enter the barracks compound. From their appearance, they were returning from an extended patrol on the surrounding roads and by-ways of the Suhl district. The lieutenant in command of the troop gave Archie a salute. He stopped and returned it as they rode past. The Marshal was a popular figure among the constabulary troopers and their officers. He often rode with them whenever he had business in areas they patrolled. Archie was willing and ready to take the same risks as did they if trouble occurred.

"How much do you need?" Archie asked Gary after the patrol cantered past and through the barracks gate.

Gary didn't reply until the last trooper disappeared into the compound. "Sixteen thousand silver Guilders to start."

Archie choked. "Boys, if you think I have that much, you're badly mistaken. I don't have anywhere near that much. I put a big dent in my ready cash when Dieter and I bought the house here in Suhl."

"No, no, no, you misunderstand," Pat protested. "That's how much we need in total for the first stage. We're soliciting investors. You can invest whatever you can afford."

They continued walking. The courthouse and mounted constabulary barracks were on higher ground than most of Suhl. The three continued walking down into the city and through the riverside flats toward the western gate. Archie's house rested on high ground along the western wall with room for a small stable in back; and was just a few streets from the western gate.

With the house in sight, Archie stopped. He needed to ask them something before he was side-tracked. "And how many stages are there in this project of yours? You planning to sell more shares at each stage? That would dilute the value of my shares, wouldn't it?"

"Well . . . maybe. We hope that after the first stage, the project will have products to sell to help finance the remaining stages. As an initial investor, we could give you a seat on the board."

"Well, I'll still need to think on that, see if there could be any conflicts of interest." They walked on. "Ok," he decided as they approached his front porch. "Since we're here, why don't you and Gary have supper with us, and then we'll talk some more. I want to hear your complete plan. Dieter may be interested, too."

"We don't mind. We're asking folks to keep quiet on this, even if they don't invest, until we have more commitments, investors and suppliers plus a few material contracts." They started walking toward the house with its aroma of fresh bread.

"You're going to have to spend a lot of time on this. What about your businesses?" Archie asked.

"Anse Hatfield is coming back, I hope," Pat said. "I've sent him some letters telling him what's been going on since he left last spring. He'll keep U. S. Waffenfabrik running for me," Pat said.

Gary chimed in. "And I have a good foreman. Gaylynn will keep a close eye on him. We're covered, Archie."

"I hope so. I don't want you to impoverish yourselves doing this."

"We won't," Gary replied. "We'll merge both of our companies into the new one once it's running. I think we'll have more business than we can handle."

Archie opened the front door and ushered them in.

* * *

The family, as the Mitchells and Isslers thought of themselves, ate jointly around a large rectangular table. The table was another piece of up-time furniture that Archie had shipped from their house in Grantville to Suhl. Marjorie had brought the basics, chinaware, silverware and cooking utensils, when she and Greta joined their men in May. The remaining furniture, items they had selected before the move, had been arriving a few pieces at a time, since then.

The table normally seated six. It could be expanded to seat more, but that wasn't necessary this time. For this evening, family and guests filled all the chairs. Little Marta sat at a table corner next to Greta. Marjorie had had a crock-pot simmering in the bakery's oven all afternoon, a mutton stew. Fortunately, there was more than enough for Pat and Gary. By family custom, no business was discussed around the table. That custom was bent when Archie mentioned that Pat and Gary had a business deal they wanted to discuss with him. After the meal was over, Archie motioned for the men to follow him into his office, the gunroom.

"Okay, now what's your game?" Archie asked when everyone was seated.

Gary talked. He recounted Pat's initial idea about the spent primers and how that idea had sparked others. "It depends," Gary Reardon said, opening the conversation. "What we want to do at first is, with Osker Geyer, to make machine tools—on a small scale. We need to make tools to provide mechanized production lines."

Dieter Issler entered the gunroom, sat and listened. "I don't understand all the issues that Gary is talking about, but it seems very expensive." He glanced at Archie sitting behind his desk. "But, I trust Archie. If he becomes involved, I'm willing to do the same . . . as much as we can. Greta and I have been saving for a long time. I missed some of your opening remarks, Gary. I need to understand what's going on."

"It's the old, *make tools to make tools*, Dieter. What we want in the near term and coming year, is to use those tools to make cartridge brass . . . ," Gary said.

"And primers," added Pat when Gary paused.

"If you are going to make brass and primers, why not go whole hog and make complete cartridges?" Archie asked.

146

"We want to do just that," Gary said, leaning forward for emphasis. "But we need to determine what is feasible and what isn't. Saying we want to make ammunition outright may not be advisable at this time. It could cost us investors if we're not careful. Too many people seem to think we don't have the ability, yet, to make cartridges in full commercial quantities, that the needed mechanization can't be made nor put into operation. I know there are some people making cartridges but they're low volume—using equipment like your single-stage press there." Gary said, pointing to Archie's reloading press bolted to a nearby table. "Each cartridge is hand made. How many can you reload with that press, Archie?"

Archie sat back in his swivel chair and rubbed his chin. High-volume throughput wasn't a feature of a single-stage reloading press. Back up-time, he used a Dillon progressive press. With it, he could load hundreds of cartridges, four or five hundred, in an hour. Still, hundreds were far from the number of cartridges needed for commercial quantities and he no longer had that Dillon progressive press. "I never counted, but maybe around fifty or sixty in an hour, somewhere around there," he replied.

"It's as I thought. I'm not a reloader myself, but I know how it's done. The number Archie quoted is about the number I'd estimated. To be commercially viable, we need to make thousands, tens of thousands, if we can, in an hour. Commercial quantities have always been a goal, but no one believes it can be done—yet. So . . . we won't mention it."

"The Hart brothers have their primers in commercial production," Dieter pointed out.

"That's true, Dieter, but they're using manual labor for their production line. Several people died last year when their plant blew up. In addition, they're using fulminate of mercury and are mostly making just percussion caps . . . only a few actual primers. I've been investigating the Hart Brothers business and manufacturing methods—as best I can from a distance. Their operation is dangerous, and I've heard they had another plant explosion. The way the Hart brothers do business is the wrong way to do it. It's dangerous and they display a callous disregard for the safety of their employees."

"We want to make primers that are non-corrosive—the French primers are corrosive—but they don't make brass brittle like the Hart brother's primers. I've heard that lead styphnate is dangerous to make and to handle, but it would be better than what the Hart boys are making."

"Hang on a minute." Archie stood and walked over to a shelf on his wall that was lined with books. He ran his finger across several titles and pulled one out. He read the table of contents while he returned to his chair. "Ah, page sixty-five."

"What's that, Archie?" Pat asked.

Archie showed him the cover. "It's the 1996 edition of *Richard Lee's Reloading Manual.* I have several reloading manuals, Hornady, Speer, and Lyman. I remember writing some notes in this one." Archie found page sixty-five, read the page, and flipped to the next one. "Here it is. Lee wrote the EPA would soon ban lead styphnate for primers because of the lead used in its production. I remember thinking, *what's next?* Lee talked about 'green' primers but I couldn't find much about them. I did a bit of research and found another primer compound that was more stable than fulminate of mercury, didn't leave a lead residue, didn't damage cartridge brass and was non-corrosive. I thought I had written some notes here, and I did— DDNP, full name, *Diazodinitrophenol.* Wow! What a mouthful. I think I pronounced it right. DDNP has been used as an explosive for a long time, blasting caps and such, but also for primers before World War Two." Archie gave the open manual to Pat, who read the page and passed it to Gary.

Gary returned the manual to Archie. "Why did they continue to use lead styphnate if this was better?"

"Well, there's better, and then there's better. I suspect that too many ammunition plants, the Army operated their own, your see, were already using lead styphnate. With World War Two on the horizon, no one wanted to change. It would be costly when funds were hard to get. Besides, the danger of lead poisoning from the primers wasn't well known, if at all."

"How is this DDNP made?"

"Beats me! I'm no chemist," Archie said as he returned the manual to his bookshelf.

"Pat," Gary said to his partner, "I think we, or one of us, should consult the Library in Grantville. I think Geyer will need some up-time data, too."

Archie interrupted. "Count me out. I can't go."

Marjorie entered the room and asked, "Archie, Dieter, can you help me for a minute? I need backs stronger than mine."

Archie nodded. "Be there in a minute, Marj. I'll be right back, boys," and with that, he rose and followed Dieter out of the room.

Pat and Gary continued their conversation. "I have some orders to fill," Pat said. "Think Geyer would want to go with you?"

"He might. I'll ask. It'll give me a chance to look for some more investors, too. How much do we have promised?"

"Umm, nine thousand Guilders. We have credit with the local money people. I haven't asked the gunsmiths yet. Some would be against it. They'd have to retool and some can't afford to do that by themselves."

"They'll have to at some point, Pat. Flintlocks are obsolete now that percussion caps are coming available in large volumes. I know the USE army is buying most of them, but there'll soon be more caps available to the public. It's inevitable that change is coming."

"True, and the timing is right for us if we can meet our business plan."

They stood as Archie returned. "I think we have discussed everything needed for the moment, Archie. You've helped us a lot. May we borrow your manuals?" Gary asked.

"Sure, Gary, just take care of them. There aren't any more that I know of."

Mike Watson

III

September 1634, Grantville

Gary Reardon and Osker Geyer arrived in Grantville in the middle of a rainstorm, a downpour. They had hired a coach for their trip from Suhl. When the rain started, the coach leaked. Rain entered through the windows, around the leather shutters they had rolled down, and water dripped from the coach roof where it had soaked through. Both were wet, cold, and uncomfortable. "This is where I grew up, Osker," Gary said when the coach rolled up before the two-story house. "Dad is in Magdeburg, but Mom is home. We'll stay here while we're in Grantville."

Osker Geyer looked at everything as they passed through Grantville. This was his first visit to the up-time town—city, now, and he appeared to be amazed at every turn. Seeing confirmed what he had only heard of. Grantville impressed him; the streets, the lights, the buildings—everything.

Gary paid the coach driver and hauled their luggage up to the Reardon front porch, out of the rain. His mother, Nancy, an elderly white-haired lady, was waiting in the doorway.

"Gary! How good to see you . . . and you've put on some weight, I see. Come inside and take off those wet coats." The two men entered the house, and she waited while they hung their coats on hooks near the door. "Come back to the kitchen and I'll fix you something hot," she said after giving Gary a strong maternal hug.

They followed her to the kitchen in the house's rear. Osker Geyer was looking at everything—the linoleum covered floor, the porcelain sink and chromed faucets, and, although he didn't understand their purpose at first, the stove and refrigerator. Nancy Reardon continued her conversation with her son as he and Osker sat at the kitchen table.

"Gaylynn is a great cook, Mom. She has to try every new recipe on me as soon as she finds one. Greta Issler is teaching her baking and Gaylynn has discovered the joys of honey-rolls." While they talked, his mother filled a kettle with water from the sink and put it on the stove to heat.

"Mom," Gary said, "let me introduce Osker Geyer. He's a business associate of mine in Suhl. We're here to consult the library."

"*Guten Tag, Frau Reardon.* I'm most happy to make your acquaintance," Geyer said.

"Glad to meet you, too, *Herr Geyer.* You are very welcome."

She turned to Gary, "I've your old room available and Dewey's room, too. He's gone with your father to Magdeburg." The kettle began to boil. She placed some loose tea in a metal ball and put that ball in the teapot before turning a knob on the stove to shut it off. While this was going on, Gary opened a kitchen drawer, found a potholder, and gave it to his mother. "Thank you, Gary," she said, picking up the kettle and pouring water into the teapot. "Will you two be staying long?" she asked. "There's no rush. I don't expect your dad and Dewey to be back for a couple of weeks."

"I don't know, Mom," Gary replied. "It will depend on what we find in the library."

The two men rose early the next morning and, after a quick breakfast at Nancy Reardon's insistence, headed for the library. Gary signed for the two of them in the registry just inside the doorway, walked past the guard, and asked the librarian where to find books on steel making and chemistry.

She directed them to the science section of the library. Geyer immediately found several volumes on the production of steel and the Bessemer process, took two volumes, and seated himself at a corner table. Osker had brought his secretary with him, a small leather case containing paper and several pencils. He had been warned that pens and ink were forbidden in the library; note cards and other paraphernalia were permitted. Absorbed, he read and made notes.

Gary wasn't as fortunate. He hadn't known that there were two kinds of chemistry, organic and non-organic. Both had several books under each category. Finally, in frustration, he found the librarian and asked her if she knew of any books on primers, specifically lead styphnate and DDNP. The librarian hadn't heard of DDNP but there had been many researchers interested in lead styphnate. She led him to those volumes.

The two men spent the morning reading and taking notes. Geyer issued a constant stream of muttered comments and hired a local researcher to help translate books from up-time English to colloquial German.

"Finding what you were looking for, Osker?" Pat asked. The hour was approaching noon, and Geyer appeared to have been successful in his search.

"Yes, and no. The Bessemer process is more complicated than I thought. I have found that my initial understanding—blow air through the molten iron, is not as simple as I thought. I want to make specialty steel and thought using the Bessemer process was the answer, but I think I was wrong . . . at least to start. I use what the books here call the puddling process. It's easier to alter the alloys than my current method. I need a hammer forge and a rolling and stamping mill, but I think I need to build, what you up-timers call, a prototype plant. I can add a Bessemer furnace later."

"You'll still be able to make tool steel and tungsten carbide steel for us, right? We need that to make the dies and other tools."

"Yes, as long as I can get the proper ores. If you can get zinc to make brass, I can get tungsten from the same place." He paused and stroked his short beard. "I think my next step is to place our orders with Schmidt Steam. Have you found what you need?"

Gary wagged his head from side to side and finally sighed. "Like you, yes and no. It's harder than I thought. I think I need an alchemist."

The trip to Grantville wasn't a total loss, not for Oskar Geyer at least. Gary, unfortunately, had to search elsewhere. He had found some information—enough to know he couldn't make primer compound by himself. He just didn't have the background, the experience or the knowledge.

IV

September 1634, Essen

Nicki Jo Prickett sat in her office in the Essen Chemical works, nursing a cooling mug of tea and staring out the window. October was approaching, and the weather had cooled earlier than expected. She should have been doing something, but . . . it just wasn't the same since last year when Tobias Ridley and Solomon des Caux had blown themselves up. She watched the wind blow through the trees in front of the building. Some had turned already, even if autumn wouldn't officially arrive for another week.

The explosion that had killed two of her researchers wasn't her fault. She knew that, and Katherine kept reminding her of that fact. She was unmotivated, and . . . just coasting. In one part of her mind, she was disgusted. She wasn't used to being idle. The rest of her mind, however, kept returning to the scene from the previous year, the scene of bodies being retrieved from the rubble after the explosion.

Katherine Boyle, the fifth daughter of Richard Boyle, the Earl of Cork, was in the outer office. Katherine and Nicki Jo were—what up-timers would call—a couple. They had been together for almost two years; discovering one another after Katherine had fled to Brussels, away from her abusive husband, the late unlamented Arthur, Viscount Ranelagh. Ranelagh had hounded Katherine all the way from England to Brussels where he apparently drown in a canal while drunk.

Tobias Ridley and Solomon des Caux had caused their own deaths, and that of others, by ignoring her instructions, trying to short-cut a process they believed could move faster. By ignoring some steps, they proved themselves wrong. The steps required to further refine and purify some ingredients were important. Tobias and Solomon thought otherwise. They were wrong, and the result was an explosion that destroyed the lab, killed Ridley and des Caux, and some other nearby experimenters.

GIGO, she thought. For Tobias, that was *Contaminants in, BOOM out.* She giggled and the sudden giggles startled her. The giggle was so . . . inappropriate. She sighed. *I should be in the lab. At least I'm not cutting myself.* Nicki Jo had a habit of punishing herself. Katherine had found her crying and cutting lines into her arm a week after the explosion. She pulled back her sleeve and glanced at the white lines of scars. The freshest one was now over six months old. That line of thought took her down one circuitous path after another. Katherine interrupted her thoughts; calling from the outer office. "Nicki Jo, you have a visitor."

"Who is it?"

"Hi, Nicki Jo," Gary Reardon said from the doorway. "It's been awhile." Gary Reardon was twice Nicki Jo's age. She knew him, a friend of her father. Brushing past Katherine, he walked over to Nicki Jo's desk and sat down across from her.

"I went to the chemical plant when I arrived," Gary said, "spoke with Banfi Hunyades, and was surprised to learn you haven't been actively working for some time."

"I've delegated much of the research to Banfi," Nicki Jo replied.

"She's lost her motivation," Katherine added.

Nicki Jo shook her head as if emerging from a fog and became aware of his presence. "Gary Reardon! Why are you here and how did you get in?" she asked.

"Ms. Boyle, I believe her name is, made the mistake of glancing toward your office door when I asked to meet you. You know me, Nicki Jo. I don't like waiting in outer offices—especially when it's an office of an old friend. As for the *why*, I would like to consult with you on a project."

"Sometimes Katy is too easy," Nicki Jo muttered. "She knew I didn't want to see anyone."

"I know it's been awhile since we've seen each other but, I have a project that may interest you."

"Ha."

"I think so, and so does Ms. Boyle."

"Call me, Katherine," Katherine Boyle interrupted from the doorway. When Gary Reardon had marched past her into Nicki Jo's office, she had followed.

"Katherine. Thank you," he said. Turning back to Nicki Jo, Gary continued. "When I entered, I found you sitting here. I've been told why you are—have been—upset, but, Nicki Jo, it's been almost a year! It's time got yourself working again. You can't continue punishing yourself."

"And you think you know how to motivate me?" Nicki Jo asked peevishly.. She saw Banfi Hunyades slip into her office, watching.

"Maybe. Maybe not. Won't know until I try."

"What do you want?"

Gary had noticed Hunyades entrance, too. He nodded to the older chemist in acknowledgement. "I want you to design and build a chemical plant," he told Nicki Jo. "A plant that is safe, using well-documented processes and able to operate with limited professional supervision and oversight."

"What kind of plant?" she asked.

"We—"

"Who's we?"

"Nicki Jo. Let me finish a sentence, please. The *we*, is me, Pat Johnson, Osker Geyer from Suhl, Archie Mitchell, others in Suhl, and perhaps some more whom I'll meet in Magdeburg on the way home. The *where* is Suhl, and the *what* is center-fire cartridge primers."

"The Hart boys are already making primers," she countered.

"Yes—using fulminate of mercury, which shortens the life of cartridge brass and is highly unstable. We want to reload our fired cartridge brass. We want you to design a facility—from end-to-end, to make non-mercury, non-corrosive, non-toxic primers. Using DDNP if possible, lead styphnate as an alternative."

"DDNP?" Banfi Hunyades asked, interrupting the conversation.

"Full name, *Diazodinitrophenol.* It's made from picric acid. I understand you all have some experience with that."

"More explosives," Nicki Jo said. For many reasons, and not just because of the explosion last year, she was reluctant to be involved with explosives.

"Has to be, Nicki Jo, if the primers are going to work. We don't want our plant to blow up in our face nor do we want to ignore the risk to our employees. That's why we need a chemical engineer, one who can design the chemical processes and also design a safe plant to make the primers."

"Do it, Nick," Katherine said from the doorway.

Nicki Jo turned her chair around to look out the window. After a moment of silence, she whispered, low but loud enough for the other occupants in the room to hear. "What am I doing here? Nothing. Maybe I do need something to take my mind off Tobias and Solomon. I really hadn't liked them all that much, chauvinists that they were."

"What about you, Katy?" she asked.

"Is this a permanent position, Mr. Reardon, or—" Katherine asked.

Hunyades straighten in his chair when she asked her question. The older chemist had seated himself in a side chair during the conversation, seemingly disinterested. Until now.

"Call me Gary, Katherine, if you would."

"Gary."

"It could be, if that is what Nicki Jo wants," he said to her. "It's an option."

Returning to Nicki Jo, he said, "I know you have a position here and I—we, our investors—wouldn't ask you to give that up. We were thinking of a consultancy. Fixed duration, explicit goals with mutually agreed upon timeline, bonuses and options to alter or extend the contract."

"How long?"

"We want to be in production in a year."

"What!"

Hunyades was nodding his head. He wasn't an idle member of Essen Chemical. He understood what it took to build a complete new chemical plant. His reaction ended one of Nicki Jo's fears.

"Yes. Full commercial production in a year producing at least a thousand primers, per production line, per day."

"Katy?" Nicki Jo asked.

"I think you should take the contract," she answered.

"I agree, Nicki Jo," Hunyades added.

"But—"

"You need to do something besides sit on your backside in your office, feeling depressed, and punishing yourself," Katherine said. "Everyone who knows you also know what you are, and aren't, doing."

"I'm not—"

"Yes, you are. What about all those fresh scars on your arms?" she countered. "What would Colette say? And Fernando, and Maria Anna?"

The names were, at first, unfamiliar to Gary. He searched his memory and realized Colette Modi was the owner of Essen Chemical; the one who had hired Nicki Jo as her Chief Researcher. Fernando and Maria Anna were the King and Queen of the Netherlands, following the separation of the Netherlands from Hapsburg Spain, and Essen Chemical investors.

"Tell them you're taking a sabbatical from Essen Chemical," Gary said, "and that we're willing to license the process to Essen chemical . . . if it works—given some constraints and non-compete—and under our brand," Gary responded quickly.

"Katy? What about her?" she asked Gary.

"She's welcome, too, Nicki Jo. We'll need you to train a staff to run the production lines safely. Katherine can help, and I'm sure *Herr Hunyades* can manage the research here at Essen Chemical while you're gone. Correct, *Herr Hunyades*?"

"*Ja, Herr Reardon,*" He confirmed. "It wouldn't be any different from what I've been doing for the last year," Hunyades added.

"I know something has to change. Katy is right. I need something to take my mind off those two—no, I'm not going there. Maybe a change of scenery, fresh faces, new . . . ," she muttered, turning around to look out her window.

"I could design the plant from end to end, Gary had said . . . and I can trust Banfi to run things here, and send reports to Suhl to keep me in the loop."

She drummed her fingers on the arm of her chair. Turning her chair back around, she exchanged looks with Katherine and Hunyades. Receiving a nod from Katherine, she turned to Gary, "It would be different, and I must have complete control."

He nodded.

This would be a competition, Nicki Jo realized. Others were involved in their own, similar projects. "Gary?" Nicki Jo asked, turning her full attention to him.

"Yes?"

"How many primers are the Hart brothers producing?"

"The best we know is 10,000 per day. Most of them are caps, not actual primers."

Nicki Jo looked down at her desk and closed her eyes. "Idiot boys. They'll kill themselves yet. Continue with your proposal." She spun her chair around and looked out her window.

Gary followed her gaze. A freight wagon was leaving the warehouse and moving toward the gate. Nicki Jo remained looking out the window, listening as Gary continued.

"We want to have several parallel production lines in operation. Higher output through parallel production."

That statement didn't surprise her. It was necessary if Gary's intent was to produce tens of thousands of primers daily. She turned from the window and asked, "Does the army need that many?"

"I don't know. We don't intend to sell solely to the army. We have other plans."

"Like what?"

"Well . . . ," he looked at the three of them, Hunyades, Katherine Boyle and Nicki Jo. "This is all confidential, you understand."

"Yes," Nicki Jo acknowledged. Katherine and Hunyades agreed.

"Okay. Let me tell you about the Consortium . . . "

Mike Watson

V

October 1634, Suhl

Archie Mitchell was alone in his office, late in the afternoon, reminiscing. The days were noticeably shorter, and his office was growing dark as evening came on. His office mate, Chief Bailiff Kurt Wagner, was assisting Judge Fross in court. It was time to light the lamps, or go home.

Dieter Issler, Archie's senior deputy, had returned from a fugitive hunt in the Wald and was taking some time off. He had returned with the fugitive, and with a little four-year-old girl, Marta, an orphan. The Issler family was adopting her.

The little girl was having a strange impact on the combined Mitchell/Issler household. After all these years, to have a child in the house was unsettling. Marta called him *Großpapa*. Marjorie was being very . . . grandmotherly. A sudden wave of longing swept through him as a memory of his long-gone daughter Lena welled up.

He calmed himself. *No time to be maudlin.*

Anse Hatfield had dropped by earlier in the day, and Archie took him to lunch at the Boar's Head Inn. Anse was in a bad way. His injuries, losing some fingers and part of his left hand, were minimal, but their loss depressed him. He couldn't do some things he had before, couldn't grip a tool with his left hand, and the limitations he now had made him feel useless. In addition, they hadn't medically discharged him from the Army, just sent home as a National Guardsman. Hatfield took the change of his status as an insult, even if it came with a promotion. *Too damaged for the army, but good enough for the National Guard,* he'd said.

Pat Johnson, keeping his promise, offered him a job. So far, Anse was resisting; he didn't want an office job. He talked about starting a small trucking company for the city, and training drivers for the National Guard. Frank Jackson was sending some small trucks, too small to be used as APCs, for that purpose. Finally, Anse told Archie about his fiancé, Leonore von Wilke. She was still in the Army, and she was another reason Hatfield wouldn't make any long-term commitments. *Whither goest Leonore, so would Anse Hatfield,* Archie observed.

Archie was about to grab his hat, cane, and head home when Pat Johnson walked in. "Hi, Archie."

"Hi, Pat. Pull up a chair. What brings you here?"

Pat walked over to Archie's desk, moved one of the side chairs in front of Archie's desk, and sat. "Have a question. Do any of your manuals describe how to form cartridge brass?"

Pat had been taking notes from Archie's reloading manuals. His question stirred Archie's curiosity. "Hmmm, I'll have to look. I know that cartridge brass is a 70/30 mix of copper and zinc and that primer brass is softer, about ninety percent copper to ten percent, or less, of zinc."

"I didn't know that. I hadn't thought about primer brass yet. My focus has been on making cartridge brass."

Kurt Moesch, one of Archie's junior deputies, walked into Archie's office, saw that he had a visitor, and left, closing the office door behind him. It must have been a minor matter. The deputies knew it was unwise to interrupt Archie when he had a visitor, unless the interruption was warranted. "Why do you ask?"

Pat scooted his chair closer to Archie's desk. "We need to mechanize the process if we are to produce the number of cartridge brass that we will need."

Archie paused, searching his memory. "As best that I recall—I read this somewhere—they made cartridge brass in three steps on three machines. You start with a small brass cup, less than an inch in diameter, and run it through three passes on each of the three presses. Each pass forms the copper cup into a closed cylinder until it's at the required length and thickness after the last pass on the second machine." Archie stopped, opened a desk drawer, and retrieved a piece of paper.

He took a pencil and drew a block diagram of the process as he remembered it. "You have to do it in stages," he drew three squares on the paper, "or the brass will split or crumple."

Next, he drew arrows from the first square to the second, and another arrow from the second to the third. "The brass is cleaned and lubed before it's passed to the next machine." He wrote *C&L* on each arrow and *Extrude/3Passes* in the first two boxes.

"The third stage, the final stage, is forming the base, imprinting the headstamp, cutting the primer pocket and an ejector groove. The last step includes cutting the brass to length and trimming the mouth. Once the tooling is set up, you can make a bunch of brass in few minutes." He drew a bubble next to the third square, drew an arrow from the bubble to the third square and wrote inside the bubble, *HS-PP-TRIM*.

"You know more than I expected, Archie," Pat said.

One of the Court's staff knocked on Archie's office door, entered, and lit the two brass lamps in sconces on the wall. Archie pulled some matches from his drawer and lit the lamp on his desk before returning to his conversation. "You're lucky, Pat. I visited the Lake City Arsenal when I was a Sergeant Major at the Army's Command and General Staff College at Ft. Leavenworth. That was just before I retired in '83," he said. "Lake City was only a short drive away on the outskirts of Independence, Missouri. The school ran a tour for every class, and I went along a few times." Archie finished his drawing and notes. "Here. Take this." He gave Pat the paper with the diagram on it. Pat glanced at it, folded the sheet of paper, and put it in his jacket pocket.

Pat returned Archie's smile. "That's good info. Gary and Osker Geyer went to Grantville to consult the library. Osker Geyer returned a couple of days ago, and Gary went on to find an alchemist," he said with a smile.

"Alchemist?" Archie chuckled. He could imagine Gary saying something like that. For all his type-A personality, Gary had a wicked sense of humor.

"That's what Osker said. I think Gary meant a chemist."

"More than likely," Archie agreed. "Where'd he go?"

"Not sure. Osker said Gary didn't want anyone connected with the government. He said Gary didn't want the camel's nose in our affairs."

Archie chuckled. "I can understand that, too."

"I'm surprised you'd say that. You're part of the government here."

"Yeah, and I'm keeping as low a profile as I can. I don't want the city and county becoming dependent on the constabulary or me. They're already loading Judge Fross with stuff they should handle themselves."

"So they can blame Judge Fross instead of themselves." Pat said. He was familiar with up-time politics and knew down-time politics weren't any different.

"That's one reason. Do you know when Gary's getting back?"

"Don't know," Pat answered. "Couple of weeks, maybe. I know he planned to go to Magdeburg to talk to some money people. I think he was going to see if some of the Abrabanel clan would be interested in investing or know some potential investors who would."

While they talked, darkness fell. "Well, if you think you can get the project running in a year, you better get moving. Winter's coming on."

"I've been busy, too. I've talked to the Wettins about buying a couple or three sections of land outside Suhl. We'll need to make the primer compound some distance away from everyone, maybe have multiple sites depending on the design of the plant."

Archie nodded. "Yeah, I remember Lake City had bunkers and production buildings scattered all over."

"The plot of land I've picked is two sides of a ridge. I figured we could put the chemical plant on the far side of the ridge, away from people and the production side . . . just in case."

"It goes boom." Archie said, finishing Pat's sentence.

"Yeah. The Wettins said they'd approve the deal pending proof of our ability to pay."

"Proof?" The request surprised Archie. That was not the way the aristocracy operated, or so he had been told. It was more like *cash on the barrelhead.*

"A letter from our financiers," Pat explained. "We now have enough funds on hand to buy the land, but I want to save that for a reserve—as much as I can—in case we hit some unexpected expenses. Osker made a deal with Schmidt Steam. He bought some smaller engines in addition to the primary ones and still stayed within budget. Our finances are better than I'd estimated for this stage."

Pat's plans seemed to come to fruition . . . at least his part of them. Archie hoped Gary would be as successful. That thought brought forth a question. "When are we going to see this master plan of yours?"

"As soon as Gary gets back. I'll call a meeting of the board."

Archie watched, through his office window, the other courthouse employees leave. It was time to cut this conversation short. "Okay, I'll go through my books when I get home. I think one of my manuals has a piece about making cartridge brass. I remember reading about Hornady's plant but I don't remember where, exactly, I read about it."

"Fine. Thanks, Archie." They both stood. Something had been nibbling in Archie's mind. Something overlooked . . . and then he realized what it was. "Uh, Pat."

Pat stopped just at the doorway, waiting for Archie to gather his coat, hat, and cane. "Yeah?"

"Don't forget to add a brassworks to your project plan," Archie said, walking up to Pat. "You'll have to make your own brass."

"Crap! I hadn't considered that. I just assumed Geyer would make the brass."

"Never make assumptions, Pat. Nothing good ever comes from it."

They walked down the hallway to the court's side door. The outside street was lit by a three-candle lamp next to the doorway. As was his long habit, Archie scanned the street before stepping completely outside. Seeing nothing to draw his further attention, he accompanied Pat down the street toward the center of town. As they walked, Archie continued explaining his thoughts about the brassworks.

"Geyer might operate it, but I think this consortium of yours should own it."

Pat thought that over. Geyer had the experience to operate the brassworks. With minor differences, it was much like operating an iron foundry. But did they—the consortium—want to give their investment to Geyer? "Yeah, you're right. Thanks again, Archie."

"Any time, Pat."

At the front of the courthouse, they separated, each heading home. Pat's questions gave Archie food for thought. He'd look through his reloading manuals after supper. *And,* he reminded himself, *write down everything I can remember about Lake City Arsenal.*

VI

Mid-October 1634, Suhl

I wish I'd thought to bring a gavel. Gary Reardon had rented a room to hold the first official meeting of the consortium. The room contained a long table encircled by cushioned chairs. One side of the room contained windows providing enough light that lamps weren't needed. On the opposite wall was a sideboard, with pitchers, mugs, and a tray of Greta Issler's pastry. Of the invitees, only a handful were present, milling about and talking. Many of the investors could not attend. The ones present, however, represented the core of the new company. Like many up-time meetings, Marjorie had brought a tray of Greta Issler's honey rolls. Someone else had filled the three pitchers with broth, tea, and one of coffee. Pat wondered for a moment where the coffee had come from. He hadn't found a source.

Time to get started. Gary took his .38 revolver from his pocket, ejected its cartridges and pounded the tabletop with the empty pistol's butt.

"Would you all sit down, please? Let's get this show on the road."

Not counting himself, there were six present for the meeting; His wife, Gaylynn, and Pat Johnson, Osker Geyer, Archie and Marjorie Mitchell, and Ruben Blumroder, who had just returned from Bamberg. Ruben was representing the gunsmiths of Suhl, and some of other local investors.

"Thank you," Gary said, as the last board member sat around the table. "I asked you here to give you updates on our progress and to formalize our . . . consortium, for want of a better word." He had a stack of papers on the table before him. He took one and passed the rest of them to Ruben, who sat next to him. "Would you take one, Rueben, and pass the rest down the table?" Pat waited until everyone had a copy of the document. "I had these copies of the project plan printed when I was in Grantville. I've included space to add more tasks to the plan as we discover something we've overlooked. Archie has already reminded Pat that we'll need our own brassworks. As first order of business, I would like to propose a name for us. I propose we call ourselves the Suhl Consortium, for the present. When we actually have some assets, I would like to incorporate ourselves and change the name to Suhl, Inc."

"Suhl Ink?" Ruben asked.

"Suhl Incorporated, Ruben. It's a legal term—a pseudo-entity who owns the assets, makes the product and takes the business risks."

"Is that legal here?" Archie asked.

"Uhhh, I don't know. I thought so, but . . . ," he stopped and wrote himself a note. "First task for me."

"It's legal," Gaylynn interrupted. "The Higgins Sewing Machine Company is incorporated."

"Let me run the question by Judge Fross—see what he says," Archie said. "Off-hand, I think we're okay, but it would be better to get an opinion from him."

"Would you do that, please?" Gary gave a sigh of relief. "You scared me there for a minute, Archie. That reminds me, we need a secretary to take minutes. Any volunteers?"

No one spoke. Taking minutes was a thankless task and later, when the minutes were published, everyone would argue that he had never said what was recorded in the minutes. Nevertheless, the consortium—corporation—was going to be a busy and potentially a very profitable business. Minutes were needed.

When no one else spoke, Marjorie said, "I'll do it, but if I'm going to be the Secretary, at least temporarily, we'll need officers."

"That's on my list, Marjorie," Gary replied.

"I nominate Gary Reardon as President, Pat Johnson as Operations Veep," Marjorie said, not waiting for Gary to continue.

"Second!" Archie said, following her motion.

"Move to adopt the motion by acclamation," Osker Geyer added. "All in favor say, 'Aye!'"

"*Aye!*"

"So moved," Marjorie finished.

Gary sat open-mouthed for a moment. Pat had a surprised look on his face. Gary nodded. "Very well. I see you all had that planned."

Gary accepted the position and addressed the group. "I had two goals for my trip. Find someone who knows how to make our primer compound and get more funding."

He paused, gathering his thoughts. In a moment, he visualized the project, a mental timeline from beginning to end. *Now, how to explain it? Do I need to do that now?*

"For the first, finding an alchemist, I left Grantville and went to Essen to talk with Nicki Jo Prickett. I had thought to hire one of her chemists from Essen Chemical. We may yet, but I talked Nicki Jo into consulting with us, to oversee our chemical plant, design the primer manufactory, and to develop the entire primer process—make it as safe as she can. She has ideas, too, for the physical layout of the site."

He paused, looking at the faces down the table. *Did they understand? Most have blank faces.* He sipped coffee, swirled it around his dry before continuing. "She will be here in a week and is bringing at least one of her people to help. I hope to hire some more of them chemists to take over after Nicki Jo's finished. She's signed a contract as a consultant for one year, with options to extend her contract if we mutually agree."

"I'd heard that Nicki Jo wasn't well," Gaylynn said. Marjorie Mitchell nodded in agreement.

"She wasn't at her best when I saw her. That explosion at her plant last year hit her hard. She lost several friends. This, uh, consultancy will hopefully be therapeutic for her. She was just coasting when I met her. Her ...uh... friend, Katherine Boyle, and Banfi Hunyades, her Chief Chemist, encouraged her to take our contract. She had lost her motivation, so they said in Essen. They hope our project will restore it."

Gary took a sip from the mug in front of him. It was a stalling tactic. His next remark could be a bombshell—or maybe not. These people had changed a lot since the Ring of Fire. "Nicki Jo and Katherine Boyle will need quarters when they arrive ... joint quarters." He paused again, waiting for someone to comment. "They'll be living together." There, he'd said it.

"For Heaven's sake, Gary," Gaylynn said in exasperation. "We know all about Nicki Jo. Marjorie and I will take care of that. Men! Get on with it!" She glanced at Marjorie, who nodded. Nicki Jo's sexual orientation was no secret. If down-timers didn't make an issue of it, neither would any up-timer.

Gary, somewhat chagrinned, continued. "On my way back from Essen, I stopped at Magdeburg and saw some of the Abrabanel family in the hope to get for some referrals for financiers who'd be willing to invest in our project. I was successful. The Abrabanels agreed to be the liaison between the money people and us. We have access to twenty-five thousand silver guilders, more perhaps, later, if we need it."

It hadn't been easy. The Abrabanels could usually be counted on to support any new technology. Here, it wasn't new technology that interested them; it was the use of mechanization that drew their attention. It was the development of the mechanization and production processes to put metallic cartridges into production that drew their attention.

"Will we really need that much?" Ruben Blumroder asked. "That's an enormous amount!"

"I hope not, Ruben," Gary answered. "We will have access to funds as we complete certain milestones on our plan. They tried to impose some time constraints on those milestones, but I talked them out of that. *And was that a struggle! I finally convinced them that tying the money to arbitrary deadlines would lead to failure. We have to be flexible, not rigid adherents to a schedule.* "The first milestone is the delivery of the steam engines for Osker. The next is his hammer mill, followed, for the third milestone, the production of hard carbon steel. There's a bonus if he produces tungsten carbide steel, too."

"What are some of the other milestones?" Ruben asked.

"There are several, Ruben. The brassworks will be one as soon as I add it to the plan. The chemical plant is another. By the way, I got a concession for a small release of funds when Nicki Jo finishes her plant design. That will help, with what we already have on hand, to fund the construction and clearing of the production site," Gary explained. "Another is the first pilot production of primers—the list has more milestones. They are all included in your copy of the project plan that I created the plan using the Grantville library's PCs. The PCs helped determine the project's critical path—those things that had to be done, in the order they had to be done, and what they required for them to be completed on time. The project plan helped convince the financiers the Consortium would succeed."

"Think we can make that one-year target?" Archie asked.

Gary looked at the others sitting around the table. Archie had asked the most important question, and it had a simple answer. He sighed, looked down at his notes and the plan, and then looked back up at the faces waiting for his answer.

"Yes . . . full end to end commercial production with a minimum of five production lines, one year from today, October 19th, 1635."

❋ ❋ ❋

Archie knocked on the study door of Suhl District Judge, Wilhelm Fross. Judge Fross didn't like the term, *office.* He preferred the term, *study,* because the law required continuous review and contemplation, studying, in other words.

The judge looked up and waved Archie in and pointed to the couch next to the Judge's desk. "What can I do for you, *Herr Marshal?*"

"I have a question for you, if you don't mind, Your Honor. A legal question."

"And what is that question?"

"Does the State of Thuringia and Franconia law allow incorporation; the creation of a legal entity for a business? Is it legal? I've been told that incorporation is legal in Grantville—the incorporation of the Higgins Sewing Machine Company, for example. Does the law concerning incorporation that is in force in Grantville apply here in Suhl County?"

Judge Fross gave Archie a long look. "I'm continually amazed at some questions that came before me. What a curious question, *Herr Marshal.* Would you give me some context please?"

Archie repeated the discussion from Gary Reardon's meeting earlier that day, and the purpose of the new corporation. "As we grow, we know there will be legal issues. It's inevitable. As we understand it, incorporation will protect individual investors from direct legal action for acts of the corporation. Do those provisions apply here in Suhl?"

"Have you been reading your newsletters, *Herr Marshal?*" The newsletter Judge Fross was referring to was published weekly by the SoTF Courts, Marshal's Service, and the Mounted Constabulary. Most of the articles were reviews of legal decisions in the rapidly evolving SoTF legal system. The rest of the newsletter contained a summary of promotions, awards and reports of criminal activity, mainly information about the various roving gangs of bandits throughout the state.

"Most of them. I may have missed one or two when I got busy. Why do you ask?"

"There was an interesting case in Grantville last month, *Murphy vs. Murphy,*" Judge Fross said. "It was a divorce case, but that wasn't the interesting part, from a legal viewpoint, of the case. The interesting part concerned the concept of *full faith and credit.* Judge Tito's decision from *Murphy vs. Murphy* was that *full faith and credit* with up-time law was applicable in the former New United States—in this case—for events that had occurred up-time. The ruling upheld the concept of *full faith and credit,* and that it was valid, now, under current law. Since the NUS constitution was used to create the SoTF constitution, and had grandfathered the previous statues of the NUS, *full faith and credit* is, therefore, applicable in the SoTF." Judge Fross stopped and waited. He expected Archie to understand what he had just said. When Archie didn't respond, he continued. "To answer your question, since incorporation is legal in Grantville, it is also legal in Suhl, in the earlier NUS and now in the SoTF. Everywhere in the State of Thuringia-Franconia."

That settles that, Archie thought. "Would you be willing to put that in writing, Your Honor? An official opinion?"

Fross thought for a moment. "Why not? It is established law, now, according to the summary in the newsletter. I'll have to get a copy of the official decision from Grantville, but that won't be difficult. Have your lawyers make an official request for an opinion, *Herr Marshal,* and we'll proceed from there."

※ ※ ※

Umph! The coach hit another pothole in the road and bounced sharply. Nicki Jo Prickett and Katherine Boyle had started their journey to Suhl the previous day. They had stayed overnight in an inn in Dortmund. Today, they were taking the northern route to Magdeburg and from there to Suhl. The troubles along the Rhine south of Essen made travel by a more direct route unwise. Colette Modi hired a squad of mounted mercenaries to travel with them to Suhl; guards against roving bands of outlaws. The war between the USE and the League of Ostend was over. Still . . . a little protection was nice. Colette was insuring her investment in Nicki Jo. For Nicki Jo, her .38 revolver, tucked inside a leather pouch at her waist, provided more reassurance.

Nicki Jo had the windows open, the leather shutters rolled up, to watch the countryside roll by. She was thinking about a trip she had taken with her parents a decade before; a family vacation. *The good times . . . before Mom started drinking.* They had driven to Philadelphia to see the Liberty Bell and Independence Hall before going to Washington, DC. She remembered sitting in the rear seat watching the fields and valleys, small towns and homes, flow past the car. The memories flowed. A demonstration about the discovery of nylon at the Smithsonian was the spark that led to her interest in chemistry.

Katherine Boyle sat across from Nicki Jo. For Katherine, traveling was not an adventure, she'd told her companion. Most of her travels had been flights from unwanted futures. One such was her flight from her, now thankfully deceased, husband. Another flight was from the political scheming of her father and his machinations. Her father planned to force her to wed someone who would increase her father's political strength, she'd recounted to Nicki Jo. Katherine had declined her father's request— forcefully. She would be no one's puppet nor brood mare for sale on the marriage market.

When Katherine first met Nicki Jo, she'd revealed her identity, that she was tired of fleeing from one place to another. The last two years with Nicki Jo had been . . . redemption, or perhaps a repudiation of her life as the fifth daughter of the Earl of Cork, the primary adviser to England's King Charles.

Nicki Jo let her gaze wander back inside the coach. Katherine was reading. *What was it?* She could barely read the title of the book . . . *Twelfth Night.* Shakespeare hadn't been well known in the here and now, before the Ring of Fire. His name hadn't spread far from England's shores, now everyone seemed to be reading him. Katherine must have picked up a copy for the trip.

She listened to the driver talking to the hired guards. They were approaching an inn where the coach would have its horses exchanged during the layover. Whoever owned this coach-line may have been copying the waystations used by the postal services. If so, she was glad he had; the waystations and frequent changes of horses reduced travel time. Fresh horses made better progress than tired horses. Moreover, she needed a nature break and some lunch.

While she looked out of the window, Nicki Jo had also been mentally working through a process for the new primer compound. She didn't want to put anything in writing yet. It would just be speculation until she had a lab set up, and could do some experimenting. Nicki Jo was a visual person . . . she could visualize processes, each step, each task for making DDNP. Documenting that process was difficult for her. Not so for Katherine. She could listen to Nicki Jo's verbal stream of consciousness, make sense of it, and write it down logically. That ability of hers was another reason why together they were better, more effective, than they were individually.

The inn appeared around the curve of the road. It occurred to Nicki Jo that she hadn't thought about Tobias or Solomon since Gary Reardon's visit the previous week. In fact, the new project occupied her thoughts. She was feeling the urge, once again, to experiment. *With precautions, of course,* she reminded herself. She had someone who was dependent—no, not dependent—someone *she* was dependent upon and whom *she* didn't want to disappoint. In her trunk was a large binder with all her notes from last year's toluene experiments. She would not repeat Tobias and Solomon's mistakes.

Mike Watson

VII

November 1634, Suhl

Gary Reardon was standing before a window, looking out upon the street and the passers-by below, while waiting for the others to arrive. Suhl had had its first snow the previous day. Most of it was gone, melted, except for remnants remaining in shadowed corners.

The consortium's lawyers had filed the new company's incorporation petition, after receiving Judge Fross' written legal opinion. Now they were waiting for him to issue his final approval. The consortium headquarters now had a few permanent employees to handle the growing administrative tasks. Gary, Pat, Osker and Nicki Jo had private; spartan offices, until the permanent corporate headquarters was finished at the soon-to-be corporation's site, now being called *the Reservation*.

Today's meeting, a lunch meeting, was being held in the Boar's Head Inn's upper meeting room. Osker Geyer walked through the door, accompanied by Pat Johnson. Nicki Jo and Katherine Boyle followed moments later. The two women had arrived in Suhl two weeks earlier.

After spending three days inspecting the Reservation, and examining topographic maps, Nicki Jo disappeared into her office. She emerged several days later, with her plant design in her hands.

When everyone had filled plates from the buffet provided by the inn's kitchen and was seated, Gary opened the meeting. "Before we start, I have some . . . information for you. There is a spy in Suhl, a stranger, who is asking some very pointed questions."

"Who is he?" Pat asked.

"I'm not sure. We know his name, Andres Zoche, and he's staying at *Der Bulle und Bär*. He says he's from Ingolstadt, but no one believes him. His accent says Leipzig."

"Who is he working for?" Geyer followed Pat's question.

"Unknown. Hart Brothers? Someone from Essen? Or Magdeburg? I just don't know, but I think we're in a race now." Gary was glad that Archie Mitchell was watching for strangers. Archie's motive, so he said, was checking for known criminals on the run. Whatever his motivation, Archie discovered Zoche, and asked the watch to keep an eye on him.

Gary's opening was a warning to them all. Others were interested in what they were doing, and a secret can only be held by one person. Too many knew, albeit bits and pieces, to keep their plans and objectives secret. Putting those bits and pieces together could reveal the consortium's goals.

When no further questions arose, he returned to his agenda and opened the meeting with a simple question. "Status?"

Geyer responded first. He always acted fast, whether eating or working, speed, to him, was an imperative, as if time was a precious commodity to be spent with extreme care. Coming directly from his foundry, he was still in his leather work clothes. Osker was a hands-on manager and took a personal interest in the foundry operation. He knew every one of his employees by face and name. "Please excuse my appearance," he said. "I had a problem at the foundry this morning."

He pushed aside his plate and placed some notes before him that he'd written earlier. "The first four steam engines should arrive in a week or less. As we planned, two are for me at the foundry, one for the brassworks and one for the final assembly plant. One of the smaller engines will drive my hammer forge. The rest are for the fabrication buildings and for Gary's tool manufactory. The engines will arrive disassembled and should be up and running before the First of December. Schmidt Steam will assemble the engines on our site and will train our engineers to operate, and maintain those engines." Geyer glanced at his notes again. "Gary, your man will be a part of that training as well."

Gary nodded and made a note for himself. While Geyer was talking, Gaylynn had been refilling cups of tea for the attendees. "By the way," Geyer said to everyone, after taking a sip of tea, "I've altered my long-term goals, but I don't think the change will affect the plan. I can't be a big steel producer like USE Steel or Essen Steel. I don't have the infrastructure to ship my product . . . yet. Not until we get a railroad into Suhl or we dredge the *Werra River*, add canals around all the mills, to allow flatboat and barge traffic. Instead, I'm focusing on quality not quantity, on specialty steel— hard carbon, carbide, and, if I can get sufficient ores, chrome for stainless steel. I may not be able to match up-time steel quality, but I want to get as close as I can. I can't match the output of USE Steel nor Essen Steel, but I'll create a niche for us. US Steel and Essen Steel can make iron and steel plates and rails; I'll make tool and specialty steel."

"What about the ore supply?" Pat Johnson asked. Iron and copper ore were available locally. The rest, like zinc, tungsten and maybe molybdenum, had to be imported from the Harz Mountain mines.

"We have contracts with the Harz mines for zinc and the other ores. We may have to extract tungsten ourselves."

The core issue wasn't surprising. Gary had been concerned about acquiring enough for their needs and had asked the Abrabanels for help. They had come through.

"There is one unexpected issue," Geyer added. "We may have to improve the road, widen it, from the mines to Suhl, building or widening some bridges. The traffic over the road will increase four-fold. The mine owners suggest using their mine tailings as a gravel source. At a price," he said with a smile. "They know how to squeeze every bit of money out of us they think they can get away with. In the future, we should consider making the road all-weather, macadamizing it."

"We have local sources for iron and copper," he continued. "They are not an issue." Geyer paused and took another sip of tea. "I have also, on our behalf, bought controlling shares in a couple of silver mines . . . just in case we need more funding," he said with a grin. "They're low producers but once we start making tools, I think I can upgrade the local mines with drills, ore saws, mechanization, that sort of thing, and make them much more productive."

Gary was glad the consortium had another revenue source. It would help pay off their debt faster if Geyer was correct. Getting back to the agenda, he asked, "Got a date for your first tool steel production run?"

"Hard carbon by the first of January. Tungsten carbide will depend on how quickly we can extract the tungsten. I hope Fraulein Prickett will advise me with that task."

"Thank you, Osker." Gary started to turn to the next member at the table, but Geyer had one more thing to say. He reached into his pocket, withdrew a purse, and threw it on the table. It landed with a thud. "This is the first revenue for our new corporation. One hundred silver guilders. I've a new profit line—making nails. The stamping machine has been working for a couple of weeks, making nails for our construction teams. The stamping machine worked so well, I just let it run, making nails of various sizes. I sold a hundred barrels of nails to a factor in Magdeburg, and the payment has just arrived. This is the consortium's share, after expenses."

No one spoke, and then a grin spread across Gary's face. Gaylynn yelped in celebration. "Thank you, Osker. That is good news, indeed." The one hundred guilders was not a large amount, as it counted in the scheme of things, and compared to their current debt. Their working expenses would make the contents of the purse disappear like smoke in a breeze. Nevertheless, it was a start. One more step to completion; one more product to be marketed.

Pat Johnson picked up the purse and hefted it in one hand. Coins faintly clinked. "Heavy," he commented.

Time to return to business, the next agenda item. Gary chose the next member to give his update. "Pat?"

Pat put the purse back on the table and picked up his notes. He skimmed them, refreshing his memory. "We've completed the purchase of that plot of land I mentioned in our last meeting. We now own two-thousand acres, a little over three square miles, and we've an option to buy twelve-hundred more acres within five years, if we need it. I had some topographic maps created when the surveyors were here. Nicki Jo has been using them to plot where to place the various units—storage bunkers, chem plant sites, primer manufactories, brassworks, assembly plants and all the interconnecting service roads—not to mention plumbing and piping for waste storage, and settling pools."

Marjorie Mitchell wasn't available to take the minutes. Gaylynn was substituting for her. Pat paused for a moment to let her catch up. When she nodded, he continued. "For security, we will add a berm around the production site, the admin building, and the bunkers. The berm won't be anything close to being a fortress, but it will give us a better defensive position if we ever need it. We're ready to start on the initial chem plant, and the brassworks. I've started making dies with the hard carbon steel that I already have on hand . . . enough for a pilot plant, I think. We'll need more from Osker for the production plants."

"I, with Wettin's approval, started clearing the Reservation last month. I sold the wood to sawmills in Suhl in exchange for seasoned wood for the Reservation. Much of the work was hand labor. With the end of the harvest season, I've recruited additional workers from the neighboring farming communities." His throat was dry. He wasn't used to talking so much. He took another sip of tea and then continued with his report. "The laborers appreciate the opportunity to make money when they ordinarily would wait for spring. A tent city has grown on a flat parcel of the Reservation. I've used some of our initial funding to buy tents and establish a logistics chain to keep the new employees housed and fed. It's a cost of doing business. I included it all in Gary's project plan."

"Good," Gary said. "Nicki Jo?"

She stood and, with Katherine's help, tacked a map of the Reservation on the wall. "As Pat said, I've started on the plant layout." She used a pencil as a pointer. Whenever she described a building and its function, she pointed to its location on the map. "The manufactory sites on this side of the ridge are the easiest to place. I'm assuming one production line per building. I don't want to put all our eggs in one basket." She moved to the other side of the map and pointed again. "I'm doing the same for the chemical and primer plants on the far side of the ridge. It's hard to see the scale on this map, but they're about a hundred yards apart with a berm in between." She pointed to two buildings on the map, separated from one another. "They are here, and here."

"What about the primer compound?" Gary asked.

She walked back to the table and sat. The presentation part of her report was over. The rest would be done verbally. "As for the primer compound," she said, "like you thought, I'm leaning toward DDNP. I'm still looking at lead styphnate because there are issues with either approach. However, DDNP is made from picric acid, and we know how to make that. The issue is a matter of keeping contamin . . ." Her voice wavered briefly. She paused, took a breath and continued, " . . . contaminants out of our materials. We may have to do further refining and purification of some ingredients ourselves to improve purity and remove any remaining contaminants."

That didn't surprise Gary Reardon. Osker Geyer had discovered he needed to add ore extraction to his list of tasks. Pat had assumed there would be additional work for making the primer compound. Nothing was as easy as planned.

Nicki Jo referred to her notes again. "There are clear-cut risks with either approach. However, I believe we can minimize worker's risk going with DDNP. The long-term plan is to have at least five primer production lines. Each line will be in separate facilities some distance from one another with berms around them. There will be three separate DDNP production lines placed along the same lines—separate buildings with berms around each plant. I'm using the same concept for the final production facilities."

"Do we need that many DDPNP fabrication plants?" Gary asked.

"I only had two, at first—for redundancy. But I had a discussion with Pat and Archie, and I think we can use any excess DDNP to make blasting caps and perhaps some industrial explosives."

That surprised Gary and it brought him up short. *Another product? Maybe two. And useful ones, too, in more ways than one.* "Good idea, Nicki Jo. Now, when do you think you can have a pilot plant for DDNP production?"

"Mid-January, assuming I've no issues with resources or raw materials, and we can finish the buildings in winter weather."

"Thank you, Nicki Jo."

The meeting began an hour earlier. Gary called for a short break before people's butts overrode their capacity to remain attentive. He noticed Nicki Jo and Katherine, followed by Ruben, leave the dining room and turn toward the private lavatory downstairs where Archie and Dieter had once lived. One of the building staff came up with pitchers of hot broth, tea, and cool beer. The innkeeper's wife followed, carrying a plate full of small pastries. Gary wondered for a moment who had planned that small courtesy; he hadn't. It was Marjorie, he decided. She was known to arraign for small items such as this dessert, even if she wasn't attending in person. The tray included, especially for Nicki Jo, cookies freshly baked by Greta Issler.

When the innkeeper's wife was gone, Gary and Geyer converged on the buffet table. Geyer filled a mug with beer and took two pastries. "I'm glad you thought of this, Gary. I always get hungry in the mid-afternoon." Gary didn't bother to inform Geyer the dessert wasn't his idea. He usually worked through lunch. Food just wasn't something he would think of on his own.

Ruben, with Nicki Jo and Katherine, returned, filled mugs and small plates of pastries from the buffet table, and, as Gary noticed, Nicki Jo added a handful of cookies to her plate. Her reputation of having a fondness for cookies had followed her from Essen. When everyone was seated, Gary cleared his throat and restarted the meeting.

"Now my report. The corporation. I expect to get conformation of our incorporation by the end of the week. To join, members will have to contribute assets and funds to the financial pool. For some, that is buying stock, for others, like Osker, it will be transferring a portion of his physical

assets to the corporation. Others, like Pat's U. S. Waffenfabrik and my Suhl
Nut and Bolt, will become wholly-owned subsidiaries of Suhl,
Incorporated. We'll own forty-nine percent of our companies. Suhl,
Incorporated, will own the rest—our contribution."

Gary took a sip from his teacup. He had expected questions, but no
one had asked any. *Have I totally confused them?*

"Ruben, how many others do you believe will be interested?"

Blumroder looked around the table and then back to Gary. "It will
depend on what they see as their benefit. I don't see any of them becoming
subsidiaries. I haven't decided for myself, but they want to have access to
your products. It's an ongoing negotiation."

"Do they understand the game-plan?"

Blumroder laughed, "Not all. I don't fully understand myself."

Okay, how to simplify this? Gary thought. "Tell them Suhl, Incorporated,
will be a holding company, a conglomeration of various Suhl industries—
of all kinds, not just gunsmiths and weapon makers. Suhl, Incorporated,
will not just be a factory. It will also be a marketing organization and will
market the members' products outside Suhl, across the SoTF and the USE.
I had a conversation just a few days ago with a cobbler, who was asking
how we could mechanize his shop. He wants to bid on making boots for
the army. He's asked if we would work with him to help design and finance
his upgrade. That request created another potential product for us—
Process and Mechanization Engineering."

He cleared this throat and took another sip from his cup. "We will
distribute expenses and risk equally across the members. Conversely, we
will also distribute profits to the members of the conglomerate in
proportion to their contributions. The same for stockholders.
Conglomerate companies will be able to buy products from one another
at cost, and that should allow them to maintain and improve parity with
their competitors outside the conglomeration. There are other benefits as
well."

Ruben appeared to understand Gary's explanation. He looked at the
other board members around the table. "Hockenjoss and Klott have said

they will buy ten blocks of shares. They want access to Osker's steel and Gary's tooling. They promised to make a new model H&K pistol chambered for the .45 Colt cartridge."

"That's good news, Ruben. They'll make a market for us and we for them. Our first products will be cartridges in .45 Colt and .45-70 calibers. We'll wait for the market to tell us what other calibers to add."

"Well," Blumroder said, returning to the conversation about the conglomeration, "many do not want to be a part of the . . . conglomerate? But they do want a business partnership."

It was a valid question. Not everyone could nor needed to join. There would still be regular business agreements. "I think we can accommodate them, Ruben. The Corporation will eventually become the elephant in the tent, but we needn't be arrogant, nor a tyrant. These people are our friends and neighbors. Without them, we'll fail."

Gary scanned the faces around the table. "I've been expanding the construction company that Pat started for the next phase, to build the plant buildings. This is in addition to those he's already hired to clear the land. I've started hiring carpenters and other construction workers. We'll break ground as soon as Nicki finishes her design. Crews have already cleared the site for the plant admin building. We can use that building as the construction office for the rest of the build-out. Questions? Comments?" Nicki Jo was nodding her head in agreement. Pat was smiling. Ruben . . . Ruben Blumroder kept his poker face. Gary knew he was excited by the light in his eyes, but Ruben wasn't prepared to display that excitement in public. Hearing no comment, Gary closed the meeting.

✱ ✱ ✱

Gaylynn followed Nicki Jo and Katherine out of the meeting. The previous week, the *Sisters*, as Gaylynn thought of the four women—herself, Marjorie Mitchell, Greta Issler, and Ursula Johnson, had greeted Nicki Jo and Katherine when their coach from Essen arrived.

They hadn't known exactly when it would arrive. Marjorie had asked Archie to let them know when the coach entered Suhl. The gate guards were the eyes and ears of the city watch, and, by extension, of Archie Mitchell, and Captain Eric Gruber of the Mounted Constabulary. When the coach passed through the gate, with its accompanying squad of mercenaries, the gate guard sent a messenger to Marjorie. The *Sisters* arrived just as the coach halted before the temporary headquarters of the consortium.

Marjorie had found a small house, with a cook and maid, to rent for Nicki Jo and Katherine. Gary Reardon reluctantly agreed to have the consortium pay the rent. Nicki Jo should be worth the expense, Marjorie argued.

With evening coming on, Nicki Jo and Katherine were heading home with Gaylynn tagging along. "How are you doing, Nicki Jo? Is the house suitable for you?" Gaylynn yammered on. She was a talker, not one to allow silence to occur when a conversation would do instead. "Marjorie found it, but we really didn't know what you needed, so we guessed."

"It's wonderful, Gaylynn," Nicki Jo replied. "I'm not much of a house-keeper. Katy is even less of one. It's big for just the two of us, but I don't think we'll spend all that much time there. But, it's really nice."

"Well, I, for one," Katherine said, "am looking forward to a nice hot bath."

Nicki Jo laughed, "You can depend on Katy, Gaylynn, to have her priorities firmly in mind."

"But, how are you doing, Nicki Jo. We'd heard . . . "

Nicki Jo didn't immediately answer. "I'm sorry, Gaylynn. My mind was elsewhere. I'm better, I think. I needed something new to do, and new people around me. Colette was nice, we got along well, but . . . I don't think I can explain it fully."

"What about the house? Need anything there? Any changes?"

"No, I don't think so. We've selected one of the three bedrooms to be converted into an office. We had the maid clear it out and had a table installed for a desk, with a chair, some storage cabinets, and a chalkboard.

The room has a western-facing window, just right to catch the afternoon sun."

The three continued down the street and turned the corner. Nicki Jo and Katherine's house was a block ahead.

"As to your question, I'm doing well, Gaylynn. Truthfully, I'm doing better than I had thought I would. I appreciate you, Ursula, Marjorie, and Greta, helping us get set up—especially the house. I love it. It's so much nicer than the one we rented in Essen."

"I'm thankful to hear that, Nicki Jo."

"You needed worry, Gaylynn," she said, smiling. She realized she had been smiling more. "I have Katy. She'll watch over me. Do you know she once forbad me to eat cookies? She said I was too . . . "

"Not anymore," Katherine interrupted. "You've lost enough weight this last year."

"Hefty." Nicki Jo finished. "You see, Katy and I have this Cheese and Chocolate company in Brussels, and one of its products is—"

"Ring of Fire cookies." Katherine said.

"I love 'em," Nicki Jo confessed. "I could eat my weight of them if Katy let me."

Gaylynn laughed. "All of us, me, Marjorie, even string-bean Ursula, have to be careful when we're around Greta's pastries. They tend to . . . disappear."

All three laughed. Nicki Jo leaned over to Gaylynn and whispered into her ear, "Do you think Greta could make Ring of Fire cookies?"

Mike Watson

VIII

Late-November 1634, RJ City

Gary Reardon and Pat Johnson walked through the devastation of RJ City, the name the residents had given the temporary tent city that had sprung up to house many of the construction workers. It had started as a small tent city in September.

The plan had called for some workers, after clearing the site, to build wooden dormitories to replace the tents. The dormitories would house the workers over the winter. It was an ongoing task. Unfortunately, half of the workers still, or had, lived in tents . . . until the storm.

The storm arrived after a weeklong period of warm, sunny weather. Construction on the chemical fabrication building was the priority, with the pilot plant milestone looming on the horizon. Moving those workers still living in tents to the sturdier and warmer dormitories had slowed. Then, without warning, the skies turned dark and near-freezing rain fell, followed by high winds, pounded the tent city.

Neither said a word as they walked. Clothing, ripped tents, broken tent poles and scattered food littered the site. As they walked, Pat saw the remnants of a cook-stove in what had been a mess-tent. The remains of wooded trestle tables and benches lay like matchsticks. Their boots squelched as they walked through the mud and water-soaked turf, their trousers wet to their knees.

A large number of people arrived from Suhl to provide aid where needed. Fortunately, no one died although many had injuries. When the storm arrived, those living in the tents fled to the existing dormitories, some only partially finished, for shelter. Anything was better than staying in the tents.

"We should have foreseen this," Pat said angrily. "It's our responsibility to see to the wellbeing of their employees. We failed."

"Yeah. My fault," Gary agreed. "I was focused on meeting the pilot plant milestone. I just didn't think—"

"About a storm."

"Yeah."

They turned and headed back toward the administration building, passing a hasty setup aid station. "We were lucky," Gary said. He saw Dieter Issler and the two junior deputy marshals on the far side of the tent city. They, along with a handful of mounted constabulary troopers, were watching for looters and insuring nothing was stolen by thieves taking advantage of the disaster. RJ City was outside the jurisdiction of the Suhl watch. Captain Gruber had assigned half-dozen troopers to assure the people of RJ City that they would be protected while they recovered from the storm. Gary had planned to create a security force for the Reservation; it was too far from Suhl for the watch to patrol. He just hadn't anticipated needing a security force this soon.

"Let's ask Anse Hatfield if he can run a temporary bus service here from Suhl. It'd save some time all around and Anse can bring in building material when he's not hauling people," Pat suggested.

Gary agreed. *We need some security people out here from now on. The Constabulary can't watch over us forever.* "Think Anse and Dieter Issler could organize our security force, too? I had planned for one, just not this soon."

Pat turned in a circle, trying to encompass the destruction. "I'll talk to them. I think they would. Dieter has a full-time job, but I don't think Archie would object as long as Dieter only worked part time, and as long as he met his duties to the Court."

The wind rose. Tent remnants flapped in the wind. "We must complete the dormitories, Gary. We can't leave our people living like this."

"Yeah," Gary agreed. "When we get back, I'll call a halt on the plant construction and divert everyone to finishing the dormitories, mess halls, and the sutlers. If we don't, we'll lose these people. They'll quit and go home. Then we'll really be in a mess."

Pat stopped, contemplating the situation and how it would be when the dormitories were finished. "We're making a company town."

Gary shook his head, looking down at his feet. Making RJ City an official village according to law wasn't in his plans, nor did he want to make it one. Nevertheless—if that was what had to be done, he'd do it. He took care where he stepped amongst the mess and mud. "Can't be helped. I didn't want one. It has so many connotations . . ."

The subject of company towns was still a sore subject for the up-time coal miners and their families. They hadn't forgotten the history—a grim history of company towns. Company towns, wholly owned by mining companies, had been a tool of mine owners to maintain control by forcing miners and their families to live in company housing. Paying miners in company script further restricted them to buying only from company stores. Company towns, company script, company stores, all had been a method to keep miners in debt to the company—economic slavery. "No company script, Pat, no company stores. I won't have it."

"Agreed." When people were paid in script, they could only use that script at selected locations, all owned or controlled by the company. *No, no company script. Period. We may have to start some stores to tie us over, but we'll invite the merchants of Suhl to take over as soon as they can.*

"I know we'll have a company town," Gary repeated, "but what can we do? There isn't room in Suhl. Some of these people traveled a hundred miles or more to come here. They brought their families, too." Suhl had grown over the last few years. Already, it was one of the larger cities in the region. The mines and local industries attracted people seeking jobs. When Suhl, Incorporated, begins production, in the next few months, the revenue that the conglomerate will create will attract more people. Jobs create money and money, used wisely, creates more jobs. Suhl will grow and it was up to city, and Suhl, Incorporated, to ensure that growth was managed carefully, lest it collapse like a house of cards.

"At least we gave families priority in housing."

"That doesn't help the singles. Many want permanent jobs, and will bring their families if they get one."

"The supply chain is still in place. We can feed them at least," Pat observed. He watched some people stacking barrels of flour and other foodstuffs taken from the ruin of a mess hall. *Should we have moved the mess halls into the new buildings first instead of people? Six of one, half-dozen of the other,* he decided.

"We lost much of the food on site. Everyone will be on tight rations for a few days but it shouldn't last more than that."

They had finished their inspection. The cleanup was progressing. Those who had been injured were being treated. More canvas had been ordered, and should arrive in a day or two. There wasn't much more they could do here. Pat turned to Gary and said, "Let's talk to Anse about his trucks, and get more folks out from Suhl to help these folks. Then, I want to check with Nicki Jo and the others and see how this affects the plan."

***

The Reservation's administration building had been one of the first buildings completed—mostly completed. Some interior walls were still unfinished, with the supporting studs still exposed. Gary and Pat arrived to discover Nicki Jo and Katherine already there, examining the workflow and manpower diagrams. "If we shift this work group to just the chem plant, we can divert the other two to work on RJ City. How will this affect the critical path?" they heard the women say. The hand-written project plan was fixed on three walls along with task-on-arrow diagrams. The critical path, the critical tasks, was underlined in red on the pages of the project plan. Gary, Pat, and Nicki Jo were the only ones who understood the full plan. A few of the construction foremen understood their portions, but only to the extent of how their work teams were affected.

"I can't tell how the critical path will change right now," Gary said as he reviewed it on the walls. *God, what I'd give for a PC and Microsoft Project.*

"I'm going to have to redo it by hand and see where, and how it's changed, but it has changed . . . I just don't know how much,"

"I'll review the plant buildings," Nicki Jo added. "Putting DDNP mixture building in, or next to the fab buildings, is not a good idea, but I think we can delay putting up the dividing berms for now. Besides, the ground will soon be too hard for more digging until spring."

"That would free up four work teams that we could use elsewhere," Gary agreed

"Yes, but they aren't skilled carpenters," Pat pointed out.

"Maybe not, but some can work under direction and do grunt work," Gary replied. "That will help."

They turned to review the project plan on the wall. Gary, without taking his eyes from the plan, said to Pat, "Zoche was hired to help build the dormitories. I figured if he worked for us, we could keep a better eye on him."

"Good idea," Pat replied. "Keep your friends close and—"

"Your enemies closer. Yeah."

The four worked long into the night before they agreed where the workflow could be altered with the minimum impact to future milestones.

Mike Watson

IX

January 1635, The Reservation

*B*ang!
    Nicki Jo and Katherine were testing another version of the primer compound. The original plan had called for a test lab, an enclosed building where the conditions they could tightly control the test. After the storm in November, they deferred that part of the plan, leaving Nicki Jo to perform her tests outdoors, exposed to the elements. The current test lab comprised a square of sandbags covered by a simple roof to shelter the testbed from rain and snow.

"What batch is that?" Nicki Jo asked Katherine.

"Number 20-12. It has passed all our tests successfully, heat, cold, shock, humidity and pressure. I think we have it," Katherine replied, giving her clipboard to Nicki Jo.

The testbed was mounted on a sturdy wooden table in the middle of the space created by sandbags piled seven feet high. The entrance to it was through a dogleg designed to divert any effects of an accidental explosion.

Nicki Jo ran her finger down the columns of test results. "How many spent primers do we have left?"

A chill wind arrived, whipping around the sandbags and causing Katherine's hair to swirl around her face. She pushed it back, out of her eyes, and replied, "Approximately a hundred. Archie Mitchell may have a few more, but not very many. Do you think we can try the new cups from the brassworks?"

Nicki Jo scratched her nose, heedful of the pointed pencil in her hand. "Yes, I think so. It's time. We need to determine if the copper/zinc ratio is good, not too hard nor not too soft. Think we could borrow one of Archie's revolvers to test the primers?"

Katherine grinned. "No need. Marjorie said we could use her Smith & Wesson. She'll carry one of Archie's single-action Colts in the meantime."

Nicki Jo laughed. She knew how protective Archie was with his, and Marjorie's, firearms. "Okay. How many cartridge cases has the brassworks made?" Pat Johnson was having trouble with his presses. The process worked when manually powered. But, when steam power was added, it hadn't.

"A couple of hundred in all. The last test run of their pilot plant ran twenty-eight cases until one crumpled and jammed the press. Pat said he thought it was a lube problem and expects to have it fixed in a few days."

Nicki Jo shivered. January in Germany was not a Caribbean vacation. Like Katherine, she wore a long woolen skirt over several petticoats. The skirt was usually warm enough unless there was a wind—like today. She had been tempted to dig out her flannel-lined jeans from her trunk. She had last worn them when she and her father had gone deer hunting, up-time before the Ring of Fire. However, she didn't want to scandalize her down-time friends. Suhl was not Grantville. "When does he think they'll move beyond the pilot stage?"

"That's up to Gary, how soon he can mechanize the presses. He said he'd like to use hydraulics to run the presses, but he can't find a good way to make hoses that will last. He redesigned the presses to be mechanically linked and belt driven, powered by the steam engine."

"Let's get back inside, Nicki Jo said. She and Katherine gathered up the remaining DDNP samples and dropped them in a water bucket. DDNP wasn't water soluble, very much anyway, but water would make DDNP useless if left in it long enough. They knew better than to carry a possibly unstable explosive in their hands, even the small samples they used in their tests. The walk back to the lab exposed them to colder temperatures and higher winds. "Will we make our milestone, Katy?" Nicki Jo asked, her teeth chattering.

"I think so if we can finalize the copper/zinc ratio for the primer cups."

"Are we still on the critical path?"

Katherine paused, thinking. "I can't visualize the plan as Gary and Pat can, but what I can say is, we are if you think batch 20-12 is ready for production."

That relieved Nicki Jo. Everyone had been working hard after the destruction of RJ City. The chemical plant was only partially finished, just those areas directly involved in primer production. A third of the chem plant was still open to the elements. The primer fabrication building was enclosed, but the interior was open, the workstations isolated by piled sandbags. It was a design change from what Nicki Jo had originally planned. However, the change worked well, much better, in fact, than she'd expected, and she had let the change remain as it was. *If it ain't broke, don't fix it.*

Good, then we start hiring and training, she decided. "Who is Banfi Hunyades sending us, Katy, for the chem plant manager?" The wind picked up again, causing Nicki Jo's skirt to lift, exposing her legs.

"I don't have his name. The last letter I received is that Banfi had a candidate, but he didn't provide his name. He's sending Georg Rohn as a candidate for Chief Chemist."

"Good, I think Georg will do. He doesn't have the usual male egotism. He'll listen to me." They walked up to the chem lab and around the corner to the main entrance. "Let's get inside," Nicki Jo said. "I'm freezing out here."

Katherine laughed. "Didn't wear your woolies, did you? That'll teach you about not being prepared."

✳ ✳ ✳

Archie Mitchell and Eric Gruber walked into *Der Bulle und Bär*. Archie hadn't been inside side the inn since he and Dieter Issler arrested Friedrich Achen the previous May. The excuse for him and Gruber visiting the inn was their habit of walking rounds in Suhl to help the local watch. Their habit wasn't required anymore; the watch had a new Wachtmeister, Johan Frey. He had instituted a new training program and had it well in-hand and organized. No, the reason Archie and Gruber were here was to watch a spy, one Andres Zoche.

"There's our boy," Gruber whispered to Archie as Zoche walked in the door. Andres Zoche had been living in the inn since the previous autumn. He worked as a laborer at the Reservation, but his wages were not enough to cover the cost of his room in the inn. He could have stayed in a dormitory in RJ City, but didn't. Instead, he lived here, in *Der Bulle und Bär*, and made the daily two hour commute on foot.

"Is he still asking questions?" Gruber asked.

"Yes, to people in the admin building and in the chem plant. He's sent some large envelopes out via the post system . . . a private courier who takes them to Magdeburg."

"And who does the courier report to, there?"

"I don't know. Nasi's replacement isn't interested. I sent word to the Abrabanels and they're looking into it."

"Has he sent any radio messages?"

"Yes, to Zwickau."

That surprised Gruber. He could understand others in the USE being interested in the Reservation. It had become common knowledge that the consortium—Suhl, Incorporated, as it was now known—would be making ammunition; ammunition all sealed into a ready to fire brass cartridges. Few, however, knew *how* the new ammunition actually worked. Gruber didn't. He was happy to just use them and not have to worry about rain and other weather related factors that prevented the use of firearms.

Zwickau was on the coast of the Baltic Sea. *Why would he send a message there?*

"And it was coded," Archie added. "I've sent copies to some interested people who will try to break it."

"Zwickau is on the Baltic coast. From there it could go to . . . "

"Anywhere. Poland, Russia, England, anywhere." Archie said, completing Gruber's sentence.

"What are you going to do?"

"Nothing . . . yet. Just monitor him. He seems to be unaware he's being watched."

"You really think that?"

"No," Archie said with a sigh. Zoche glanced at the two lawmen, spoke with the barmaid, received a stein of beer and walked up the stairs to his room.

"I know some people who can toss his room and no one would ever know."

Archie thought for a minute. "Do it."

✳ ✳ ✳

A week passed before Archie and Gruber met again over steins of beer. Gruber had one of his men, a former burglar, search Zoche's room. He found nothing suspicious except a small book of commentaries by Francis Bacon, the former Lord Chancellor of England. Gruber didn't know why Zoche would have a copy until Archie Mitchell suggested the spy could use it for code keys. Gruber sent a radio message to Magdeburg asking if they could find a duplicate copy of the commentary. It was unlikely, since few of the commentaries had been printed.

"I have discovered another spy, Archie," Gruber added to his report on Zoche. "He doesn't appear to be allied with Zoche, more of an independent."

That statement didn't surprise Archie. He doubted Zoche would be here alone. No, there would other groups spying as well. "Name?"

"Otto Mohr. He applied for a job with Gary Reardon's Nuts and Bolts. He didn't get hired, so he applied next for a job at the brassworks."

Archie Mitchell was the unofficial security officer for Suhl, Incorporated. Zoche seemed to be interested in the DDNP compound.

Mohr seemed to be more interested in the mechanization of making cartridge brass. "Was he hired?"

"Still pending, I think."

"Okay. I think we need to talk to Gary and Pat. I'm more concerned with Zoche. He is more interested in DDNP, and could cause us more trouble. Let's finish this beer and go find Gary."

The conversation with Gary Reardon was short. Hire Mohr, but keep a close eye on him. They'd keep him away from the seeing the presses unassembled. The internal design was hidden when assembled. They'd let Mohr think he could ferret out the secret of the presses while insuring he never had access to the details.

X

February 1635, The Reservation

Nicki Jo was in her lab in the chem plant when Katherine walked in. "Nicki, there's been an accident."

"Where? Anyone hurt?" Nicki Jo asked.

"DDNP fab number two. Nothing serious, just some cuts."

Nicki turned off her alcohol burners, halted the process she was working on, and followed Katherine out of the lab.

They found Georg Rohn talking to one steward at the accident site. "He's lucky," the shop safety steward was saying. "Idiot. He should have called for help. It's in the protocol." Georg Rohn hadn't been on the job very long, and he was shadowing the production process with the safety steward. He needed to know exactly how to make DDNP, and understand the process and protocol Nicki Jo had created for its manufacture.

"I didn't expect this would happen when I wrote them," Nicki Jo said as she was told how the accident occurred. "I'll have to add another paragraph. At least he wasn't hurt, and the damage was minor," Nicki Jo said.

"Yes, the sandbags and steel plate saved him," Georg Rohn replied.

"Run me through it again."

"He was working through step twenty-three. He had just dipped some picric acid when he felt the sneeze coming on. Instead of following protocol and laying the ladle down, he froze. The first feeling subsided and then came again. This time he followed protocol, too late perhaps, and was lowering the ladle when he sneezed and shook the ladle. That set off the picric acid in his ladle. Fortunately, there were no sympathetic detonations, and the sandbags around the picric acid crucible absorbed the shock."

"Hmmm. Suggestions?" Nicki Jo asked.

"I think we should separate the individual workstations further apart, and add more sandbags between stations," the safety steward said. Further separation would add more isolation and help prevent one explosion from setting off a chain reaction down the other workstations.

"Isolate the stations more, and add some blow-out panels," Nicki Jo added.

The safety steward looked at the damaged workstation. The explosion ripped some sandbags open and others slid to one side as the sand ran out of the ripped bags. The station's protective steel armor plate was scratched, but the damage was minimal. Nicki's design had sand bags and steel plates placed in a fashion to redirect the force of an explosion away from the worker, the workstation, and, as much as possible, from the other chemical reagents. Her design had worked. This station could be back in production as soon as cleanup was finished.

"I agree," the steward said. "We can fix the other fab buildings now, move to one and retrofit this one later."

Nicki Jo nodded. "Write it up for me, and I'll sign it. What about the worker? How is he?"

"Shaken, scared, embarrassed . . . ," the safety steward answered.

"He should be."

"And, he has a couple of cuts, but none need stitches. I'll have the plant medic paint the cuts with an antiseptic, and bandage them where needed. I've put him on suspension with pay for five days per the safety rules. We'll have the accident review in a couple of days, but I don't see any willful negligence. A lack of training?" he asked Nicki Jo.

She pondered the question. She hadn't thought about what could happen from such a simple thing as a sneeze. Picric acid was touchy, but it was necessary for the process to make DDNP. *Could I change the formula to make the picric acid less . . . hazardous?* No, not and keep the DDNP usable and meet the requirements for a primer. *No,* she decided, *no change of the formula. Leave changes to formula to version two,* she decided, *if there is one.*

"Maybe. I'll have Katy review the training plans." She turned to the Safety Steward, "Recommendation on the worker?"

"Well, he makes a good training example," the safety steward said. "I'll think about it, but my first impression is that we should move him to a less . . . dangerous job."

"He won't like that," Katherine observed.

"I know, Katy," Nicki Jo said, "but we need to set precedence. We pay high scale, plus a hazard premium, for this job, and will pay his family a large compensation if he is killed or disabled. But his monetary loss in future income will teach the others to keep focused on the job."

"What was his rotation?" Nicki Jo asked the steward.

"He was in his second day. Week-on, week-off." Job stress was a risk that had been discussed before starting up the DDNP fabrication line. The work schedule was six days on, Monday through Saturday, followed by a week off the production line. They would work in a safer job for a week before returning to the line. Workers needed time off, time to be with their families, time to de-stress from a potentially lethal job if the worker didn't pay attention. Nicki Jo designed the fabrication process to be safe and reliable. However, no job, no process, was idiot-proof. Fortunately, this worker wasn't an idiot. He just sneezed . . . at a most unanticipated time, an unanticipated occurrence.

"Should we change that? Shorten the time-on to five or four days? Longer time off to de-stress?"

"No, I don't think so," the safety steward replied. "I'll watch for stress buildups, but I don't think it's a problem with this crew. Others . . . maybe, but we should wean out the weak ones during training."

"Okay. I'm depending on you and the other shop and safety stewards to tell us," she reminded him, "the management, whenever you think there's a problem. If our employees kill themselves, or even get hurt severely, no one will want the jobs. We need good workers and we're willing to take the steps needed to keep them."

"I understand and I'll report this to the steward's council at our next meeting."

"Good." Nicki Jo made one last inspection of the workstation and walked out. She had work to do.

✿   ✿   ✿

It was time for their weekly meeting. Gary wondered how necessary they were. Everyone talked with each other almost daily. He had asked several that question, and their answers were unexpected. They wanted the meeting! Apparently, Gary's staff meetings were the only time they were all together in one spot and able to receive information about the entire project. Without the staff meetings, they isolated themselves in private fiefdoms. "Status reports. Pat, how are we on construction?" Gary asked. This meeting was in the new administration building. It was so new the smell of sawdust still hung in the air. He had covered the walls of the conference room with diagrams of the plant site, drawings of the buildings, the down-time version of blue-prints, project diagrams and task-on-arrow process flow diagrams. Gary had temporarily conscripted the conference room as a working room for the meeting because it was the only one with interior walls instead of exposed studs.

Most of the members of the Board were present—Pat, Gary, Osker Geyer, Ruben Blumroder, and Archie and Marjorie Mitchell. Marjorie had her pencil and paper ready to take the meeting minutes. When everyone was seated, Gary began, "We finished RJ City in mid-December, and returned to the chemical and fabrication buildings. All the tents are gone, and everyone has a roof over their heads. Nicki Jo changed her process design and cut out a lot of work from the original plan. Still, we're about a month behind where I'd hoped we'd be."

"The primary issue on the critical path is the jamming of the cartridge presses," Pat said. He was first on the agenda.

Gary sneezed. The free-floating sawdust tickled his nose. *Have to get this place cleaned. Wet rags should pick up all the remaining sawdust. Ahh, don't get sidetracked.*

"There were two causes for the jams in the presses," Pat continued. "The first was the thinness of the cartridge walls. The second was the carbon-steel dies we were using. We replaced the dies with the new ones made from tungsten carbide now that Osker has that available for us.. We have just enough on hand to make dies for the prototype presses. The new dies will leave a thicker cartridge wall. We have also improved the lube and cleansing system. Our last run made 1,200 cartridge cases without a stoppage. We halted the run because we ran out of copper cups."

"What about the composition of the primer cups?" Archie asked.

"Well," Pat said hesitantly, "Nicki borrowed Marjorie's Smith and Wesson to test them."

Archie glowered at Nicki Jo and muttered, "Without asking me first."

"Marjorie's Smith & Wesson Model 25 is stronger than Archie's Colt single action revolvers, so it was a good choice. We popped a hundred caps and only had one failure. That was a cap that had no anvil," Nicki Jo responded. "There will be a QC check in the production system to watch for that."

"QC?" Ruben Blumroder asked, puzzled about the term.

"Quality Control, Ruben, finding manufacturing defects during production before they get passed to the customer." Nicki Jo answered.

Ruben thought for a moment and nodded. "I know about manufacturing defects. Looking and planning for them ahead of time was something I hadn't considered."

Pat knew Ruben well enough to see him berating himself about his oversight. "Osker, how is the copper smelting going? Can you meet our production quotas?"

Geyer had had his hands full, but he was still on schedule. His part of the plan was clear-cut, make steel and make brass. Once he had determined what needed to be done, it was easy to implement changes in his steel processes. Brass was easier than steel. "Short answer, yes. I'm still building stockpiles of ores and product, but I have sufficient material on hand to meet your needs."

"Does anyone have, or see any issue, that would prevent a full run of the pilot plant?"

"What is the target number again?" Ruben asked.

"One thousand primed cartridge brass per line per day. We have one line ready."

"Let's go for it," Pat said.

"All agreed?" Gary asked. He waited. No one spoke. Geyer, Nicki Jo and Katherine were nodding agreement. "Okay. Let's cleanup the site first. Remove anything that might affect the test. How about . . . ," he glanced down at his calendar, "next Tuesday for the run. Objections? Issues? Alternatives?" He waited again. "Sobeit."

They started to stand when Archie cleared his throat. "I have something to add—not about the test."

"Go ahead," Gary said.

"Our resident spy has applied for a job in the chem plant. I had his application put on hold. I think that approving him would not be a good idea. Gruber agrees."

"Is he a danger?" Nicki Jo asked. She certainly didn't need a saboteur in a place where he had explosives readily available.

"I don't know, but it's a possibility. We believe he is working for a foreign country, Poland, Russia, France or England. We don't know."

"I don't want him around if he's a danger. So far, we've been using him as a carpenter. The buildings aren't a secret. It's what is inside those building that is the secret. Let's cut him loose." Pat said.

"I agree," Gary chimed in.

"There's another factor. Four others have joined him. Four strangers arrived last week. One claims to have been a chemical student at the Imperial College in Magdeburg. According to the college, there was a chemical student at the College last year. But, his description doesn't match the man here."

"What do you suggest we do, Archie?" Pat asked.

"First, make no formal decisions yet. If any ask about being hired, stall them. Second, Gary, get your security guards in the loop, and start patrolling the grounds at night."

"That's doable," Gary answered.

"And start mounted patrols of the perimeter. I assume that squad of mounted mercenaries that guarded Nicki Jo and Katherine are still around?"

"Yes, Anse Hatfield hired them to help train his security force."

"Use them, and have them train more mounted guards. In the meantime, we'll keep watch on these five."

XI

Late February 1635, The Reservation

The pilot plant consisted of several buildings; the chem plant, where the DDNP was made, the primer plant, where the DDNP was injected into the cups to make a finished primer, the brassworks that made primer cups on one small production line, and the brass cartridge cases formed in another line. The remaining building was the assembly plant where the primers were inserted into the brass; a separate building for safety. Nicki Jo was adamant about separating the fab plant from the chemical plant. She wanted to prevent the possibility of a sympathetic detonation if the chem or primer facility went up.

All stages of production had been tested individually. Now it was time to test the entire production line from end to end. The test run would start at 7:00AM and run until they were out of materials. In other words, they could make no more primer cups, no more cartridge brass, no more live primers, no more primed cartridge brass.

The crews were ready. They had been training for a week, walking through each step of their piece of the process under supervision. The workstations were completed, and where they were handling explosive material, surrounded by sandbags and armor plate.

The facilities were ready.

Pat looked at the group—officers, stockholders, managers, professional staff, Nicki Jo and Katherine. The employees were at their positions, waiting for the signal to start. He pulled a handkerchief from his pocket and waved it. The fabrication plant steam engine operator was watching for the signal. When the operator saw Pat waving a handkerchief, he followed his instructions and pulled the lanyard on the brass whistle on top of the engine.

The whistle sounded, echoing across the Reservation. Everyone, except for the company officers and stockholders, dispersed.

Archie watched them leave. He turned to Pat. "Is it gonna work?"

"Yeah, it should—it will," Pat answered. "We reached this milestone sooner than I estimated. I thought Nicki Jo was going to have more problems making DDNP safely. I knew she'd be paranoid about that. It's one reason Gary, and I wanted her. Everyone knows about the explosion at Essen Chemical. Her paranoia is what we wanted."

"We're still behind schedule, though?" Archie asked.

"Yes, a month," Pat agreed. "It would have been worse if Nicki Jo hadn't altered her design. That saved us several weeks. She thought it would introduce additional worker risk, but after that accident in the chem plant a couple of weeks ago, she now thinks she was too cautious in her original design."

"Let's get inside, Pat. I'm getting cold out here."

They were now alone on the reviewing stand. It wasn't much of a stand, a hastily constructed platform a couple of feet above the ground. They stepped down and headed for the admin building. The test run would last most of the day, and both of them had jobs to do.

As they walked, Pat mentioned, "I've already had requests from employee committees asking if, when, they could buy stock. I've assured them we will have some kind of profit-sharing program once we're in full production and selling our product. That's satisfied most of them."

Archie nodded in agreement. He, as a member of the board, had received queries, too.

"Gary and I," Pat continued, referring to the upcoming initial sale of stock, "along with our financiers, have restricted the amount of shares to be sold on the open market. We have enough financing that we needn't sell more shares. We may make some concessions to our existing partners, like H&K. They've just bought another 10 blocks."

The two continued walking across the graveled driveway to the front steps of the admin building. "We thought to sell shares to our employees, but we now think a simple profit-sharing plan is better. That will still allow our employees to have a stake in the corporation."

They reached the main door of the admin building. Archie held the door open for Pat. "How much for a block?"

"Fifty silver guilders for one block."

"So H&K's initial investment was five hundred guilders?" Archie asked.

"More, actually."

They passed through the double front doors, past the receptionist's desk, and down the hallway toward Pat's office. "Our financiers suggested we convert to USE dollars and declare one share equal to USE$100, or roughly two and a half guilders. I argued against that. I want us backed by silver, not paper. In the end, the financiers appreciated that view. We need to repay them, buy out their investment and they'll want a profit for investing and risking their capital. If all goes well, we can be free and clear of them in a few years. This will allow us to remain a closely held corporation and still allow us the leeway to sell more shares in the future if we ever need to do so."

They reached Pat's office and went inside. Pat hung his coat and hat on a coat tree next to the door while Archie draped his coat over the back of a side chair and pulled a second chair closer to Pat's desk and asked, "What is the total investment at this point?"

Still standing, Pat walked to a side-table, poured two mugs of hot broth, returned to his desk, and gave one mug to Archie. He sat and continued the conversation. "Not counting the initial cash on hand, we have about thirty thousand guilders total investment; the actual asset value is half again more. I've asked the financiers to send an auditing team. They'll arrive later this month and will be our assurance to the investors that we're really doing what we say we're doing."

"Any money worries?" Archie asked.

"Surprisingly, no." Pat leaned back in his swivel chair and stretched. He hadn't noticed how tense he had been that morning. He shouldn't have been. All the trial runs had performed well, and we've fixed all found bugs. If the test went well, they would have passed a major milestone and the possibility of failure would be reduced. From this point forward, research would be finished, and development nearly so. Pat closed his eyes for a moment, and then opened and looked at Archie. "You know, there was a real risk it would all collapse if we hadn't gotten enough initial funding, if the Abrabanel clan hadn't come through for us."

"Are they directly invested?" Archie doubted any obvious direct involvement. From what he knew and had heard, the Abrabanels preferred to work behind the scenes, not out in public.

"No," Pat confirmed, "Indirectly? You can count on it."

＊ ＊ ＊

Gary Reardon blew his whistle. It wasn't needed. Everyone was already present, standing in the shadows of the western peaks. His watch read 4:35PM. The individual managers gathered in front of the reviewing stand. "Report!" he bellowed.

Pat Johnson stepped forward. "Four thousand, seven hundred, thirty-two cartridge brass manufactured."

Nicki Jo spoke next, "Eight thousand, two hundred seventy-six primers manufactured."

Gary reached into his pocket, extracted a piece of paper and read the figures aloud, "Four thousand, six hundred and ninety-three primed cartridge cases." The managers and supervisors clapped. They knew they had done their jobs. "We would have primed all the brass," Gary said, "except for one box of primers that was spilled. Those are being picked up at the moment . . . carefully," he added, to the laughter of some of the employees.

He turned to the rest of the officers and stockholders. "I'd call that a success. We overran our goal by a factor of four—and that was just one production line that was only semi-mechanized."

Later than evening Gary Reardon walked into the radio station and told the attendant, "I have some messages that I need sent."

BEGIN: SUHL TO BMBG
TO: ABEL ABRABANEL
FROM: GARY REARDON
DATE: FEBRUARY 23, 1635
MESSAGE: TEMPLATE   3   STOP   MILESTONE   43 SUCCESSFULLY COMPLETED STOP 4693 stop 9 DOT 5 HRS STOP 400 PERCENT STOP

"Send that same message to these people and addresses, too," Gary ordered, passing the list to the attendant along with a silver guilder to insure confidentiality.

I think I'll have a little celebration, Gary thought as he left the station. The Boar's Head Inn was out of his way home, but not all that far. Gaylynn would understand. The proprietor had received some superb brandy from Amsterdam and Gary thought he'd try it. He wasn't a drinker, but today . . . *Yes, today was special.*

***

"We need to track down who Zoche is working with here in Suhl and up the line to Zwickau," Archie said. He was sitting in the Reservation's new boardroom with Gary Reardon, Constabulary Captain Eric Gruber, and Nicki Jo Prickett and Katherine.

"Francisco Nasi, in his private capacity, is interested in our situation and has promised to watch Zoche's couriers from Suhl to Zwickau. When the courier passes our secret data, he'll sweep in and gather them up.

"But he doesn't have any authority now," Gary said.

"Well . . . yes and no," Archie said. "He still has contacts in the government and the military. If he finds evidence of foreign espionage, it falls into the area of responsibility of the military."

"So we've been told," Eric Gruber added.

"What do you plan?" Nicki Jo asked.

"We have hired Zoche as janitorial staff from the admin building. We were thinking if you, Nicki Jo, left some altered documents covering the DDNP process—processes that don't work—out where he could find them." Archie looked at Nicki Jo. He needed her cooperation for his plan to work. "We could watch him steal them and pass them on to the courier. When Nasi tells us he's closed on the other end, we pick up Zoche and his friends. Nasi believes we can charge them with treason if they are working for a foreign nation. They all claim to be USE citizens."

Archie wasn't sure about the treason charges. As long as he had proof of theft, it would be enough to charge them. Then he, Gruber and the watch, would arrest them, and the prosecutors could take it from there.

"Can you do that, Nicki Jo?" Pat asked.

"Easily. We had a number of failures, some very spectacular, before we reached our final formula. Some go boom very, very easily."

"What about the other one, Mohr?" Gary asked. Mohr was trying to steal his drawings for the mechanized brass production and ammunition assembly system. Pat was very protective of those designs. He'd worked extremely hard to develop and test them, and he didn't care to give all that work away without some profit.

"We believe he is working for some competitors in Magdeburg. If we can prove that, we can sue them and win."

Pat interrupted, "As long as I—we get paid for our work, Archie, I'm satisfied,"

Archie nodded and continued, "If our plan works with Zoche, we'll try something like it on Mohr, Gary."

XII

March 1635, Suhl

"*What!*"

Gary Reardon was working for himself today at his Suhl Nut and Bolt works. He had spent little time with his business for the last seven months. He had an excellent manager, but sometimes he just had to be there. That excellent manager, his wife Gaylynn, was passing Gary's office and heard his outburst. She paused at his open door and gave him a look. Gary returned her look with a frown. Gaylynn returned the frown, held it, and then nodded to Gary and proceeded down the hallway. Gary understood that look—*keep your voice down!*

"They refuse to deliver any black powder, Gary, under the terms of our contracts," Pat Johnson reported, sitting in front of Gary's desk. He had just given Gary the news. Their black powder suppliers had reneged on their contract. "They raised their prices by four hundred percent, and they won't deliver any more powder than one ton per week. We can take or leave it."

"How can they do that? They agreed last November they would be our supplier. Ten tons per week. We have a contract with each of them!" Gary stood up. He needed to pace. It was one of his stress relievers. Unfortunately, his office wasn't big enough to pace, and what little free space it had was now occupied by Pat Johnson.

"I don't think they can make ten tons a week even if they combine all their output," Pat said. "They are small producers and only make enough for local customers . . . until now. They didn't expand their mills, expanding would cost them money."

"But they'd make more, more than enough to pay back their investment in a short time," Gary countered. "We would even provide financing for their expansion if they needed it."

"They don't see it that way and please sit down. You're putting a crick in my neck standing there." Pat said. "They think they're in a controlling position, and claim they have pre-existing commitments to other clients."

Gary sat, stared at Pat, looked away, and then hit his desk with his fist in frustration. It was one of his rare expressions of anger. He couldn't pace, he couldn't relieve his growing anger and frustration. The project was still behind. They'd gained a week, and now this—a new job and an expensive one. With no outlet for his anger, it seethed and continued to grow.

"Where's Nicki Jo?" Gary asked. There was a solution. It wasn't one he liked, but she was coming free. "We've got another job for her."

"Out at the site, probably."

Gary expected that answer. If she weren't home in the house Marjorie had found for her, she'd be in her lab. "I need to think about this. Would you go get her and bring her back here? Katy, too, of course. We need to put our heads together on this."

With Pat gone, Gary stood up and left his office. He needed to pace. He had to moderate his temper. They thought they could act like robber barons. They were wrong. *Oh, they'll pay,* he promised himself.

✳ ✳ ✳

"I know it's not in your contract, Nicki Jo," Gary said, "but we're in a bind. Can you do it?"

"Make a powder mill?" Nicki Jo responded, "Sure. It's just mechanics. Once you have the mill wheels set up, it's just a construction job. I hadn't planned for one, so there's no place in the current plant design. We'll need an additional site, mill and bunkers."

"Fortunately, we have workers available." Gary muttered. He had planned to turn some laborers loose now that the major construction phase is over." *God, the cost!* "Would you manage this—the design of the mill and oversee its construction?"

Nicki Jo didn't mind building the mill. It was a simple construction job, but it affected her plans. She was about to wrap up her contract, having finished the DDNP fabrication plant and the primer manufactory. All she had left was some final documentation and training reviews. She glanced at Katherine. *Objections?* She mentally asked. Nicki Jo knew that if Katherine had objections, she would not hesitate to speak. Apparently, she had none since she remained silent. "I'll do it, Gary. Shouldn't be a big deal, just supervision."

"Thank you, Nicki Jo. Would it be okay if I work with Katy on your contract change?"

"Go ahead. She's better than me on contracts."

Katherine and Nicki Jo left Gary's office to return to the Reservation. When they were out his office door, Gary turned to Pat. "You have a list of these people—the ones who are holding us up?"

"Right here," Pat said, laying the list on Gary's desk.

"I wanted to keep Suhl, Incorporated, a friendly affair. We'll deal fairly with the people of Suhl, provided them with new jobs, improved their economy and the overall prospects of the entire city. But there's always some sons-of-a-bitch who have to screw things up. *Damn it!*"

"Gary—"

"I'm gonna screw 'em, Pat. I'm going to nail their asses to the wall. I'm going to find out who their suppliers are, where they get their saltpeter, their charcoal and sulfur, and put those sources under an exclusive contract with us. We'll out produce 'em and undersell 'em—even at a loss if necessary. *No one stabs me in the back!* And when they come to us begging for relief, we'll buy them out for pennies on the dollar."

"Gary, there's more."

"More?" Gary asked, his eyebrows leaping upward.

"I think Zoche bribed them."

The pressure to meet the October deadline was growing for everyone involved in the project. Gary was usually an even-tempered man. A type-A personality and driven to meet his self-designated goals, but he'd forgotten that Gary, when his anger was aroused, held a grudge.

"I think it's time for Andres Zoche to go away."

"Gary!"

"Oh, nothing physical . . . ," *but I can still imagine beating the shit out of him,* " . . . just insure he's jailed and no longer a factor. Let's get Archie's plan in motion. I'm tired of Zoche's interference."

"What about Mohr?" Pat asked.

"He's working for some interests in Magdeburg. I'm not all that concerned about him. We'll keep him from finding any drawings of our tools and presses. Eventually, some will get out, but we'll have our head start and the people in Magdeburg will play catch-up."

XIII

April 1635, Suhl

"**N**icki Jo, a letter from Banfi Hunyades, arrived today," Katherine announced, walking into Nicki Jo's home office. Nicki Jo often did her writing, documentation, and process plans, here, in the quiet of their home. Today, she sat at her desk writing in her daily diary. The diary was a recitation of her activities for the day, the details of the issues and resolutions that she was documenting for her reports to the Suhl, Incorporated's Board of Directors.

"What does he want?" Nicki Jo replied, looking up.

"I didn't read it. It's addressed to you." Katherine gave Nicki Jo the sealed letter and sat in the chair at the side of the desk.

"Katy. I've told you before, I have no secrets from you. I want you to read my mail."

"Only if I want, Nicki, and I see no need. You'll tell me what I need to know." Katherine propped her elbow on the edge of the desk and rested her cheek in her palm. "I'll wait while you read the letter. Then, you can tell me what was in it."

Nicki Jo sighed. With the letter in hand, she broke the wax seal, opened the letter and read it through while Katherine waited. When she finished, she handed it to Katherine. "I think you need to go back to Essen for a while. I don't know if what we're doing here has gotten out, but this may be something we can leverage."

Katherine read the letter and looked up, "Nitrocellulose?"

"Yes, the stuff for smokeless gunpowder."

"But—"

"I know. I've said it's too dangerous but I've been rethinking that."

"Picric acid and DDNP are dangerous, too," Katherine mentioned.

"Yes. Some differences but not all that much." Nicki Jo drummed her fingers on her desk and looked out the side window. She could see Suhl's rooftops and, in the distance, the ridge that blocked her view of the Reservation. The view from the window had become a welcome sight. She could just see the top of the tower next to the Rathaus.

"You know where this leads." She said, continuing to look out the window. After a few moments, she turned from the window and said to Katherine, "If we do this, we'll need to tell the others. They'll be interested, too."

Katherine read the letter again, "There's no mention of confidentiality."

"Oversight? Deliberate?" Nicki Jo asked. "What do you think?"

"Don't know, Nicki."

Nicki Jo looked out the window again. She tapped her teeth with the pencil, a habit she'd had since grade school. She looked at Katherine. There could only be one course of action. "That's why you need to talk with Banfi. We need to know what constraints are in this contract, the clients, the project scope . . . any conflicts of interest?"

Katherine looked down at the letter and, for a moment, contemplated what she should do. Nicki Jo was right. Someone had to go back to Essen. That meant . . . "Oh, Nicki . . . I don't want to go. I like it here. We've made new friends here."

"I can't go, Katy, not now. There's still the mill to build."

The two women looked at one another. They'd not been apart more than a few days for nearly two years. Katherine feared Nicki Jo would get depressed again if she weren't here to help her. She knew Nicki Jo's weaknesses—Nicki Jo didn't do well being alone. Katherine didn't understand the term *bipolar cycle*, it being an up-time concept, but if she had, she would have recognized its effects on Nicki Jo. The method Nicki Jo used to keep that cycle at bay was work. She could immerse herself in work and ignore the outside factors that could trigger a cycle. On the other hand, Nicki Jo had had no depressive episodes since they arrived in Suhl late last September. That change was welcome. But could Nicki Jo continue to fight her recurring depression without her?

"I know what you're thinking, Katy. Marjorie's here . . . so are Gaylynn, Greta, and Ursula. I'm not alone."

Katherine sighed. She knew when her objections had been reviewed and rejected. Truth be known, she wasn't as concerned as she had been in Essen. "Very well."

"I'll come, too, as soon as I've finished the powder mill," she said.

"But that's . . . "

"Yes, a couple of months."

Katherine's eyes were moist. "Very well, I'll leave on the next coach north."

"And take those mercenaries with you," Nicki Jo added. The squad of mounted mercenaries had liked living in Suhl. They were being well paid, well fed, and no one was shooting at them. It was time they earned their keep once again.

May 1635, The Reservation

"Any word from Nasi?" Nicki Jo asked Archie as she entered his office in the courthouse and sat in the chair in front of his desk. She was getting anxious. They'd sprung the trap a week ago. She and Archie had watched Zoche find the doctored file in her admin building office. Her office there held nothing more than correspondence with suppliers. That information wasn't critical. She kept all her important documentations in her safe in her house in Suhl, watched by a trusted guard, a mounted constabulary trooper on medical leave for an ulcer.

The trap wasn't complicated. On the day they would set it, Nicki Jo would be in her office with her chief chemist, Georg Rohn. Their roles were to wait for Zoche to come to clean her office. When Zoche walks in, they would discuss the DDNP process and accompanying documents on.

Then, having completed the conversation, she would file the documents, but be called away and would forget to lock the cabinet. That would give Zoche the opportunity to steal the altered formula.

Zoche arrived. Nicki Jo gave him a nod in acknowledgement and continued her conversation. "Do you need this anymore, Georg?" she asked, taking the folder from Georg's hands.

"No, Nicki Jo. I've noted the last change. It's all up to date now and you can store it all in the archives down in the strong room." Georg Rohn had practiced his part in the scene being played for Zoche. He was careful not to look at Zoche, to ignore him. Nicki Jo took the folder with its red strip across the cover and walked over to the filing cabinet. Standing next to the cabinet was a long iron bar. When the bar slid through the metal handles of the cabinet, an up-time pad lock would secure it.

She opened a cabinet drawer, thumbed through some folders, and slid the striped folder in place just as Pat Johnson walked into her office. "Nicki Jo—Georg, you too—would you join me in my office? I want you to review my idea to speed up the primer assembly line. I'm concerned about the pressure being applied to the compound and I don't want any self-detonations."

Nicki Jo slid the drawer shut. "Sure Pat." She and Georg followed Pat out, leaving the cabinet unlocked as planned. Archie Mitchell was watching through a pin-hole from the next office. When they were gone, Zoche opened the cabinet, removed the red-striped folder and one other. He switched the contents and put the red-striped folder back. The other folder, now containing the altered DDNP process, he hid inside his shirt and walked out.

That had been a week ago. When Zoche returned to his room in Suhl, he sealed the folder inside a weather-proofed pouch and delivered it to a private courier. Two of Gruber's troopers followed the courier to Erfurt, where the surveillance was handed over to Francisco Nasi's operatives.

"Nothing yet, Nicki Jo. It's not dark yet, so I doubt anything will come in on the radio net until then. Why don't you go home? I'll let you know as soon as I do—after I have Gruber and the watch arrest Zoche.

Nicki Jo didn't want to go home. Her cook and maid were waiting for her, but they weren't Katherine, and she missed Katherine. She still needed six more weeks to finish the powder mills on the Reservation. Once that was done, she could go to Katherine. She puttered in Archie's office, doing nothing, and whiled away another half an hour before deciding not to waste any more of Archie's time. She stood to take her leave when a messenger from the radio station arrived.

The messenger handed the paper to Archie, who read it. "Tell Captain Gruber that I said it's time," he instructed the messenger, who left the office to find the mounted constabulary captain.

"Nasi got them," Archie told Nicki Jo. "They were Poles. Nasi let the package go on. He thought they'd blow up their lab at least once before they got wise that your formula wouldn't work."

Nicki Jo sat back down and sighed. "I'm so relieved. I've been worrying about this for months."

"Well, you can quit now. We'll grab Zoche and his friends. I expect the people in Magdeburg will want to talk to them."

"What about the other one, Mohr?"

"That turns out to be domestic espionage. He is working for a group in Magdeburg. Nasi has identified them all. We'll sue them and recoup more than if they had just licensed our process. We'll all win from this."

"Except for the Poles."

"And the people in Magdeburg."

XIV

July 1635, Suhl

Nicki Jo pointed to her bags, designating which ones the porter was to load on top of the coach and which ones she would keep inside with her. A number of people were gathered to say goodbye. The *Sisters*, Marjorie, Gaylynn, Ursula ,and Greta, were lined up to give her departing hugs. Pat, Gary, and Archie had hoped she'd stay, but she had fulfilled the terms of her contract, and had done so months earlier than planned. Nicki Jo was a whirlwind when motivated. Moreso, when her primary source of motivation was in Essen. The time spent in Suhl let her resolve most of her personal issues. Perhaps the new surroundings, new people, had been more therapeutic than anyone thought. Whatever the reason, Nicki Jo had returned to her *pre-explosion* self, and any thoughts of self-punishment had vanished. Permanently, everyone hoped.

Katherine had resolved the contract issue in Essen, but the political situation along the Rhine was deteriorating. Colette Modi was offering a deal. Essen Chemical would accept a contract with Suhl, Incorporated, to operate the Suhl chemical plant. She would also move parts of Essen Chemical to Suhl, away from the armies marching near Essen. That move would safeguard her company and expand Collette's operations in the SoTF.

No one knew where that would go. Behind all the military maneuvering, Suhl County was a peaceful island in a world of turmoil.

The black powder mills, Nicki Jo's last task, were in full operation. Gary paid her a sizable bonus for her achievements. She had met every milestone, either on time or earlier than planned.

"We'll keep your house waiting for you, Nicki Jo," Marjorie said.

"Thank you. I expect I'll be back in a couple or three weeks. I'm meeting Katherine in Magdeburg, and we're spending a few days with the people at the Imperial College. I just don't know, at this time, how long we'll be there."

"I'm glad Katherine got out of Essen. I've been worrying about her all the while she's been gone. It will be good to see her again."

"I'm not sure how she managed that, Marjorie. I think she may have taken a ship to Lubeck and from there on to Magdeburg."

The three men stood back from the fray. Finally, at the urging of the coach's driver and guards, Nicki Jo entered, and the porter closed the coach's door. She waved to her friends as the coach moved out toward the north road, accompanied by hired guards, to Erfurt and on to Magdeburg.

"Well, I need to get back to work. See ya," Gary abruptly said to the other two men and walked off.

BEGIN: SUHL TO BMBG
TO: ABEL ABRABANEL
FROM: GARY REARDON
DATE: JULY 7, 1635
MESSAGE: TEMPLATE 27 STOP MILESTONE 132 SUCCESSFULLY COMPLETED STOP 6 TONS PER WEEK STOP ENTERING PHASE 4 STOP

The radio station operator looked up. "More messages, *Herr Reardon*?"

"Yes. Just like before, Karl. Here's the list of recipients."

The station operator glanced at the clock. "These will go out in about six hours on the evening net, *Herr Reardon*. I can barely hear Grantville right now and they can't hear me at all."

Gary knew the propagation effects of the Maunder Minimum restricted radio transmissions, usually, to the evening and morning hours, at dusk, and at dawn. The operators called it the *grayline* effect—that period before and after dusk and dawn. "I understand. If you can't send them tonight, please send me a message?"

"Certainly, *Herr Reardon*. If not this evening, we'll try again in the morning. I'll let you know whenever they are sent."

"*Danke*." Gary placed a silver guilder on the counter, " . . . for your efforts."

The radio operator smiled at the sight of the coin. He swept it off the counter and slipped it into his pocket, nodding respectfully. He would have insured *Herr Reardon*'s messages were sent as quickly as possible, and privately, too. But it was nice for *Herr Reardon* to acknowledge and reward that confidentiality.

An hour later, Gary rode up to the Suhl, Incorporated, administration building. He had taken Archie's advice and had bought a horse for his daily commute. It was much better than the hour-long walk it would normally take to reach the Reservation. *Should we provide a shuttle service?* Another item for his to-do list to think about.

Portions of the admin building, the upper floor, were still empty. He entered and greeted the receptionist, who sat behind a counter just inside the main door. He was a new hire and had been on the job for only a week.

"You have some visitors waiting for you, *Herr Reardon*. They're in the waiting room."

"Their names?"

The receptionist glanced at the register that every visitor had to sign, "*Herr Lang, Herr Thalmann und Herr Exel, Herr Reardon.*"

Gary recognized the names. They were the three who owned the black powder mills in Suhl. Each one had promised to supply Suhl, Incorporated with black powder. Each had signed a contract. But after being bribed by the spy, Zoche, they had each reneged on their contracts.

"Give me five minutes and then escort them to my office. Send a security guard to my office first."

"Jawohl, Herr Reardon."

Gary turned left and walked down the hall to his office. He reached Pat Johnson's office, which was next to his, and saw Pat was inside. He opened the door. "Pat, would you join me in my office?" he asked. "Lang, Thalmann and Exel are here."

Before Pat could answer, Gary closed the door, walked a few more steps down the hall, and entered his own office. He had just seated himself behind his desk when Pat walked in through a connecting doorway between their offices. Gary gestured for Pat to sit in the chair that would give him a view of the visitor's chairs, and of Gary.

As Pat was sitting, a security guard, one of Anse Hatfield's men, entered. "Just stand over there along the wall, cross your arms, if you would, Eric. I want you to be visible and intimidating. I don't think our visitors will get violent, but I think your presence will help keep them in control of themselves."

"Jawohl, Herr Reardon." The guard positioned himself along the wall, spread his legs, crossed his arms, and stood guard.

The receptionist knocked on Gary's office door, opened it and announced, *"Herr Lang, Herr Thalmann, und Herr Exel, Herr Reardon."*

"Thank you, Mattheus. Show them in."

The three men walked into the office. Lang strode in, looked at the chairs before Gary's desk, walked over, and sat before Gary could invite them to sit. *Herr Thalmann,* and *Herr Exel,* were more hesitant, but followed Lang's lead.

So that's how it's going to be. So be it. No reconciliation, just snub me from the start. If they had been more—respectful, he might have cut them some slack. Maybe. Not now.

"What do you want?" Gary asked bluntly.

Thalmann opened his mouth to speak and then stopped. He glanced at Lang and shut his mouth. There was a moment of silence before Lang spoke. "You will stop stealing our customers, or we will sue you, and shut you down."

Gary smiled and said nothing. Pat's face was expressionless.

When Gary gave no response. Pat Johnson spoke instead. "Stop? We aren't stealing anything. We're selling a better, cheaper product. If your former customers prefer us over you, that's just too bad—for you."

Lang opened his mouth to refute Pat's statement, but Pat silenced him by pointing a finger at Lang and continuing. "We didn't want to build a powder mill. We wanted to help existing Suhl merchants—you. Each of you promised to supply us with black powder and then refused. You failed to deliver and refused to do business with us. Not we, with you. If anyone has a complaint, it is us. You broke your contracts. If you are unhappy that we're making our own black powder, selling powder that is better, and cheaper than yours, you have no one to blame except yourselves."

Lang sputtered. Thalmann and Exel glanced at one another, but remained silent. "Do you have anything else to discuss?" Gary asked. "No? Then *Guten Tag, Meine Herren.* Eric, please escort these gentlemen off Suhl, Incorporated property."

"*Jawohl, Herr Reardon.* This way, *meine Herren.*"

The three rose and walked out. Thalmann and Exel had not said a word. Obviously, it was Lang who led the group. As they left, Lang stalked off in the lead.

"Think they'll be back?" Pat asked.

"Not yet, but yes, they will. Our powder mill is now operating and we've a surplus to our needs. We can increase the amount we sell to their customers and drop our price another ten percent to put the squeeze on them."

Pat nodded but said nothing. He wasn't as vindictive as Gary was, but he agreed a lesson had to be made. Suhl, Incorporated, would treat any honest businessman fairly. But try to screw Suhl, Incorporated—and you'll be screwed in return.

"Have you received their current valuation?" Gary asked.

Pat stood. He nodded, and replied, "Several times. It keeps changing—downward. They're not being underwritten by Zoche anymore."

"I'll give them another month," Gary stated.

"That sounds about right."

"What will be your price?" Gary asked. He preferred to let Pat be the dog in this fight. Pat was more . . . conciliatory, no, that wasn't the word; Pat would put them out of business, and do it in such a fashion that everyone would know why it was being done, and everyone would approve the manner it was resolved.

Gary could not do that. Oh, he'd put them out of business, in the same way Pat did, but the citizens of Suhl would consider Gary a tyrant, arrogantly imposing his power on three small factors. No, Pat was the better one to handle this.

Pat didn't immediately answer. "I'm feeling generous, Pat. I think ten cents of the dollar would be fair," Gary said, smiling at Pat.

Pat looked out the window and watched the three climb into a coach for the trip back to Suhl. "Some people are so short-sighted." He turned from the window. "Are we back on schedule?"

"Almost. The production lines are all working. We're continuing to stockpile ores and materials for the primer fabrication plant. We have four bunkers full of .45 Colt cartridges, sealed, crated, and ready to ship. Plus, we've another three bunkers of .45-70 cartridges. We're still playing catch-up, finishing the interiors of the brassworks and the chemical plant. As work teams get finished, we're putting them to work building the remaining berms."

"Good," Pat responded.

✳ ✳ ✳

"Gary, Lang has closed his doors," Pat said, walking through the interconnecting door between his office and Gary's. "Ruben just sent me the news. He thinks Thalmann and Exel will close within a week, too."

Their meeting with Gary and Pat had occurred a month ago. The three had lasted longer than either Pat or Gary had thought.

Gary looked up at the news. A smile spread across his face. "Think it's time to make them an offer?"

Pat rubbed his jaw. "No, not yet. We can do that after the lawyers swoop in to collect their debts. Then we'll deal with the lawyers. Lang, and the rest can take it, and be glad to get it. If not from them, then from the new owners."

"Who is our property lawyer?" Gary asked.

"Ahh, I can't remember his name at the moment. He's new."

"Put him on it. Tell him what we want, why, and turn him loose when you think it's time."

"Will do."

Gary ticked another item off his mental to-do list, returned to his desk, and began reading the next report from the stack before him.

* * *

Archie Mitchell woke to the shaking of his house. Small objects and crockery fell and shattered in the next room. Marjorie was awakened, too. From the squeaking of the floor above them, Dieter and Greta were stirring upstairs, and Marta was crying.

"What was that, Archie?" Marjorie asked.

He wasn't sure. Something had shaken the house. Earthquake? No, he had felt those before when he had been stationed at The Presidio in San Francisco. What could have happened—the Reservation!

"I think something blew up at the Reservation. Go upstairs and tell Dieter we need to head out there."

Archie was saddling his pinto when Dieter ran up. "I'll be right with you," he said as he passed by to saddle his horse.

Archie tightened the pinto's belly-band, led him out of the stable, and mounted. Dieter joined him and they headed for the Reservation. The Reservation was three miles outside Suhl, to the west. Archie and Dieter lived close to the western gate and the road to the Reservation. Pat Johnson and Gary Reardon would be coming, too, but they lived on the other side of Suhl. Archie and Dieter would arrive first.

The ride to the Reservation only took twenty minutes. The administration building came into sight, and lamps were visible inside. That was normal. The security guards worked out of the admin building. This evening, there should be ten guards patrolling the grounds and buildings. "Let's stop here first, Dieter. Someone should know what happened," Archie said, riding up to the front door. They dismounted and tied the horses' reins to the hitching rail in front.

The security shift supervisor met them at the door. "I thought you would be coming, *Herr Marshal.*"

"What happened?" Archie asked.

"A bunker blew up, Number 9. We're checking the other buildings and bunkers, but other than some broken windows, and some minor roof damage, the damage isn't bad . . . except for that one bunker."

"Where is Bunker 9?"

The supervisor walked over to the map of the Reservation mounted on the wall. There was an index on one side. Each building and bunker was numbered. The supervisor looked at the map and pointed to one bunker. "Here," he said. It's on the edge of the storage area, almost two miles from here. That's why the damage was so slight."

What could cause the bunker to explode? "What was stored there?" Archie asked.

The supervisor walked over to the central desk and took a binder from a drawer. In the binder were a list of the bunkers, and what was stored within each. Some contained finished ammunition, others had finished primers, and some, like Bunker 9, contained DDNP.

"DDNP," he replied.

Archie turned to Dieter. "Let's go," he said.

Before he and Dieter rode off into the darkness, Archie told the supervisor, "*Herr Reardon* and *Herr Johnson* will be here soon, as well as *Herr Rohn*, I suspect. Tell them we'll be at the bunker site."

Jawohl, Herr Marshal!

It was a short ride to the bunker site. The moon provided some light, appearing after the evening's earlier overcast had dispersed.

They smelled the odor from the explosion before they reached the bunker. It had been a standard bunker, a sunken stone and concrete building covered with earth and surrounded by a twenty foot high berm. The entrance had been through a dog-leg designed to keep most of the force of any explosion within the berm. From Archie's visual examination, it had not worked. The dog-leg was gone. Two security guards were present. One was sitting on the ground. The other was tending to his partner.

"You okay?" Archie asked, riding up to the pair and dismounting. He recognized both of the guards. One was a former gunsmith apprentice who joined the security force for its higher wages. The other was a militiaman.

The one sitting, the former apprentice, said, "The explosion knocked me off my horse. I broke my arm, I think."

"What about you?" Archie asked the other guard.

"I'm all right. We were a half a mile away and had several berms between us when it exploded. My ears are ringing, though."

"Mine, too," said his partner.

"Glad you're okay. Do you know what happened?"

"There was an intruder. We found some wagon tracks coming in from outside—not through any of the entrances. We were following them when it all blew up." The protective berm around the Reservation was one task still uncompleted. There were gaps here and there, along the furthest side from Suhl. The intruder had driven a wagon through one of those gaps.

The bunker was a smoking hole in the ground, and the grass on the sides of the berm was gone, blasted clean by the force of the explosion. Gone, too, was the dog-leg entrance, completely erased. Archie sniffed the air. He had popped enough primers to identify the odor of exploded DDNP. But . . . there was another smell, one he couldn't quite identify. "Do you smell that, Dieter?"

Dieter sniffed, sniffed again. "Black powder, I think. It's faint but . . . "

That was it. Archie walked around, examining the scene. There wasn't much left inside the berm. The berms directed most of the force of the blast upwards, just as Nicki Jo had planned. "Let's check outside," he said to Dieter.

They walked outside the berm in time to see Pat Johnson ride up with Gary Reardon. "Got an injured man inside," he told them.

"Check the ground, Dieter. That powder didn't come here by itself. Our powder mill and bunkers are on the other side of the reservation."

More mounted guards arrived with lanterns. Archie gave them instructions to check the ground around the nearby berms looking for anything suspicious. Any nearby tracks outside the bunker had been wiped clean by the blast. The search would have to spread out if they hoped to find anything.

✳ ✳ ✳

Archie and Gary looked at the splintered wagon, illuminated by the light of a dozen lanterns. "Damn fool," Gary muttered. The remains of the wagon, two horses, and the driver were only two hundred yards from the exploded bunker. Most of the force of the explosion had been directed upwards . . . but not all. The dog-leg entrance to the bunker had been blown out, allowing some of the explosive force to vent horizontally—directly toward the bunker and berm where the wagon driver had stopped to watch.

"You know him?" Archie asked. The body was mixed in with the wagon, in several pieces. The head was intact. Mostly.

"Yeah, Joseph Lang. I put him out of business. Zoche bribed him to break a contract with us. He's the reason why we built our own black powder mills."

"I don't know what he was thinking. He was too close. A bunker full of DDNP makes a much bigger explosion that a keg of black powder," Archie observed.

"Is that what he did?" Gary asked.

"I think so. There was a keg still on the wagon when the bunker blew. It blew, too. I think he rolled a keg of black powder against the bunker door, lit a fuse and took off."

"Why didn't he go further away?"

"He didn't know the explosion would be so big. It would have been a safe distance for a black powder explosion."

"Stupid."

"Yep," Archie agreed.

Georg Rohn walked up. He had been checking the scene as well. "How much DDNP did we lose?" Gary asked him.

"I'll have to check the records, but I think about seven hundred pounds. We have more stored in other bunkers," Rohn answered. "We had enough empty bunkers that I spread the DDNP storage as far from one another as I could."

"Will this affect our production lines?"

"No. We've more than enough for the primer line. This bunker was for the new blasting cap line."

Gary watched the guards carry off what the explosion left of Joseph Lang, what they could find of him. The remains of the two horses, and the wagon, would be removed later.

"Dieter and I will write up a report for Judge Fross and the Suhl Watch," Archie told them. "I'll send you an official copy, too, Gary. I'll label Lang's death as *Death by Misadventure*, as our former British compatriots would say."

"Death by Idiocy," Gary replied.

"Yeah, that, too."

Mike Watson

XV

September 1635, Suhl

"Well, Anse, it's not quite Labor Day, but it'll do," Archie said into Anse Hatfield's ear. Hatfield was wearing his *third hat*, as he liked to call his part-time job, overseeing the corporation's security force. He divided his time between working with Ursula Johnson, reviewing the books of U. S. Waffenfabrik, supervising the foremen of his trucking company, training drivers for the Suhl National Guard, and building Suhl, Incorporated security force with Dieter Issler. The noise from the crowd made conversation difficult, especially for old soldiers whose hearing wasn't all that good to begin with.

"I'd forgotten, Archie. This *is* Labor Day, isn't it?" Anse Hatfield swept his gaze across the crowd. "No parades, and no politicians speechifying, though." His wife, Leonore, was somewhere in the mass of people, likely with Marjorie Mitchell or Gaylynn Johnson. Leonore had arrived unexpectedly last autumn and married Anse Hatfield not long after.

Servitors hired for the event circulated with trays of drinks, pitchers of beer, and platters of finger food. The administrative building's lawn was littered with open tents and long tables and chairs positioned under the few trees remaining after the previous year's clearance. A wagon rolled up to one tent, and the carters unloaded several barrels of beer. Everyone appeared to be having a great time. Here and there, Anse's security guards were visible, wandering through the crowd, keeping the peace.

"Maybe not the *old* Labor Day, but we have the picnic, and Suhl, Incorporated, is picking up the tab. Have you reported all this to your boss?" Archie asked.

"Pat? Why should I? He's right over there." Pat Johnson was conversing with a man just ten feet away.

"No, your other boss, Francisco Nasi," Archie said.

Anse turned to look at Archie. "So . . . you know about that." He wasn't asking a question, he was confirming a poorly kept secret.

"I get copies of every message sent and received by the radio station, Anse. The Court administers the station, and guess who supervises the operators?"

"Does anyone else know?"

"No, why should they?"

"Then why do you . . . "

"You forget who I work for—Judge Fross and I keep him in the loop whenever I think it's appropriate. I may be on the Board of Suhl, Incorporated, but my primary loyalty is to the State of Thuringia-Franconia. I've asked Judge Fross, and he's found no conflict of interest. That said, speaking as one of the Board of Directors, Suhl, Incorporated doesn't mind Nasi knowing what we're doing. He's known officially since he helped us collar that spy. I suspect he is one of our original investors, and gets copies of our progress updates from the Abrabanels. I wouldn't be surprised if Nasi won't be one of our better marketeers."

On the far side of the crowd, under one tree, musicians started playing, and Archie could see couples dancing to the music. "As for our competitors," Archie continued, "like the Hart boys . . . Well, we prefer to keep our business to ourselves, keep it all a secret until we're ready to announce the news—like now."

He saw Pat Johnson, Gary Reardon, and Ruben Blumroder head for the reviewing stand. He knew what was coming next. Archie grinned. "I think the show is about to start," he said, changing the subject. "Shall we join them?"

* * *

The weather was warm, perfect for an outdoor gathering. Anse Hatfield left to join his wife and members of his National Guard unit. Archie estimated that most of the corporation employees were here. So were others from Suhl who had a connection with the company and the project, in one form or another, including those who had helped when the storm had ruined RJ City the previous year. Maps of the Reservation were on display at several locations showing the layout of the plant, the fabrication buildings, the brassworks, the powder mill, and the storage bunkers.

Displaying those maps had initially given Archie some concern, but on reflection, everyone in Suhl already knew the layout. As far as outsiders—spies—they could easily get a copy of the Reservation map. The Reservation contained forty-seven buildings and bunkers, in all. The black powder mill was Nicki Jo's last project. It was in a separate area of the Reservation, comprising five buildings and bunkers.

Everyone was dressed in their finest. Marjorie, and the other wives, had plotted and planned to help those who couldn't afford any expensive finery. Archie couldn't help but compare Marjorie with the other wives. She had a fashion mind of her own, as the down-timers discovered. She and Archie were dressed alike, more or less. Marjorie had altered one of his black suits that had come with them through the Ring of Fire. She had his suit jacket shortened to waist length, and the buttons replaced with silver ones. The alterations allowed him to wear his 'Church' regalia—black polished cowboy boots, black pants, and a silver and turquoise belt buckle he had bought on their last vacation in Arizona. Added to that was a white shirt, black bolo tie with silver and turquoise clasp, hand-tooled leather holster for one of his Colt .45 revolvers, and topped off with his freshly cleaned and blocked off-white Stetson.

Marjorie wore a short black Bolero jacket similar to Archie's, including matching silver buttons, with a long, ankle length black pleated skirt that left her silver-toed black boots exposed. Like Archie, she wore a white blouse. Hers was ruffled, with a silver and turquoise brooch at her throat. She also wore a tooled leather belt and holster around her waist, holding her Smith and Wesson Model 25 in her customary cross-draw position on her left hip.

Her pistol gleamed brightly. It had been polished and blued in Pat's gun shop as compensation for its use during the research and development of the primers. The Mitchells stood out from all the Seventeenth Century dress as if they were Hollywood celebrities at a premier showing of a movie.

The other up-timers present wore variations of their up-time suits, except for Pat Johnson. He joined the locals, dressed in stockings, knee pants, buckled shoes, frock coat, and ruffled shirt. All he needed to be mistaken for a down-timer was a sword. Instead of a sword, he wore his Colt revolver, freshly hot-blued, like Marjorie's Smith & Wesson revolver. Several pistols had been reblued after Pat had finally gotten around to building his hot-bluing tank. That was the reason Archie was wearing his revolvers. His matching Colt Commanders were in Pat's tank being reblued.

"If I may have your attention, please!" Gary Reardon called. The crowd was so large that he used a speaking trumpet to allow everyone to hear. He turned in a circle, repeating his call.

When the crowd quieted, he began, "Thank you all for coming." His voice sounded hollow through the megaphone. "Today is our celebration. The Project, as some of you have called it, is finished. I hope all of you have received your performance bonuses. You finished a month ahead of the plan and you came in ahead of schedule despite the storm that hit RJ City last year. That storm put us behind a month. But you—every one of you—buckled down, and didn't let that stop you. You met and exceeded your goals at every stage—even when coming from behind! Not only did you make up the time after the storm, but when we had to build our own powder mill, you chipped in and built it in two months! You all are to be congratulated," he said amid the applause.

"I would like to announce the completion of two last tasks before you rejoin the celebration. First, I've sent out a press release to Grantville,

Bamberg, Magdeburg, to Nicki Jo and Katy, and a few other places. The press release announces the creation of a new, wholly-owned subsidiary of Suhl, Incorporated—SMC! The Suhl Metallic Cartridge company!"

He waited again for the applause and shouting to subside before he continued. "Some members who worked on this project deserve some special recognition . . . Marjorie Mitchell, would you come up here, please?"

Marjorie appeared surprised at the request. She and the other wives had been busy preparing for the celebration. It had grown to be a much larger festival than they had planned, but nothing in the party agenda had included her.

When she walked up and joined Gary, he motioned her to stand at his side. "Marjorie has been one of the most important people on the project. Not because she is some technical expert, not because she provided some special knowledge, although we're very happy she lent us her pistol for some of the testing. No, Marjorie is special because she was there for all of us right when needed. When the storm hit RJ City, Marjorie organized the emergency kitchens to keep everyone fed until the mess halls were repaired. When Katy Boyle went back to Essen, Marjorie stepped in to fill her spot. Nicki Jo told me how much that helped before she left to join Katy. When Jurgen Holtz fell and broke his leg during the construction of the chemical fabrication building, Marjorie, and some of the other wives, helped the family care for their kids, and Jurgen, too, so Jurgen's wife could take a job in our headquarters. When someone needed help, Marjorie was there."

"For that, and many other reasons, we have something for her. Ruben—do you have it?"

"Right here," Ruben answered from the front of the crowd. He walked up to the steps of the reviewing stand, carrying a large case of polished wood under his arm, and joined the two on the stage. From the way he carried the case, it obviously had some weight. One of the party workers set up a portable table next to Gary, and Ruben laid the case on it.

Gary continued, "I know all of you can't see this. It will be on display here for the rest of the evening. Ruben, will you make the presentation?"

Ruben stepped forward, glanced at the crowd, nodded to Gary Reardon, and turned to Marjorie. "Gladly. Gary. Marjorie, I, and some others—Hockenjoss and Klott, and Georg Bohn over there, had parallel plans running with the project. It was all well and good to produce .45 Colt cartridges, but there were few existing pistols chambered in that caliber. To sell ammunition, there needed to be a market, something that would shoot the ammunition. Suhl, Incorporated, is announcing a new revolver. One we'll place on the market, as of today. It is a copy, as close as we can make it, of Marjorie's Smith and Wesson Model 25. The SI Model 1 will be chambered in .45 Colt. It will be available in various barrel lengths, and is a six-round revolver with swing-out cylinder. We're including a cleaning kit, fifty rounds of .45 Colt SMC ammunition, and four speed-loaders with every pistol."

Ruben cleared his throat while the crowd clapped and cheered. He held up his hand to quiet them. "In this case, is a special SI Model 1 revolver. It is one of five," he explained. "The first to be produced by Suhl, Incorporated. We gave these five some . . . special treatment. My people engraved each one. We've engraved the model and serial number on the barrel and inlaid with gold script. This one says, "*SI Model 1, .45Colt, Number Five*. Georg Bohn built the case and carved the oak grips. Another contributor provided the speed loaders. The case contains the engraved pistol, cleaning kit with rod, and one hundred rounds of SMC ammunition. That's why the case is so heavy."

The crowd laughed. Many of them knew about the special pistols. They just didn't know who would get them.

"Serial number One goes to Emperor Gustav Adolf, number Two goes to Ed Piazza, number Three to Mike Stearns, number Four . . . well, I can't disclose that yet. I think you all will understand when it's finally announced."

Archie stood watching the presentation. He had been told earlier that afternoon about Marjorie's pistol. It wouldn't have been possible if Osker Geyer hadn't been able to improve his steel to be near up-time quality. He was extremely proud of his revamped company, Geyer Steel. He had borrowed several of Archie's manuals and had used them, along with the information he'd acquired from the Grantville library. With that, he'd been able to produce a close copy of 4140 and 4150 ordnance steel. Geyer hadn't been able to get enough chrome and molybdenum to match the amount called for in the up-time formula. But, he had experimented, and found an intermediate compromise, one that would do until he found a better source for the two ores. Using Geyer's steel, the new SI revolver weighed almost the same as Marjorie's original revolver. Geyer had other plans, too. He had told Archie that he was opening a steel and copper wire drawing plant in a few of months. Osker said he already had orders for copper wire of several gauges, and for steel cable.

Pat Johnson appeared from within the crowd, walked up to Archie, and joined him, watching the rest of the presentation. When the presentation was over, Pat turned to Archie, "I have something for you, Archie." He placed a wooden box in Archie's hand, a smoothly finished and varnished box with polished brass hinges. Overall, it was slightly larger than his hand.

"Open it, Archie."

Archie unlatched the lid's catch and opened the box.. Inside were rows of shiny, new .45 Colt cartridges . . . ten rows of ten cartridges. Pat had the inside of the lid engraved with a logo of the letters *SMC* imposed over crossed SI Model 1 revolvers, and the company name, *Suhl Metallic Cartridge Company*. Under that was a line that said, *Wholly owned subsidiary of Suhl, Inc.*

"Take a closer look," Pat instructed.

Following Pat's orders, Archie pulled one of the fat cartridges from its felt-lined hole. He had to squint to read the headstamp. It read, *SMC, .45* and *Suhl 35*. At first, Archie wasn't sure what was so special about the cartridges—then it hit him. He looked at the bullet. It was copper-clad! And its nose had a hole in it! "*JHPs!*" he exclaimed,

"Yep, Jacketed Hollow Point," Pat said, when Archie discovered the surprise. "When I was figuring out how to draw brass, I came across a page in one of your manuals about swaging lead to make jacketed bullets. After that it was simply a matter of drawing the copper over the lead and molding the hollow-point and cannelure."

"Thank you, Pat. I appreciate this."

"These are black powder, but I hope for something better in the coming year."

"Better?"

"You heard why Nicki Jo sent Katy back to Essen?'

"Yeah, something about a contract."

"To safely make guncotton . . . nitrocellulose."

"Oh!"

"Yeah, just a short step away from smokeless powder. I think *Poudre B* was made from nitrocellulose. I gave her a cup of each of your smokeless powders that you used to reload .45ACP and .30-06 cartridges. I hope you don't mind?"

"No! If she can make smokeless powder, I don't have to worry about running out of .45ACP ammo."

"I thought that, too. That's why I had her sign an option to make smokeless for us, when she thinks it's feasible."

A burst of clapping erupted from the crowd.

"You haven't been keeping this secret, have you?" Archie asked with a wave of his hand toward the crowd.

"Well, secret from some, not from some others. We have a head start with SMC, and I want us to stay that way, ahead of all the others."

"You have orders in hand, don't you?"

Pat grinned. "I received one today from Abel Abrabanel for ten thousand rounds."

"Of .45 Colt?" That order surprised Archie. *What would the Abrabanels want with ten thousand rounds of pistol ammunition?*

"No, .45-70," Pat explained. "U. S. Waffenfabrik is announcing, today, in partnership with Suhl, Incorporated, of course, our new rifle, the Model 1635, a takeoff of Remington's rolling block rifle in .45-70 caliber. We have two versions, a sporter-hunter version, and the M1635 military version. The military version comes complete with a ladder-sight marked out to 500 yards, a bronze cleaning rod, a cleaning kit in the butt, and a bayonet with scabbard. Abel ordered ten M1635 military version rifles."

Archie chuckled, "Beating all the competition," he repeated. "I always knew you were a sneaky one, Pat."

"But the best part is the other orders I've received."

"Oh?"

"From the USE Army and another group. All told, they will take about all of our current stockpile and up to eighty-five percent of our production for quite some time."

"Eighty-five percent of what?"

"Just about everything. I don't know if we got an order for SL Model 1 revolvers, but I did for the M1635."

"I thought you said you didn't want to sell to the army?"

"No, what I said is that I didn't want to sell *solely* to the army. We aren't."

"God, Pat, if I didn't know you better, I'd say you were a Jesuit. You parse your words like them."

Pat Johnson laughed, waved at Archie, and walked back into the celebrating crowd.

Mike Watson

THE FIFTH INTERVIEW

Suhl, June 12, 1636

Maria D'Angelo sat quietly in the Mitchell-Issler family room, letting the men talk. The story about the formation of Suhl, Incorporated and SMC, Suhl Metallic Cartridge, as Archie had taken pains to explain, had taken several interview sessions. He had introduced her and her brother to other up-timers, Gary and Gaylynn Reardon, Pat and Ursula Johnson, Anse and Leonore, née von Wilke, Hatfield. Ursula and Leonore were down-timers as were other invited Suhl residents, Osker Geyer and Ruben Blumroder. This gathering was again in the Mitchell-Issler household.

The story about the new corporation revealed how well up-timers and down-timers worked together toward a common goal. One of the more unfounded complaints—usually from competitors—was that up-timers were seizing control of the new products and technology to the exclusion of down-timers. The creation of Suhl, Incorporated, proved that accusation untrue.

Archie and Dieter had taken pains to minimize their roles in the corporation's creation. Dieter's involvement was less visible. However, when he and Anse Hatfield formed the corporation's security team, their efforts had as much impact on the overall success as that of Archie on the board of directors.

With the first interviews, the stories from Archie Mitchell, Harley Thomas, and Dieter Issler exposed a new culture growing inside the Marshal's Service and the Mounted Constabulary; a culture of integrity, honor, dignity, and reliability—concepts that did not always sit well with some down-timers. Corruption, bribery, and treachery were absent in the court system, and in the subordinate services of the marshals and constabulary. The developing culture was evolving to maintain that integrity and to block outside attempts to counter it.

Bloem's original concept, how down-time was affecting up-timers, changed. Even away from Grantville, the center of up-timer activities, their influence spread far beyond that city. These few people, up-timers, all alone—and mostly unintentionally—were changing the course of history, the New Time Line some called it.

* * *

Archie glanced at Maria in time to see her eyes grow large and round. She had been taking notes, *or perhaps a letter to Karl Mohn?* Turning around, he saw their two cats, Elsa and Kari, enter from the kitchen.

Archie crossed the room and sat next to her. "Ah, you've seen Elsa and her daughter, Kari." Archie said. He made a clicking sound, and Elsa walked over and butted his thigh. Archie reached out to scratch her ears, eliciting a loud purr. "Elsa appeared last fall during the plague scare. She helped us identify a potential health risk with rats in the city. Kari is six months—seven months old, I think. She's Marta's cat."

"W—what kind of cat are they?" Maria asked. She appeared fearful, given the size of Elsa and Kari.

"We don't know exactly," Archie answered. "Elsa was the Swedes' cat when they had a garrison here. They left behind her when they moved out. We believe she's a hybrid between a Swedish *Skogkatt* and a lynx. That's just a guess. Elsa and Kari have long tails. Elsa's other kits, from the same litter as Kari, don't. They have short stub tails like a lynx. I haven't weighed Elsa lately, but I think she's up to thirty pounds. Kari weighs almost twenty pounds and will grow to match her mother, I expect. Elsa had four kits when she joined us. The other two are with friends here in Suhl."

"B-b-but. They're big! Aren't they dangerous?"

"Not to us. I wouldn't expect a burglar to escape unscathed, however, if one attempted to break into our house. The Suhl City Council has issued a proclamation protecting Elsa and her kits. All cats by Suhl City Council orders."

"Why?" Maria asked.

Archie glanced at Elsa, then to Marjorie and Greta. "Well, I came home one day . . . "

Mike Watson

PART V: PURR

Suhl, August–September 1635

Marshal Archie Mitchell was hot, sweaty, and tired. Today had been a court day. He had to testify in a case before Judge Fross, the Chief Magistrate of the First District Court of the State of Thuringia and Franconia. An August heat-wave had turned the courthouse into an oven. Across Suhl County, a front brought winds, but did little to lessen the heat. Walking home, southeasterly winds blew grit into his eyes, and, not the least, blown his best Stetson off his head into the dirt. Twice.

During his last uphill trek home, he'd fought a headwind. The incline made his leg and hip hurt, and he'd been forced to lean on his cane to lessen the ache. He was looking forward to sitting in his recliner with his feet up; relaxing with something cool to drink . . . maybe some of that new wine Pastor Weber had given him.

Archie arrived at the house he and his wife, Marjorie, co-owned with the Dieter and Greta Isslers. Dieter was a close friend and his senior deputy. His wife, Greta, operated the bakery in the front of the two-family house, assisted by Marjorie Mitchell.

He trudged up the steps and across the covered porch to the bakery door. The shaded porch was welcome and its cool shadow was more welcome. Removing his Stetson, he walked inside and had only taken a few steps inside when he halted—something caught his attention from the corner of his eye.

Sprawled out on the floor, along the wall of the bakery, out of the way of foot traffic, was the biggest, hairiest cat he had ever seen. Archie estimated it was, from its nose to the black tip of its long hairy tail, over a three, maybe four feet long, with tannish-gray fur and black tuffs rising from its ears. It also had faint, dark tiger-like stripes running along its body and tail.

The cat returned Archie's look and dismissed him by raising a front paw, licking the back of it, and swiping it across its ear and jaw.

Marjorie Mitchell entered the bakery from the kitchen in the rear. "I thought I heard you come in." She noticed Archie was looking at the cat on the floor. "I see you've met Elsa."

"Elsa?"

"Her," Marjorie said, pointing to the cat. "She's been around here the last few weeks. Today, she left seven rat-tails on our back step. Greta thinks she's been living in our stable."

"Why is she here?"

"Greta suggested we bring her inside. She reminded me that rats and mice carry fleas and fleas carry . . . "

"Plague . . . yeah." Outbreaks of plague had been breaking out all along the Rhine and around Lorraine in France since the previous spring. The SoTF Public Health Service had reported no cases near Suhl, nor in Thuringia. *So far.*

"Yes," Marjorie affirmed.

While the two had been talking, Elsa rose, stretched, and walked over to Archie. Seeing that she didn't have his attention, she head-butted his leg just above his knee. On her feet, Archie could see her long legs. She stood nearly two feet tall. Her long tail and fur aside, she reminded Archie of a lynx. A long-tailed lynx, true, but she still appeared very much like a lynx.

"She likes you, Archie."

Elsa head-butted Archie again and then stropped her body around his legs. *That's an enormous cat. She must weigh twenty-five or thirty pounds. Maybe more!*

With one more circuit around Archie, Elsa ambled out the inner door and down the hallway toward the kitchen.

"What kind of cat is she? I've never seen one that big," Archie asked.

"*Frau Juncker* next door said she is a *Skogkatt*, a Swedish or Norwegian cat. She said Elsa probably came with the Swedes and was left behind when the garrison left. She's been around for some time, according to *Frau Juncker*."

"Umm," Archie replied as he watched the cat disappear into the kitchen. "She seems to be too friendly to be wild. I'd bet someone has raised her from a kitten."

Marjorie nodded in agreement. "She's big. What's the name of that big long-haired cat from up-time?"

"Maine Coon?"

"Yeah, that's it. They're big cats."

"Elsa's not a Main Coon. Her legs are too long . . . and Maine Coons aren't that big."

"She could be a hybrid." Marjorie said after a moment's reflection.

"Could be. What do you want to do with her? I doubt she's cat-box trained—do they do that here?" Archie was uncomfortable with inside pets.

"I don't know. Greta suggested we let her roam inside during the day and then put her out at night. Folks up-time did that."

"Yeah." Archie thought it over and agreed. He still didn't like having a housecat—a giant housecat at that. However, he knew he couldn't win an argument with both Marjorie and Greta.

✳ ✳ ✳

This is strange, Archie thought. *Everyone is carrying on as usual, but everyone is aware of the cat wandering under the table, waiting like a dog, for any piece of food that was dropped. Little five-year-old Marta Issler is paying more attention to Elsa than she is to her food.*

Greta gave Elsa half a sausage. The cat looked at the sausage as if thinking, *What strange thing is this?* She sniffed it and in the next moment, the sausage was gone. Whatever else she is, Archie observed, Elsa is not a slow eater.

After a few licks of her paw, she walked over to Archie's chair and slumped to the floor beside him.

"I think you have a friend, Archie," Marjorie said, with a hint of laughter in her voice.

"Umm," Archie replied. He and Marjorie had, once upon a time, pets, up-time dogs—a beagle or two and a couple of white, black, and tan foxhounds. But they'd never had an inside pet. *Certainly not a big hairy cat.* They had some itinerant mousers that had stayed in their barn along with the Mitchell horses. *If she's a pet,* Archie mused, *she'd better pay her way, or she'll be an outside cat.*

Between Meiningen and Suhl, August, 1635

Mounted Constabulary Corporal Adam Haan waited at the rendezvous point with Constable Peter Engel. Haan's six-man patrol had split into three pairs earlier in the week; each pair continued with their assigned patrol routes. This week, Corporal Haan's team was patrolling out of Meiningen and points west to the border of Buchenland. He had chosen the shortest route for himself and his partner; wanting to return to the rendezvous site early in case any of the other pairs needed help.

They made an overnight camp west of Meiningen, in the ruins of a small abandoned farming hamlet. The site had a good well with clean water and a stone storehouse that, while missing its roof, provided protection against the wind.

By noon of the following day, the other constable pairs arrived, and the assembled patrol rode toward Meiningen. Later in the day, they passed through Meiningen and continued on the road east toward Suhl.

They were riding through a forested valley when Constable Pflueger, riding two hundred yards ahead as scout, returned at a gallop. "Something strange up ahead, Corporal," he said excitedly. "There're wagons camped off the side of the road. There's no movement—and I saw a body."

Corporal Haan removed his wide-brimmed hat and wiped his forehead with his sleeve. He had been looking forward to getting to barracks at Suhl, to a bath, and a friendly evening at his favorite inn. Removing a cloth from his pocket, he wiped his hat's interior headband and placed it back on his head. The act gave the constable-scout time to calm down.

"Tell me exactly what you saw, Pflueger. How do you know it was a body? What else did you see? Make a clear logical report, Constable."

Pflueger straightened in his saddle and repeated his report. After several questions, Haan decided his report was accurate. He doubted the site was an ambush, but it never hurt to take precautions.

The patrol neared the campsite. Haan halted the patrol, ordered the troopers to encircle the site at a distance. He reminded them to check for any tracks arriving or leaving the campsite.

The camp appeared to be normal . . . if you set aside the lack of movement and no visible damage or evidence of pillaging. No fires burned, nor was there any lingering smell of wood smoke. Whatever had happened, Haan concluded, occurred at least a day before. The corporal, remembering the news of pestilence in the Rhineland, suspected a cause. "Constable Heiger!" he called.

"Here, Corporal!" Heiger answered, riding up from Haan's right.

When he arrived, Haan asked him quietly, lest the others hear. "You had the plague and survived, didn't you? And know what it looks like?"

"*Ja*," was the soft reply.

"The up-timers say that surviving gives you some immunity. Check out the camp. Touch nothing, just look and return."

✳ ✳ ✳

Heiger acknowledged the order and walked his horse to the camp. It appeared normal, with four wagons in a circle. A dozen hobbled horses grazed along the edge of the meadow. The constable stopped. There were more bodies inside the circle of wagons. He walked his horse around one wagon and past another. The bodies all displayed the telltale signs of plague. One victim showed small signs of life, but shuddered as the constable approached and was still. The other bodies hadn't been dead long enough to smell and frighten the horses.

A dozen bodies, he counted; eight men, two women and two adolescent boys. He remembered an old refrain about the plague, *Breakfast with your family, dine with your ancestors.* He knew the plague could arrive, quickly kill, and depart.

The constable recognized death by plague. He had seen it before.

✳ ✳ ✳

Haan watched Heiger while mentally reviewed his limited orders concerning plague victims. The common remedy to prevent further spread of the disease was burning. He'd heard reports of homes, entire villages, being burned to stop the plague. Sometimes it worked, sometimes it didn't. He didn't have any specific instructions, but he knew what had to be done. He glanced at the horses on the far side of the campsite. *Them, too,* he decided. The up-timers said fleas spread the plague. Horses can be flea-ridden. The corporal didn't like killing, man nor animal, but. . . needs must.

Heiger returned and reported, confirming Haan's suspicions. The entire group had died of the plague. Hann wondered if they were coming from Suhl. *Please, no!* he prayed. Or from Meiningen.

Haan called the other troopers to him. "Heiger says they died of the plague. He's a survivor and knows the signs." The corporal pointed to one constable. "You. Ride back to Meiningen and tell the Wachtmeister and Bürgermeister what we found. We don't know if they passed through Meiningen or not. Tell them to prepare as best they can."

He pointed to another constable and said, "You ride to Suhl and tell them the same."

The two constables rode off as instructed. Haan turned to the rest of his troopers. "Heiger will put the bodies inside the wagons and then move them together. I want the rest of you to gather all the dry wood you can find, cut down small trees, too. We need to build a big fire." He looked at the grazing horses and reconsidered. "Make that two big fires."

"You will burn them?" one trooper asked. Burial, not cremation, was the current practice. Many thought cremation to be repugnant; to burn people like a pile of trash and garbage.

"Yes. I don't like it," Haan said, "but I don't want to let the plague to spread from here. Burning everything will help. I just hope no one else has been here before us—and I don't want you to get the plague, either, understand?"

The trooper gulped and the rest nodded their heads in agreement; everyone had had someone, some family member die from the plague. "Up-timers say that fleas carry the disease. If these people have infected fleas, so will the horses," he reminded the troopers.

Haan wondered if these people were from the Rhineland, refugees fleeing the plague spreading in that region. This group may have evaded the quarantine.

When all was ready, Heiger used his revolver to kill the horses. The troopers used their horses to pull the dead ones together and covered them with brush to create another bier. Before lighting the fires, Haan recited a passage from the Lutheran bible, ending the service with, "May God keep you." The constables lit the biers, performing their last duty to the dead.

The troopers continued to keep the fires burning for two more days until the fire reduced everything to ashes. On the last day, the constable Haan had dispatched to Meiningen returned.

"I told them, Corporal. They checked the inns and chandlers. No one remembers seeing them. The Meiningen council promised to take all necessary action," the trooper reported.

When the last embers of the biers died, Corporal Haan gathered his troopers and continued their ride to Suhl.

Suhl, Mid-August 1635

Archie and Chief Bailiff Karl Wagner decided, no court being held today, to declare a Range Day. They were not needed at Court, it would not be open. Judge Fross was holding a conference for local and county magistrates. With the court out of session, Archie and Karl Wagner arranged for his deputies and Wagner's bailiffs to go to the range for pistol training.

Judge Fross, from his first day as the SoTF District Judge, insisted that everyone who worked for his Court to be competent with a firearm, and armed. Suhl's recent history had not been a peaceful one.

In the case of the bailiffs and deputies, the issue weapon, an H&K cap and ball pistol, was being replaced with the new SL-1 .45 caliber cartridge revolver. The change in the manual-of-arms was small but decisive. The deputies and bailiffs needed practice for the transition from the older, single-action cap and ball revolver to the new double-action cartridge revolver.

Archie and Dieter rose early and walked to the stable in the rear of their house. They had been working on it since spring, replacing the stable's front door, rebuilding the stalls, fixing the roof and closing gaps that would allow drafts through the walls. Winter was coming in a few months and it was important to protect the six horses, four owned by the Mitchells and two by the Isslers, from the winter elements.

The previous winter, Archie had the six horses stabled with the Constabulary horses, a benefit of being employees of the District Court. Archie was uncomfortable using his position for special treatment. The building behind their house was closer to home than the stable at the constabulary barracks.

When Archie opened the stable door, Elsa was inside, waiting, peering down at them from the hayloft above the stalls. On the hard-packed dirt floor, just inside the door, were the bodies of four rats and a mangled, brown-furred predator.

"Elsa has been busy," Dieter mentioned when he noticed the dead rats. "That's an *Iltis*," he said, pointing to the brown corpse. "It's like a weasel or Marten. Stinks," he proclaimed.

"Yeah," Archie agreed. "With the ones she killed yesterday plus these," he said nodding toward the dead rats, "that just seems to be a lot of rats."

Dieter rubbed his chin, the rasp of his beard audible to Archie. Dieter only shaved every other day and on Sunday. "Greta said Elsa has been bringing rat-tails to the rear door every day. But she didn't say how many." He paused. "From what she said, and those we see here, that seems a lot . . . I've not seen much evidence of rats around here, not that I've thought to look. Regardless, she's proved herself to be an efficient mouser."

Archie nodded. "She didn't eat these—wouldn't the *Iltis*, anyway. We must be feeding her too much." They saddled their horses and led them outside while Elsa watched from the loft above.

"Archie," Dieter said after mounting his horse, "I just remembered, there is a trash dump not far from here."

"Oh? That's interesting. I wonder if that's the source of our rats?"

✳ ✳ ✳

Marjorie watched, through the kitchen window, the two men had ride off. Moments later she saw Elsa drop from the loft and disappear from view. A minute later, the closed door moved. *Elsa is pushing against it.* A gap, large enough for the cat to slip through, appeared in the doorway. Elsa trotted to the rear step of the Mitchell-Issler house, sat on the rear step, and called *Eerrooow!*

Marjorie opened the door and looked down at the cat. "Hello, Elsa. Hungry, are you?" Elsa slipped past the woman and came inside.

The woman looked at the step and around it. *No rat-tails today.*

Inside the house, Greta Issler was preparing meat turnovers she called *Fleischkühle* to be sold in the city market later in the day. Elsa walked up and stropped herself around Greta's legs, causing her to look down at the cat.

Meerooow.

Greta laughed. "That sausage last night didn't last long, eh, Elsa? Here, try this." Greta ladled shredded pork into a cracked bowl and put it on the floor next to a bowl of water.

While Greta was mixing the filling for the meat turnovers, Marjorie was using a rolling pin to roll out dough for the turnover crusts. "I think I'll need more eggs for the next batch of dough."

Greta nodded. "I gave *Frau Juncker* two loaves of bread yesterday. Would you go see if she has any extra eggs? She owes us and I really don't want to go to the market right now."

Frau Juncker, their next-door neighbor, was a widow with three children, one of whom, her youngest son, was still living at home while attending Latin school. The other two were grown and married with their own households. The widow raised chickens in a large coop behind her house to supplement her income as a seamstress. She sold most of her eggs to Greta and a nearby inn, but also kept a few behind for herself and her son.

Marjorie found her at her chicken coop. "Come. Look at this," *Frau Juncker* called, pointing to the ground near the chicken fence as Marjorie walked up.

The ground showed signs of a battle with tufts of tannish-gray hair and bits of bloody brown fur scattered around. Marjorie picked up a tuft of hair, examined it and said, "This looks like Elsa's fur." She looked at the other brown, bloody fur. "I don't know what that is, though. Stinks." The foul odor emanating from the brown fur reminded her of a skunk. Skunks had been common in West Virginia, but not here. *Are there skunks here?* She didn't know, just that she'd not seen nor heard of any since the Ring of Fire.

"From the fur and blood on the ground, it looks like there's been a fight. I've checked my chickens and they are all safe." She looked at the bloody fur. "I wonder if Elsa stopped something from getting at my chickens. I've not lost any since she appeared."

"She was waiting at our door this morning. I'll check her and see if it has hurt her when I get back," Marjorie replied. "Before I forget, do you have any extra eggs? Greta and I are making *Fleischküßle* for the market and we've run short of eggs for the dough.

"*Natürlich.* I know Greta always underestimates her needs . . . do you think she may have a few *Fleischküßle* left over?"

Marjorie chuckled. "I'm sure she will."

"*Gut!* Let's get those eggs for you."

* * *

The bakery was hot. The oven in the kitchen added to the heat from the summer sun outside. In fact, the entire house was hot. On days like this, the heat wore Marjorie down and she was feeling her sixty years. With the day's baking done, she retreated to the Mitchell apartment and opened the windows to allow a cooling breeze flow through the room. She relaxed in Archie's recliner while Greta and Marta went to the *Marktplatz*.

Just as she was about to doze off, she heard a noise and opened her eyes to see Elsa sitting on the windowsill. The cat jumped down to the floor with a thump. Her wraith-like appearance startled Marjorie. The windowsill was a good six feet above the ground and she hadn't thought Elsa could jump that high—but she had—and the initial noise she heard must have been the sound of Elsa's claws on the side of the house.

"Come over here, Elsa. Let me look at you," Marjorie said, sitting up in the recliner. She hadn't expected a response and Elsa didn't move until Marjorie patted her lap. The cat walked over to the recliner and head-butted her arm and rested her head in Marjorie's lap.

"Have you been fighting, Elsa?" She ran her fingers through the cat's fur, dislodging several clumps of fur. *You need a combing. I'll borrow one of Archie's currycombs.* During her examination, she found places where Elsa's fur was thinner. "Maybe protecting *Frau Juncker*'s chickens?" Her fur gave off a foul odor reminiscent of the bloody fur *Frau Juncker* found.

263

Elsa purred and moved closer, rubbing against the recliner and Marjorie's leg. Marjorie, with a grunt, picked her up to stroke and examine the cat. Elsa must have been someone's pet—a well-cared for pet. She was too friendly and comfortable with people to be feral. It didn't take long for Marjorie to discover that Elsa was a mother—a mother still nursing kittens, she noted.

Elsa had enough of Marjorie's ministrations. The cat got off her lap and walked through the doorway to disappear down the hallway toward the kitchen.

I wonder where she's hidden the kittens. She reclined and grew drowsier. As she slipped off into sleep, she thought, *I'll mention them to Archie tonight.*

* * *

Archie's deputies and Karl Wagner's bailiffs finished qualifying with their new revolvers. Archie was pleased to note that Dieter, not known for his rifle marksmanship, was the top scorer of his three deputies. His score embarrassed Karl Wagner. Archie reminded himself, Karl was not, nor had ever been, an armsman. He'd never owned a weapon for his own protection beyond a small belt-knife. That had changed with the coming of Judge Fross. Archie assured him his score was high enough to satisfy him and if Archie was satisfied, so would be Judge Fross.

Each new revolver was issued with a flap belt holster and two .45 caliber speedloaders carried in molded leather pouches carried on a belt. The speedloader held six cartridges grouped in a circle to allow them to be loaded into the pistol's cylinder all at the same time. The last practice session was reloading their revolvers using speedloaders.

"Captain Gruber's troopers won't get the new pistols for a few more months. When that time comes, he and I will organize pistol matches between you and his constables. I want you to beat their time reloading. *Herr Wagner* and I will watch the match between you and the constables very closely," Archie announced.

Everyone laughed. They knew his implied threat was baseless. If Archie Mitchell hadn't been a member of the Board of Suhl Incorporated, they'd get the new revolvers sometime around the turn of the next century. Fortunately, for the bailiffs, deputies, and troopers, Archie and Judge Fross convinced Bamberg, the SoTF capitol, to allow Suhl District to evaluate the new pistols for the rest of the court system.

With that last word, Archie said, "Let's go home. It's been a long day." The bailiffs headed for the wagon Wagner had borrowed from the Constabulary to transport them. Archie and his deputies walked to their hobbled horses grazing in the shade of nearby trees.

The deputies mounted and rode back to Suhl. Dieter leaned over to Archie. "Let's ride outside the wall and look at the trash dump I mentioned this morning. I'm curious to see if there are more rats there than usual."

✳ ✳ ✳

Archie wasn't sure what he had expected. He'd not thought much about trash. The city of Suhl picked up their trash and night soil each day. Just as when they were still up-time, he'd never thought about where it went. The city took human and animal waste to the city's nitrate beds, where the city extracted saltpeter. However, trash went to rocky ravines outside Suhl. The Mitchell-Issler household was less than a quarter of a mile away from one, albeit on the other side of the city wall. Archie wondered if this dump was the source for all the rats Elsa had been killing.

They smelled the dump before they reached it. The strong, sweet, sour smell of decay made worse by the summer sun was not enough to deter scavengers who walked through the dump.

Archie and Dieter sat atop their horses, watching the scavengers . . . and listening to rats scurrying in the trash whenever a scavenger came close. "I'm not sure what I expected," Archie admitted to Dieter. "I can hear the rats, but are there more here than usual? What is usual?"

"I'm not sure what it is for Suhl," Dieter replied. "I've seen more rats elsewhere. Magdeburg had a real problem before Tilly arrived, and I've heard that conditions are worse in the Rhineland, France, and England . . . but that's just hearsay," he admitted.

Archie nodded. "Let's talk to Wachtmeister Frey tomorrow. Maybe we need to have a killing to thin out the rats. I'd think it'd be a health-measure."

"Frey's a Suhl native. He should know if there're more rats in the dumps than usual."

"Good. Put it on our agenda for tomorrow."

They were about to ride off when one scavenger began to beat the trash around his feet. He bent over, picked up a dead rat, and threw it over his shoulder.

"Yeah," Archie repeated, after watching the scavenger kill a rat, "I think we need a rat killing."

* * *

When they got home that afternoon, the sun was still visible above the city wall. Archie and Dieter unsaddled their horses and spent a half-hour giving them a curry and rubdown. Archie was gratified to see that Johan, *Frau Juncker*'s son, had already cleaned out the stalls and replaced the muck with fresh straw. They had hired the boy to help with the horses. Every day, he mucked out the stalls, replaced the soiled straw, added fresh hay in the feed trough for each horse, and prepared their daily allotment of grain.

Johan had left a note saying the hay and grain stores were low. Archie checked the grain bin, noted the level of remaining grain, and nodded. *Time to get more.* As he closed the lid, he noticed that something had been gnawing at one corner of the bin. *Rats.*

He straightened, put his hands against his back, and stretched. Dieter was already walking toward the house. Archie was about to follow him when he paused—he heard something, something beyond the still present ringing in his ears from pistol practice.

I wonder . . . he thought he knew what the sound was and climbed the ladder leading to the hayloft. His suspicions were confirmed. Elsa was lying on her side while four mewing kittens nursed. The cat raised her head to stare at Archie as if deciding he whether he was worth more attention. Judging him harmless, she laid her head back down.

Three of the kittens looked like smaller versions of Elsa. The fourth was different, more tannish than gray, and spotted. *A little lynx, with a long tail. I wonder if Papa was a Lynx.* Hybrids had happened, he knew.

✳ ✳ ✳

Dieter had beaten him to the tub, Archie discovered when he entered the house. Instead of turning left to the Mitchell apartment, he turned right toward the kitchen to find Marjorie stirring an iron pot on the stove.

"What's for supper, Marj?"

She turned her head to look at him, smiled, and said, "Your favorite. Goulash. I made noodles today."

Archie nodded his appreciation. "Guess what I just found."

"What?" Marjorie said, returning her attention to the pot of goulash.

"Kittens. Four of them in the hayloft. I heard mewing and found Elsa nursing them. Three look just like her. The fourth looks more like a little, long-tailed lynx."

Marjorie looked over her shoulder. "I was going to mention that Elsa had kittens somewhere. I was over at *Frau Juncker*'s this morning, and she thought Elsa had killed something that was trying to get at her chickens."

"Dieter and I found four dead rats in the stable, and something he called an *Iltis*." He remembered what he was going to tell Marjorie. "I think Elsa may be part Lynx."

"Are there lynx around here?"

"Yep. I've seen some. They're a little smaller than the ones back home, but the coloring is about the same."

"Well," Marjorie said, considering the information, "She could be part lynx, I suppose."

"I had that thought, too . . . I suppose a lynx could crossbreed with a cat, or whatever a *Skogkatt* is."

"What should we do," Marjorie asked, "about the kittens?"

"Why should we do anything?"

"Well . . . "

"They aren't our kittens, nor is Elsa our cat."

Marjorie put her wooden spoon down next to the iron pot and turned to Archie with her fists on her hips. "Archie. We've fed her. She's been in and around the house for two weeks. She has her kittens in our barn . . ."

"Stable. It's too small for a barn," he countered.

"Okay, stable, then. Sometimes, Archie, you can be a real pain in the ass," Marjorie said. "It appears she's adopted us. She's our cat. She is the Mitchell and Issler cat. Get used to it."

"Okay, okay, don't get riled."

"*Humph!* Marta likes her, too, and she likes Marta. Don't forget that."

Archie sighed. He knew when he was in a losing argument. He rose and started for the hallway to the bathroom to see if Dieter was finished when his deputy entered the kitchen with fresh clothes and wet hair. "Your turn for the tub," Dieter announced.

"I think we have plenty of warm water left," Dieter added, sitting in the same chair that Archie had just vacated. "You can run a fresh tub."

"Thanks. I just might." Archie said, heading for the bath and loosening his gunbelt as he walked. He hung the gunbelt, holster, and pistol from a peg in easy reach while he bathed, a recent habit. The scene of John Wayne in the tub in the movie *Big Jake* flashed through his mind. He'd not needed a weapon while bathing. Yet. But you never knew when you might need one.

* * *

Marjorie was glad they had hauled her parent's old coal stove to Suhl from Grantville. She didn't like cooking over an open fire or the bakery oven. Her stove easily fit into the cavity that was the building's original fireplace. The iron stove burned wood just as easily as it had coal. It also heated the kitchen very well last winter, better than the bakery's big in-wall oven.

Elsa scratched the outside of the rear door when Marjorie was setting the table. When she opened the door, Elsa marched in with a kitten in her mouth and trotted into the Mitchell bedroom to disappear under the bed. A moment later, she reappeared and trotted out of the bedroom, down the hall to the kitchen, pushed the unlatched rear door open, and headed to the stable. A minute later, she reappeared with another kitten. She repeated the process until she ensconced all four kittens under the Mitchell bed.

Marjorie stood and watched until she remembered the goulash was still simmering on the stove. *Oh, boy. Archie's not going to like this! Elsa is a quiet cat, but will the kittens be as quiet?* She didn't think so. Archie can make that discovery all by himself. *I had better look for something to keep the kittens in instead of under our bed.*

Stirring the goulash one more time, she lifted the pot and poured its contents into a large, thick-walled ceramic tureen. She carried the tureen over to the table, capped it with a thick matching lid and covered the tureen and lid with clean towels. Covered, the tureen would keep the goulash hot until everyone was ready to eat.

Greta entered the kitchen from the bakery in front, carrying two fresh loaves of bread. She placed the loaves next to the tureen and wrapped them in another thick cloth to retain their warmth.

"Elsa just brought in four kittens and stashed them under our bed," she told Greta.

"*Really!* Oh, I have to look!"

"Archie doesn't know yet," she called as Greta headed for the Mitchell bedroom. "He's in the bath!"

✻ ✻ ✻

Archie finished his bath and wrapped himself in an old bathrobe. *I'll miss this old robe when it wears out. Too bad terrycloth hasn't been reinvented yet.* He walked into their bedroom and was about to toss the bathrobe aside when he saw Greta on her hands and knees, looking under the bed.

"Uh, Greta?"

"Hush, Archie. Don't scare them."

"Scare who, what?"

"The kittens! Get down here and look."

"Uh, well . . . .all right."

Archie's hesitation wasn't about getting down on the floor. His concern was getting back up again. Since he'd been wounded two years before, he didn't have the strength in his left thigh that he once had.

He got down next to Greta and looked. Elsa was under the bed, curled around four kittens. Two kittens were asleep. The one that looked like a miniature lynx wasn't and started stumbling toward the two people.

"They can't stay there!" Archie said.

"Why not?" Greta asked.

"They'll get squished when Marj and I get in bed."

"Ummm, good point. I'll see what I can find to make a cat bed."

* * *

Archie shooed Greta out of the bedroom and dressed. He entered the kitchen to find Marjorie climbing up the stairs from the cellar with a woven basket in her hand. "Cat bed, Archie," she said, heading for the bedroom. The basket was large enough for Elsa and her four kittens. Archie followed into their bedroom and found her searching through the cedar chest her father had made for her.

"This will do," she said holding old flannel pajamas that once had belonged to one of their daughters. She placed the flannel on the bottom of the basket and got down on the floor.

"Easy now, Elsa. I'll not hurt them." She reached and retrieved the small, lynx-like kitten, scooted back from under the bed, and put the kitten in the basket. "Don't let it get out, Archie." She moved under the bed again and reached for another kitten.

Rrrooooow, Elsa growled softly.

"I won't hurt them, Elsa, but they can't stay here."

Elsa didn't contest Marjorie picking up another kitten, but she still growled. Before Marjorie could return for another kitten, Elsa picked up a kitten by the scruff of its neck and scooted out from under the bed, leaving the remaining kitten for Marjorie. The cat stalked around the bed until she saw the basket containing two kittens. The little lynx was standing up, paws on the rim of the basket, watching everything going on. After a moment, Elsa walked over to the basket and dropped her kitten into the basket to join its two siblings, just as Marjorie emerged from under the bed with the fourth kitten.

"I think this basket would be a better place for them than under the bed," Marjorie told the cat. "Let's find a nice, quiet spot for the basket and the kittens."

Marjorie picked up the basket and headed for the kitchen. "There's a spot in the kitchen, a niche near the wood box that's out-of-sight and out of the way," she told the big cat following at her heels. When she and Greta first saw the house, they found a rotting cabinet in the corner next to the oven's wood box. Its removal was one of the first items on the family's to-do list. The spot where it had once stood was just the size and just the place for the cat bed-slash-kitten basket.

Greta watched the procession. Marjorie, with kittens in a basket and Elsa following, entered the kitchen. Marjorie stooped and placed the basket in the corner.

"Think Elsa will let them stay there?" Greta asked.

"We'll just have to wait and see. I hope so," Marjorie replied.

Elsa walked over to the basket and appeared to be counting noses. The cat moved the kittens inside and curled up in the basket. Her position blocked the exit to keep any of the more adventurous kittens inside the basket.

"Elsa seems to accept it," Greta commented.

"Yeah. Let's get back to work. We can play with the kittens later."

* * *

By habit and agreement between the two men, Archie sat at one end of the family's trestle table, and Dieter sat at the other. The two lawmen, both armed, placed themselves to guard the Mitchell-Issler family if it was ever required.

Suhl was not a peaceful city. Not yet, at least, although it was more peaceful now than when he and Dieter arrived the previous year. The city had rebelled when the Swedes still garrisoned the place. When the garrison left, a gang of thugs took over, and they did not welcome the two lawmen. Few of those thugs remained.

Archie had a good view of the front of the house, past Dieter, while Dieter could see the rear door and the hallway toward the Mitchell apartment and the bathroom. When they had first agreed upon the seating arraignments, Archie had told Dieter, "I was surprised once. I'll not be surprised again." Dieter agreed; a degree of professional paranoia could be a lifesaver.

Marta sat on Dieter's right, between him and Greta. Marjorie sat on Archie's right. The big tureen was in the middle of the table with hand-cut slices of bread surrounding it. A tub of fresh butter was on one side of the tureen and a tub of berry preserves on the other side. Since Marjorie was closest to the tureen, each diner passed their plate to her. She filled the plate with goulash and added a thick slice of bread.

Elsa had been watching from the basket in the corner. When four kittens had finished nursing, she disentangled herself from the kittens and walked over to Marjorie's chair, where she patted Marjorie's leg with a paw to get attention.

"Oh, you want some, too, eh, Elsa?"

Merrooow.

Marjorie scooted back her chair and walked over to the cupboard to retrieve a cracked bowl. *This should do for Elsa's dish. I wonder if she'll eat goulash. Guess I'll find out.*

She filled the bowl with goulash and put it on the floor. Elsa peered at the bowl, sniffed it, and drew back. She bent over the bowl, gave it a lick, considered the taste, and continued to eat its contents.

"I guess Elsa likes the meat in the goulash," Marjorie said, returning to her place at the table.

"She better," Archie muttered. "There's no Petco around here filled with cat food."

* * *

"Three girls and one boy," Marjorie declared. After supper and its cleanup, everyone wanted to see the kittens. Two of the Elsa-like kittens and the little lynx were females. The other Elsa-like kitten was male. Marta wanted to name the kittens, but the adults decided to wait.

"We don't know yet if they will all live," Greta explained.

"And until they're bigger," Marjorie added, "we'll have trouble telling one kitten from another."

"Not that one," Marta said, pointing to the little lynx. "That's *Kari*," she proclaimed, defying anyone to object.

Kari was a Nordic name. "Where did you hear that name?" Greta asked.

Marta walked over to Greta and leaned against her. "*Mutti*," she said. Marta had never spoken her mother's name since the time Dieter found her in the burning remnants of a small hamlet the previous year. Raiders had attacked the small village and killed everyone, her parents, and friends, everyone except for Marta, who hid in the brush outside the village. Marta's mother must have had Nordic ancestry.

"*Kari*, it is, Marta," Greta agreed.

Kari and her siblings had been exploring the kitchen in kitten fashion. Elsa's people played with them for a while until Elsa, deciding it was time to go out, picked up each kitten and deposited it in the corner basket.

"I think Elsa is telling us it's time to go to bed," Dieter said to Greta.

Archie raised an eyebrow at Marjorie. They both knew the Isslers were trying hard to make another addition to their family. Marjorie saw the raised eyebrow and chuckled.

"Time for us, too, Archie."

✻ ✻ ✻

The meeting with Suhl's Wachtmeister, Johan Frey, was informative. Neither Archie nor Dieter knew that Suhl had three more trash dumps outside the city walls besides the one that the Archie and Dieter visited.

Frey said he'd have some of his watchmen check the other dumps for unusual numbers of rats. He was skeptical about rats causing the plague, but he admitted, the up-timers knew much more about plague than did he. They even had medicine and treatments that reduced the death rate of the disease, *so he had heard*.

Killing rats was a reasonable act, but he remained skeptical. He had heard too many wild claims of up-timer miracles.

"The first obstacle will be the city council," Frey said. "They will have to approve the rat killings," he reminded Archie and Dieter. "Some of them do not believe the plague comes from rats. They think it is Divine Retribution on the sinful."

"Arrange the meeting, if you would," Archie said. "Some plague victims have been found near Meiningen. Captain Gruber briefed me on that case. A constabulary corporal reported the discovery of eight dead yesterday. His patrol cleared the site. This is the only incident I know of, and those are the only proven plague deaths near us or Meiningen.

The victims were on the road to Suhl. Captain Gruber said he suspects a family evaded the Rhineland quarantine. If they could get this far, others could have too."

Frey agreed. Captain Gruber and Corporal Haan had met with him, too; warning of what they had found. Frey didn't need additional warnings on the consequences of an outbreak in Suhl.

Archie continued, "I'll have one of the EMTs lecture the council on disease control and preventive measures first. Then I'll remind them of all the lost revenue to the city if there's an outbreak of plague here like there is in the Rhineland. I hope that will convince them." Frey was skeptical about two council members being in favor, but he agreed that a rat killing was needed. Anything to prevent the plague from coming to Suhl.

* * *

Suhl's city council agreed to the rat killing. The decision wasn't by acclimation, two of the six councilors voted no. However, fear of the plague goaded the rest of the council into action. Outvoted, the two contrary council members left the meeting, allowing others to plan how the rat population could be eliminated or reduced. When the meeting resumed, Archie announced a bounty of two pfennig per rat-tail. Suhl, Incorporated would sponsor the hunt. The conglomerate was as eager to keep its workforce healthy as were the EMTs and the Suhl branch of the SoTF Public Health Office.

* * *

Frey's plan called for volunteers to surround the trash dump armed with hoes, shovels, and clubs. Suhl's watch would dump dead brush on the dump and light it. When the fire made the rats flee, the men and boys around the dump would kill the rats as they emerged. Women and girls, in an outer circle, would kill those rats that escaped through the cordon of boys and men.

Archie was skeptical that dead brush, when lit, would ignite the trash in the dump. To his surprise, it worked much better than expected. He and Dieter were armed with shotguns to kill any rat that escaped the two lines of rat-killers. Gruber volunteered several of his off-duty constables to assist them.

Archie had replaced the double-ought buckshot shells in his pump-action shotgun, with new, all brass, black-power shells, filled with #6 shot. Dieter carried his double-barreled coach gun loaded with the same brass shot shells. The constabulary troopers had to be content with their sabers. Captain Gruber thought the rat killing would give them saber practice.

The watch fired the dump in mid-morning. Not long after, rats appeared, and the battle commenced. Leather leggings, tied over their shoes and boots, reaching up to their knees, and leather gloves, covering their arms up to their elbows, protected the volunteers.

Some rat-killers dismembered the rats with hoes and shovels. Others smashed them with clubs. The best tactic, it seemed to Archie, was used by some men. As soon as a rat emerged from the trash, a man stomped it.

By mid-afternoon, the flow of rats had ceased. Any remaining in the dump would be dead from the fire and smoke. Frey's watchmen would stand guard for two days until the dump stopped burning. Then, after the dump was cool, the remaining trash would be turned to see if any live rats remained. Any found would be disposed of.

Archie saw men and boys running to a spot on the far side of the dump. He leaned over to Dieter and said, "Looks like a rat breakout. Let's ride over there. They may need help."

By the time they arrived, the breakout attempt was over. Some boys were tossing dead rats, minus their tails, back into the fire while others returned to their places around the dump. Few rats make it past the first line of rat-killers. Women, girls, and Gruber's troopers accounted for the rest. No rats escaped.

Archie, as a board member of Suhl, Incorporated, the new conglomerate that owned SMC, U. S. Waffenfabrik, and Suhl Nut and Bolt, set up a field desk at the dumpsite to issue chits to the rat-killers as they presented their rat-tails. The chits were redeemable, in cash, at the Suhl conglomerate's city office the following day.

As he wrote up the chits, he discovered that several boys and girls had earned a larger bounty than he expected. *Did Suhl, Inc. just create another cottage industry?* The bounty would continue until all the dumps were burned and cleaned of rats.

* * *

"How was your day?" Marjorie asked as she greeted Archie and Dieter that evening, still smelling of smoke and dead rats. Dieter waved and continued up to the Issler apartment, leaving the Mitchells alone..

"Productive," Archie answered. "If my count was correct, we killed over three hundred rats out of that dump and we still have three more dumps to go."

"That's . . . that's a lot of rats in just that one dump," Marjorie murmured. *I wonder how many are in town outside the dumps?* "I'm glad they're gone. Nothing good comes from rats."

Archie nodded. "Where is everyone?"

"Greta has gone to the laundry and Marta is taking a nap with Elsa and the kittens."

"Oh?"

"Look in the family room," she said. The family room was one of the two common rooms in the Mitchell-Issler household, the other being the kitchen. Archie walked in and saw Marta asleep on the floor; her head resting on Elsa's stomach with three kittens asleep snuggled up to the cat. The fourth kitten, lynx-like *Kari*, was lying on Marta's stomach. Elsa opened an eye as Archie looked into the room and then shut it.

"I think Elsa has adopted Marta," Marjorie whispered.

They returned to the kitchen. "What's for supper?" Archie asked.

"Leftover *Fleischküble* from yesterday," Marjorie replied, "Go take a bath. You stink!"

"After my day, I would think so."

"Off with you!"

* * *

The city burned and cleared the last trash dump of rats ten days later. The Suhl city council issued a proclamation forbidding the killing of cats and encouraged residents to keep felines and rat killing dogs. Inns and *gasthaus* of the city complied, too, to help keep the rat population under control.

Dieter was sitting in the kitchen with Greta one morning after the last dump burning, watching his wife take baked bread out of the oven. "Greta, have you seen any rats lately?"

"No, but I haven't thought to look, Dieter. Elsa hasn't brought in any rat-tails these last few days."

"That's good. I'll check later and see how many 'tails are being brought in."

Greta nodded and handed him a slice of warm bread and slid crocks of butter and preserves to him. "Good. No one wants plague here."

"The city is continuing the rat bounty for the ones inside the city walls," he said. "There're bands of boys and girls roaming the alleys and backstreets of Suhl looking for more. Wachtmeister Frey said the numbers of rat-tails turned in for bounty has dropped to a score or two per week.

"I hope it's enough to prevent the plague from coming here, Dieter."

✻ ✻ ✻

The chicken predator returned. *Frau Juncker* lost a hen a few days after the last dump burned. She had a wicker fence around her chicken coop to allow her chickens a bit of daytime freedom. Each evening she shooed them into the coop and each morning her son released them. One morning, Johan had found a dead chicken outside the coop, or rather what remained of a chicken. One must have escaped during the night or had not entered the coop the previous evening.

Elsa had been spending nights inside since moving her kittens from the stable to the house. When Frau Juncker mentioned her dead chicken, Greta and Marjorie decided to put Elsa out in the evening in the hope she would catch the chicken killer.

Each evening, after they put the cat outdoors, but nothing happened. Nothing killed any chickens, nor had anything tried to gain entry to the coop. Elsa still found late night meals and left the evidence, rabbit heads or squirrel tails, on the rear doorstep.

One evening, a week after Frau Juncker lost the chicken, Elsa was lying next to the threshold of the rear door. Darkness had fallen early, but it was not yet time for her to be placed outside. With her people watching her kittens, she appeared to be content to let others take care of them.

Archie watched the scene. They had already received several requests for the kittens. Everyone agreed *Kari* would stay. *Kari* was Marta's kitten.

While Archie mused, Elsa stood and went to the rear door. *Meerrow!* She seemed to be asking to go out. Archie opened the door and Elsa slipped out into the near darkness toward the stable. The horses seemed to be nervous, restless in their stalls. *Something's out there.*

Trusting Elsa's senses more than his own, Archie retrieved his shotgun, still loaded with the #6 shot from the last rat killing, and followed the big cat. Marta was standing in the open rear door. She, too, had known something was prowling behind the house.

"Go tell your father something is outside, Marta," Archie told her. When she didn't respond, he said, "Now, Marta!" more sharply that he'd intended. With a surprised look on her face, she fled to the family room, calling for her father.

Archie had only taken a few steps when Elsa found the prowler. Archie heard high-pitched squalls from Elsa and hisses, lower-pitched, huskier growls from her opponent.

Dieter, hearing the fight, arrived with a lantern and his shotgun. The two men trotted to the stable but found nothing. The fight had moved toward the neighboring home of *Frau Juncker.* Archie saw the widow standing silhouetted in her doorway.

Elsa was in a battle using teeth and claws against . . . a badger! Archie had never seen a badger since the Ring of Fire. Both of the fighters were showing blood, and Archie couldn't tell who was winning. Elsa had the badger's neck in her teeth and was shaking it furiously while attacking its torso with her claws. The badger couldn't get its teeth onto Elsa but its claws were raking her along her ribs and legs. Both were rolling around on the ground, each trying to get an advantage over the other.

When Archie and Dieter arrived, Elsa loosened her hold on the badger and it escaped into the darkness. She looked, for a moment, as if she was about to give chase. Instead, she looked up at Archie, mewed, and turned back toward home.

Frau Juncker arrived as Elsa slowly walked home. "Put up a fight, she did."

Archie nodded, watching the big cat. *She's hurtin'*. Dieter had stepped forward with the lantern. The badger was gone, or hiding just outside the lighted area.

"I think it's gone," he said.

"Elsa saved my chickens," *Frau Juncker* announced. "She was protecting them."

Archie wasn't so sure. *I think she was more curious about what was scaring the horses. But, no matter, the badger's gone.*

✳ ✳ ✳

Elsa was waiting for them when they returned to the Mitchell-Issler house. Archie sat on the stoop, while Dieter hung the lantern beside the door.

"Let's look at you, Elsa," Archie said. The cat moved next to Archie and sat on the step. She had blood on her in several locations and around her muzzle. Badger blood, Archie decided. She had blood in places on her flanks. Badger blood covered her paws.

Her thick fur protected her like armor, Archie decided. *She doesn't appear to have any serious injuries. I think the badger came off the loser in this fight.*

By this time, the rest of the household had arrived. "What was it?" Marjorie asked.

"A badger. I think it was nosing around the stable and spooked the horses. Elsa went to investigate."

"You're a regular watch cat, aren't you, Elsa? Let's see how much you're hurt," Marjorie said, leading the big cat back to the house.

"*Frau Juncker* thought Elsa was protecting her chickens," Dieter said as he followed the Mitchells inside.

"I kinda doubt that," Archie replied, "but it won't hurt if that is what she thinks. I hope she tells others. There are still too many people who want to kill cats."

"That's true," Greta added. "Let's take care of our ferocious watch cat."

✳ ✳ ✳

Frau Juncker upheld Archie's expectations. Within days, the story of Elsa protecting her chickens circulated throughout the local neighborhood. An innkeeper, a couple of streets from the Mitchell and Issler residence, acquired two cats and installed them in his stable.

Frau Juncker repeated her request for a kitten and Greta had relented. *Frau Juncker* would get a kitten when it was older and weaned.

Marjorie and Greta had been teaching Marta her letters and numbers. Marjorie was teaching her English and Greta, German. Growing up in a bilingual household, Marta was already proficient in both languages, at least as proficient as one could expect a five-year-old.

Not long after Elsa's big fight with the badger, Archie and Dieter returned home from the courthouse to find a new hand-lettered sign posted next to the bakery door: *Premises Protected by Watch Cat Security.*

Archie grunted when he read the sign. Dieter just smiled and shook his head. Greta, Marjorie, and Marta, Marta most likely judging by the crudity of the lettering, had posted the sign for all to see.

The sign made Archie consider a question. *Did the rat killings halt the plague? Would anyone have thought of that measure if Elsa's back-door rat trophies hadn't exposed the large and growing rat population?* After considering the question, Archie decided that, no, without Elsa exposing the rat problem, nothing would have been done. People had known rats were in the dumps, but no one had thought of the consequences and ignored the issue. That failure could have given the plague an inroad into the city. Elsa deserved credit for the warning. *Complacency is always an enemy,* Archie reminded himself.

Given their ages, it was unlikely he or Marjorie would have survived the disease if it had arrived. They had been immunized during Archie's army years. But those immunizations were decades old and likely no longer effective.

Suhl, September 1635

A month passed since the constabulary reported the plague deaths on the road between Suhl and Meiningen. There had been no further reports of plague cases. Meiningen had closed their city gates, allowing only local farmers in to sell produce. Strangers were barred. Many of the closest farmers stayed inside Meiningen's walls, leaving only during the day to work on their nearby farms. Archie couldn't remember how long an incubation period the plague had, but surely, it was less than a month.

The SoTF Public Health Office reported no other outbreaks within Franconia or Buchenland. The Office's opinion was that the city had nipped the outbreak in the bud. Everyone fervently hoped so.

Pastor Weber and the other Suhl clergymen approved of the increased attendance in their churches. They all scheduled special services of thanksgiving for the plague passing them by.

Returning home on the first day of September, Archie proceeded back through the house to the kitchen, where he rummaged in the cooler for the wine that had been a gift from Pastor Weber of the Holy Cross chapel. Marjorie and Greta, today being market day for the bakery, were gone on various errands, leaving Archie and Dieter alone in the house.

With the bottle in hand, Archie continued to the Mitchell apartment, where, after hanging his hat and gunbelt on a nearby coat stand, he poured himself a small glass of deep red wine and sat in his recliner. Archie took a few sips and set the glass on the lamp table next to his recliner and closed his eyes and leaned back; he'd had a tiring day.

He was almost asleep when he felt a nudge on his shoulder. Archie opened his eyes to see Elsa sitting on her haunches next to the recliner. She head-butted Archie's shoulder again.

He sighed. Elsa wanted attention and she wouldn't stop until he responded. Archie reached over, scratched her ears, between her ears, and rubbed under her chin. She rewarded him with a loud purr. After a few minutes, she laid her head on his arm, turning her head to one side to see him better.

Meeerroow.

"What do you want, cat?" Archie asked. For days now, she had been following him whenever he was home. Yesterday, she had followed him when he took his pinto to Christian Zeitts to have a shoe replaced. *What does she want from me?*

"Okay, cat, what it is?" he asked, not expecting anything like an answer. To his surprise, Elsa stood, put a paw on the edge of the recliner, and jumped up onto Archie's legs and lap.

Ooof! "Jeez, cat, you're heavy! Move!"

Move, she did. She laid down, rubbed the side of her head against Archie's belt buckle while purring, and stretched her body down between Archie's legs to the end of the recliner.

Her weight had shifted the balance point of the chair. The recliner teetered precariously, her weight close to tipping it..

Okay, okay, you've made your point. You're the Mitchell and Issler cat. Archie scratched her ears. *That doesn't mean you're my cat. You're the family cat.* Elsa raised her head to look at him, and Archie could almost hear her reproof. *That's what you think, old man.*

He sighed, listened to her purring and conceded the argument. *All right. You're my cat, too.*

THE LAST INTERVIEW

Suhl, June 16, 1636

During the ten days Thomas Bloem and his sister had been in Suhl, they had interviewed most of the resident the up-timers. The brother and sister had rented rooms in the Boar's Head Inn and were now writing the draft of their article. Maria was sitting alone, writing in her journal in the main room of the inn, a now common sight. They had been pestering Gary Reardon, Pat Johnson, and Osker Geyer the last few days on future plans for Suhl, Incorporated, and Pastor Weber for his views on the local impact of the up-timers.

Archie's stomach growled as lunchtime approached. Marjorie and Greta had left early for the market, and he'd overslept. In his mad rush that morning, he'd left his lunch sitting on the kitchen table. Briefly, he wondered if Dieter had picked it up. But, looking at his deputies' schedule, Dieter wouldn't be in the office until later this afternoon.

"Archie," a voice called.

He looked up to see Constabulary Captain Gruber standing in his office's doorway. "Yes?" he replied.

"The Bamberg and Erfurt weekly couriers arrived this morning. I've some letters and the court newsletter for you." The courier system made rounds to all the SoTF buildings and sites; an internal mail system of the state government. Gruber dropped three envelopes on Archie's desk and laid more on Karl Wagner's, the court's chief bailiff, desk.

One envelope remained in his hand, and Archie, ever curious, wondered who it was for. His stomach growled again.

Gruber laughed. "I've one more letter to deliver. How about lunch at the Boar's Head Inn sound to you?"

"Works for me," Archie said, reaching for his cane, leaning against the coatrack, and his Stetson. "You're going to deliver that envelope at the inn?"

Gruber smiled, "What's that up-time saying, *Neither rain, nor shine, nor dark of night, will stay the delivery of the mail.*"

Standing, ready to go, Archie hitched his gunbelt into a more comfortable position and said, "Something like that."

The Boar's Head Inn was a twenty-minute downhill walk from the courthouse. The heatwave that had camped over the city had broken overnight, bringing cooler breezes to Suhl. Archie tried, unsuccessfully, to see whose name was on the envelope. Gruber teasingly shifted it from one hand to the other as they walked. Finally, Archie could no longer stand the suspense. "Who is the letter for, Eric?"

"No, no, no. That's private until I deliver it. All I'll say is that it came from the north."

Karl Mohn, Harley Thomas' deputy, was in the north, in Erfurt. If Harley, Karl, and the two constabulary troopers had good weather, they were due to pass through Suhl today or tomorrow on their way back to Bamberg.

Archie grinned, and Gruber just shook his head. He was smiling, too.

"Think they'll be back today?" Archie asked. He needn't explain who he was speaking of.

"This afternoon, I think. The road north is dry, according to the courier. He left the same time they did."

"Hmm." Archie and Gruber both smiled.

Innkeeper Otto Hersch met them at the door. "Welcome," he said. "Your usual table?"

Archie, Eric Gruber, and Suhl's Wachtmeister, Johan Frey, often met in the inn. "Yes," Gruber replied, "but first I need to deliver a letter. Is *Frau D'Angelo* here?"

"She's in the main room, in the corner."

"*Danke.*" With that, Gruber strode forward into the main room. Spying her writing at a corner table, he advanced upon her.

"*Guten tag, Frau D'Angelo.* I have a letter for you. It just arrived from the north."

Archie had followed Gruber. He wanted to see her reaction, and was rewarded by seeing her eyes grow bright when she saw the envelope in Gruber's extended hand.

She took the envelope, read its return address, and smiled. "*Danke,*" she said, slipping the envelope into her bag sitting on a chair next to her.

They were disappointed when she didn't open and read the letter. Both were also experienced reading people's faces and body language. But not this time.

Innkeeper Hersch approached. "I'm sorry, *meine Herren*, your usual table is occupied. Would you like to choose one here?"

Ah ha! "Yes, Otto," Archie said. "That one," he said, pointing to a table that gave a clear view of the room's two entrances, and, by chance, of Maria D'Angelo's table.

"*Ja,* that will do," Gruber agreed, making it clear he would have chosen the same table if Archie hadn't spoken first.

After placing their order and taking a sip from the steins Hersch's barmaid placed on their table, the two discussed the latest events of the court system. Maria still hadn't opened the envelope. Archie and Gruber watched her surreptitiously. Finishing her writing, she blew on the page to dry the ink and placed it on a stack of paper on her table.

When the barmaid brought their lunch and set it on their table, Maria slid the envelope out of her bag and slit it open with a small knife she carried up her sleeve. She slid several pages from the envelope, spread them out before her, and began to read.

"What a poker face," Archie muttered. He couldn't read anything from her expression.

"*Ja*," Gruber agreed.

Maria finished reading the letter and was about to re-read it when her brother entered the room. She folded the letter and slipped it back into the envelope. Thomas Bloem saw her and asked about it. Archie and Gruber were too far away to hear the exchange. Whatever her response, Thomas Bloem appeared to be surprised.

When Thomas began to read the draft pages Maria had written, Archie knew he and Gruber wouldn't get any more information.

After finishing their lunch, Gruber rose to his feet. "I need to get back to the barracks." Pointing at the brother and sister with his chin, "If you discover anything, let me know."

Archie grinned and nodded. Gruber was a notorious gossip. *So am I*, he reflected. He finished the remnants of his beer and was about to leave when Harley Thomas and Karl Mohn walked into the room.

Harley, seeing Archie sitting in the corner, walked over and sat. "Did I just see Captain Gruber leave?"

"Yes, and I was about to do the same. Gruber said you may show up today."

"Good weather, dry roads. We made good time," Harley said, waving to the barmaid to take his order.

Karl Mohn, instead of following Harley to Archie's table, walked over to Maria's and Thomas' table, bowed, and greeted them. After a brief exchange, he joined them.

The two marshals watched. "Karl wrote a page a day when we left here and sent them to her via the court courier."

"I know. It just arrived. Gruber delivered it an hour ago. It didn't beat you here by much."

Harley laughed. "A state-of-the-art communication system." He watched Karl and Maria for a moment. "Think what they'd do with email."

Seeing Harley and Archie together at the corner table, Thomas Bloem rose and walked over to the two marshals. "*Guten abend, meine Herren*." Turning to Harley, "May Maria and I accompany you as you return to

Bamberg? We've finished our interviews here and our publisher lives in Bamberg. He wants us there. Maria can ride on horseback, if that's an issue," Bloem said.

"No, not an issue. We'll leave in the morning at six. You can meet us at the constabulary barracks. You have horses of your own?"

"Yes, two older ones. They were the only ones I could afford. I'll recoup my expense in Bamberg."

"Before you all leave," Archie interrupted, "Why don't we all meet for one last get together. I'll give Marj and Greta a heads-up."

Thomas smiled and nodded. "We accept. I like their cooking." He looked over his shoulder at his sister, who was in conversation with Karl Mohn. "Three years a widow," he muttered and sighed. Shaking his head, he turned back to Archie. "What time?"

"Six. That work for you and Karl, Harley?"

"Fine with us. We'll be there."

✶ ✶ ✶

Archie was standing on the Mitchell-Issler front porch when Harley, Mohn, Bloem, and his sister arrived. Karl Mohn was walking alongside Maria D'Angelo while Thomas Bloem walked next to Harley Thomas.

Interesting. Karl seems to be aggressively courting the young widow. Neither he nor Harley, he expected, would object. The unofficial view of the service was that married marshals and deputies were more stable than unmarried. He hadn't championed the viewpoint, but he agreed with it. *The service should be a family.*

Archie waved them inside and directed them to the family room. Maria ignored him and proceeded down the hallway toward the kitchen. Karl and Harley followed him into the family room where Dieter, Pat Johnson and Gary Reardon sat, deep in conversation about Pat's latest idea.

"Archie, what would you think about Suhl, Incorporated making a new rifle—a lever-action repeater like your Winchester '73."

"Like? What would be different from my Winchester? You know its weak point."

"Yeah, the tube magazine. I remembered I had fixed yours when you dented it. My idea has two options. First, extend the forearm to cover the entire tube, or use a stacked magazine like the Winchester Model 1895 . . . like an SKS—top-loading—with stripper clips."

"Would this be for the military? The USE hasn't deployed the M1635 rifles they bought from us."

"Ah." Pat sat back as if he hadn't considered that point. "If it weren't for black-powder fouling, I'd go for a semi-auto," he said, lapsing into thought.

Harley laughed. "You're just impatient, Pat. Isn't Nicki Jo working on smokeless powder?"

"Yeah, but she's going nowhere. She's still in Magdeburg, and whenever she gets some time to work on it, she gets side-tracked. I wrote to her that their house here is still waiting for them whenever she and Katie want to come home."

"Who's keeping her distracted?" Marjorie asked. She'd just come into the family room to call the men to the table.

"Colette. I think she wants Nicki Jo there until Colette's ready set up the Suhl site of Essen Chemical."

"Regardless," Gary said, speaking for the first time since the marshals arrived, "smokeless powder is still a year or more away."

The six men stood and followed Marjorie down the hall after she said, for the second time, "Dinner time."

When Archie reached her, she said, "I had to add two leaves to the table to fit everyone. Glad I had thought of that when we had it built." She turned into the dining area of the kitchen that contained the long trestle table. The rest of the men followed.

Greta, with Maria helping, had already placed the food on the table, two tureens of goulash, bowls of mashed potatoes and other vegetables, and two platters of sliced bread and rolls.

"What a feast," Karl Mohn said, looking at the food spread down the table.

Greta smiled. "*Danke.* I'll always accept a compliment."

Marta, who had been helping her mother, asked, "Can we eat now? I'm hungry."

"We all are, Marta." Turning to the rest, Greta gestured for them to gather around the table and sit.

* * *

Harley groaned. "I don't think I'll need to eat until we get to Bamberg."

Greta laughed. "Just in case, I'll send a basket of snacks with you in the morning. Just a little something to remember us by."

The women cleared the table. Greta and Marta washed the dirty plates and utensils while. Maria and Marjorie returned to the table. Once seated, Maria reopened the discussion. "Since this will be our last opportunity to ask questions, I have one," she declared.

"And?" Marjorie asked, sitting next to her.

"What are you going to do next? I'm asking *Herr Mitchell* and *Herr Thomas* specifically."

Archie looked at Harley and shrugged his shoulders. "I can't speak for Harley, but . . . Marjorie and I are getting long in the tooth. I'm sixty-three, Marj is sixty-one, Harley, you're fifty-nine, if I remember right, and Max is sixty-two. We will not be around for long—the up-time medical science that extended our lives doesn't exist now."

"And won't for years, yet," Marjorie said.

"What Marj and I have decided—we've not even told Dieter and Greta yet—we staying here in Suhl. As long as I can do the job, I'll stay here as the Marshal. When I can't walk up the hill home . . . it'll be time to retire. We're making enough as shareholders of Suhl, Inc. to be comfortable as we grow older."

"Greta and I have decided to stay here, too," Dieter announced.

"I didn't know that," Archie said, turning to him. "You're next in line for a marshal slot when they open the new court in Fulda."

"I know. But we'd have to move, again, if I took it." He shook his head. "We've moved enough. We like Suhl and have friends here. It's enough." He grinned and winked at his wife. "Maybe I'll take your job when you retire."

Archie laughed. "You would, too."

When the laughter died, Bloem turned to Harley Thomas. "And you, *Herr Thomas?*"

"Truth be told, I've not thought much about it. Vina, my wife, is in Bamberg helping Max Huffman. He's not well—health-wise—last I heard from her. I've been on the road a lot recently—like this trip to Erfurt. It's getting tiresome. When Karl is ready," He pointed to his deputy who was talking to Bloem's sister and ignoring the conversation at the table, "I'll send him out on the road, and I'll stay closer to home."

"I think all of us are settling in place," Ursula Johnson said, speaking for the first time from her husband's side. "Pat has his friends here, as do I. I'm sure the same is true for Gaylynn."

"That's so," she said, sitting next to Gary. "Gary can go galumphing all over the country, but I'm staying here. Besides," she laughed, "I have the Nut and Bolt business to run. Gary's too busy with Suhl, Incorporated."

"There are some," Gary said, "not us I don't think, but others who want to uplift everything to the twentieth century level." Gary shook his head. "I was like that once . . . but no more. It can't be done. There's too much resistance; people, politics, history even. All we can do is what we can do. Pat had the idea that grew into Suhl, Incorporated. Archie had the core knowledge and reference material, and I . . . had the drive." He sighed. "I'm tired. I'd like to get Nicki Jo away from Colette and make smokeless power. But Colette doesn't seem to want that. Don't know why. Anyway, I think we all have our place and that place is here. In Suhl."

CAST OF CHARACTERS

Max Huffman. SoTF Marshal, badge #1, Bamberg.

Harley Thomas. SoTF Marshal, badge #3, Bamberg-Granville.

Vina Thomas. Wife of Harley Thomas, Bamberg.

Archie Mitchell. SoTF Marshal, badge #2, Suhl.

Marjorie Mitchell. Wife of Archie Mitchell, Suhl.

Dieter Issler. SoTF Deputy Marshal, badge #4, Suhl, Deputy to Archie Mitchell, Suhl.

Greta Issler. Wife of Dieter Issler, Suhl.

Marta Issler. Adopted daughter of Dieter and Greta Issler.

Karl Mohn. SoTF Deputy Marshal, badge #12, Bamberg-Granville. Deputy to Harley Thomas.

Judge Charles "Chuck" Riddle. Chief Justice, SoTF Court, Grantville and Bamberg.

Dan Frost. Chief, Grantville PD.

Frank Jackson. General, NUS/SoTF National Guard.

Judge Wilhelm Fross. Presiding Judge, 1st SoTF District Court, Suhl.

Karl Wagner. Chief Bailiff, 1st SoTF District Court, Suhl.

Eric Gruber. Captain, SoTF Mounted Constabulary, Suhl.

Johan Frey. Wachtmeister, Suhl.

Ruben Blumroder. Suhl representative to the SoTF Legislature, Master Gunsmith, Suhl.

Osker Geyer. Iron factor, Suhl.

Pat Johnson. Owner, US Waffenfabrik. Chief Operations Office, Suhl, Incorporated, Suhl.

Ursula Johnson. Wife of Pat Johnson, Suhl.

Gary Reardon. Owner, Suhl Nut and Bolt. Chief Executive Officer, Suhl, Incorporated, Suhl.

Gaylynn Reardon. Wife of Gary Reardon, co-owner/manager of Suhl Nut and Bolt.

Anse Hatfield. friend of Pat Johnson, Gary Reardon, and Archie Mitchell. SoTF National Guard, Suhl.

Thomas Bloem, Maria D'Angelo. Journalists, *Thuringia Times*, Bamberg.

Nicki Jo Prickett. Protégé of Colette Modi. Chief Chemical Engineer, Essen Chemical, Suhl Chemical.

Katherine Boyle. Fifth daughter of Richard Boyle, the Earl of Cork. Companion of Nicki Jo Prickett.

Printed in Great Britain
by Amazon

81953337R00169